The Bakersville Dozen

The Bakersville Dozen

KRISTINA McBRIDE

Sky Pony Press
New York

First Edition

This is a work of fiction. Names, characters, places, and incidents are from the author's imagination, and used fictitiously.

Sky Pony Press books may be purchased in bulk at special discounts for sales promotion, corporate gifts, fund-raising, or educational purposes. Special editions can also be created to specifications. For details, contact the Special Sales Department, Sky Pony Press, 307 West 36th Street, 11th Floor, New York, NY 10018 or info@skyhorsepublishing.com.

Sky Pony® is a registered trademark of Skyhorse Publishing, Inc.®, a Delaware corporation.

Visit our website at www.skyponypress.com
Books, authors, and more at www.skyponypressblog.com

www.kristinamcbride.com

10 9 8 7 6 5 4 3 2 1

Library of Congress Cataloging-in-Publication Data available on file.

Jacket photo by iStock
Jacket design by Sammy Yuen

Hardcover ISBN: 978-1-5107-0805-1
E-book ISBN: 978-1-5107-0806-8

Printed in the United States of America

THURSDAY
JUNE 1

THE AMERICAN NEWS-REGISTER

A Time to Remember

If you haven't yet viewed *The Bakersville Dozen*, you've at least heard of it. With over two million hits, the video-gone-viral features a compilation of thirteen girls—all members of the senior class of Bakersville High School in Bakersville, Ohio—showcased in a variety of situations, while provocative titles highlighting each girl's alleged sexual prowess play across the screen.

The video has garnered national attention as a result of the disappearances that have followed. Five girls featured in the video have gone missing in as many months.

Police are asking the public to report any information related to these disappearances.

After its release, the three-minute montage sparked outrage across the country, igniting a fevered dialogue in the national news and daytime talk shows circuit, alike. Last fall, just after hitting several hundred thousand hits, a spoof was featured on *Saturday Night Live*. The president's wife also weighed in, calling the video "a horrific example of the objectification of women in America."

Nobody knows who is behind the video, which hit the internet via an encrypted

REPORTED MISSING

EMILY SIMMS	JANUARY 2
LEENA GRABMAN	FEBRUARY 1
BECCA HILLYER	MARCH 5
JJ HAMILTON	APRIL 4
SUZE MOORE	MAY 6

server late September last year. The local police and FBI have worked together to take the video down, but their efforts seem fruitless. As soon as the video is removed from one host site, it appears on several others.

A spokesman for Adele has stated that the Grammy winning artist is seeking damages for the unlawful use of her hit song, "Rumor Has It," as the tune is featured throughout the video and is quoted in the opening segment, which claims:

"Some girls put out. Others don't. One thing you can always count on? Guys talk. Here's the score at Bakersville High—a guide to the most sexed-up and sexed-down girls of the senior class—as 'Rumor Has It.'"

The disappearances remain as much of a mystery as the video's creator. In a recent press conference, Kegan Gray—lead detective on the case—stated, "We are considering all possibilities and following up on all leads. Our main concern is to find these girls while keeping the people of Bakersville safe. We ask that you remain vigilant and report anything suspicious to the local police."

With graduation season upon us, this is a monumental time for high school seniors across America. But the graduating class of Bakersville High will be celebrating amid the tragic absence of five of its classmates.

Authorities are requesting that anyone with information relating to either the video or the missing girls call 1-800-BAKER13.

THE BAKERSVILE DOZEN:

LEENA GRABMAN – I LIKE IT HARD

JJ HAMILTON – JUICY FRUIT

KELSEY HATHAWAY – SHAVED, 'NUFF SAID

BECCA HILLYER – HOT FOR TEACHER

CARRIE HIXON – PANTS ON FIRE

BAILEY HOLZMAN – LIKE A VIRGIN

SUMMER JAMISON – SPICY

BETH KLEIN – SQUEAKS, SQUEALS, SHRIEKS

AMY LINTA – ANYTHING GOES

SUZE MOORE – I'M SEXY AND I KNOW IT

BRITTANY SANFORD – LIKES TO BLOW

EMILY SIMMS – TEASER NOT A PLEASER

SYLVIE WARNER – EASY

CHAPTER 1

2:13 PM

"So have you decided what you're doing about the party tomorrow night?" My best friend, Hannah, looped her arm through mine and gave a little squeeze as we made our way down a crowded hallway leading to the front entrance of Bakersville High School.

"Nothing to decide." I shrugged, guiding her around a throng of cheerleaders, all in various stages of primp-mode, and past a batch of techies, who were leaning against their lockers like it was just any other day. "There's no way I can go. My parents would kill me if they found out. I think they're afraid someone might deflower the only virgin in the Bakersville Dozen."

"We both know it's a little more than that," Hannah said.

"Obviously." I elbowed my friend. "It was a joke, Han."

"There's not much to laugh about when it comes to that video, Bailey," Hannah said. "Or anything that's happened since it went live. I can skip Jonesy's to hang out at your house. We can watch movies in our PJs and eat ice cream out of the carton. Totally therapeutic."

"Really? You'd do that?"

"Um. Yeah. That's what best friends are for, right?"

I sighed, catching a flash of white-blonde curlicues up ahead, which meant Sylvie Warner was stalking the entrance to the atrium. She was the last person I wanted to deal with. I tugged Hannah to the side, sliding behind a pair of unnaturally tall basketball players.

"That sounds perfect," I said. "My only other option was getting together with the girls, which is just depressing. Reminds me of who's missing and makes me worry about who could be next."

"There's not more to it?" Hannah asked, eyebrows raised. "Like avoiding Sylvie Warner?"

I groaned. "Am I that easy to read?"

"It's more that you're human, and there's only so much a person can take. I wondered when you'd snap. I expected it to happen a long time ago." Hannah offered a sad smile. "It might make me awful, but I've been waiting. I miss you. Since everything started, you've been spending more time with them than me."

"Aww, Han. It's just the circumstances." I tossed my hair out of my eyes. "I love the girls, okay? All of them. We're in this together—that stupid video and all the unknowns? No one else can really understand how it feels, and that kinda makes them like family."

"Even Sylvie?" Hanna snorted.

I laughed, the sound so free and natural, it startled me. "That girl has made herself the center of everything. She's controlling, obsessive, and—"

"Freakishly annoying?"

"Exactly! But we both know Sylvie's not the only issue. The whole thing pisses me off. I should be celebrating, not hiding."

that being part of the notorious Bakersville Dozen had ruined my life.

Hannah said something else, but her words were lost in the roar of the crowd. I pulled her along, past the main office, noting the two police officers standing in the doorway. Their presence only made me walk faster. I'd talked to the police too many times in the last few months, answering enough questions to last me the rest of my life. There was no way I would let them steal my Last Day Ceremony.

Elbows and shoulders jabbed us as we made our way toward the center of the atrium. All I wanted was a few minutes of normalcy. A few seconds where the weight of the missing girls wasn't pressing me into the ground.

And then, just like that, my wish was granted. I heard him before I could see him—the chanting of his words twining through the current of bodies—the perfect distraction.

"We made it, freaks, geeks, and Barbie dolls!" His voice pinged off the angled brick walls. "It's the *last*, the *final*, the *closing* day for seeeeen-yours!"

He stepped up on a platform that had been planted in the center of the atrium, and I could finally see him—gorgeous him—a ripple of silky brown hair falling across his left eye as he turned in a circle, one hand pumping the air, the other holding a microphone up to a pair of lips that I knew, firsthand, often tasted like spearmint.

"Juuuuude," someone called, voice deep and drawn out. Others joined in. From his spot on the stage, Jude smiled. To most of the crowd he was leader of the spirit committee, honorary host of the Last Day Ceremony, or maybe party boy with a wicked sense of humor that could liven up any situation. To me,

"You don't have to convince me."

"Since January, I can't even leave the house without m
ents flipping out. They're even debating whether they'll l
leave for college in the fall."

"No way. And you didn't tell me?"

"Telling you makes it real. I don't want any of this to b
Except for Jude, my entire senior year has been a bust."

Hannah gave me an irritated look.

"I shouldn't have to mention you, Han." I rolled my
"Nothing compares to you."

"I should hope so."

I grabbed Hannah's hand as we were swept into the c
No longer shielded by the tallest guys in our class, Sylvi
a clear view of me as I rounded the corner. The bodies ai
me spilled into the atrium—a two-story, octagonal space, f
four main hallways that resembled spokes on a bicycle v
The bodies stalled out a few rows in front of Sylvie. She i
her eyebrows, her lips moving, as she waved me toward her.
my hand to my ear to let her know I hadn't heard a thing
said, and twirled, riding a well-timed surge of classmates
from her.

"Sylvie's in full-blown tracking mode." Hannah had to
to be heard over the chatter.

"I know," I shouted back. Ignoring Sylvie was mean,
didn't care. I needed some space from her and from every
she represented.

"She looks like she's about to explode," Hannah said. "A
Type-A energy can be combustible, you know?"

"She wants us to stand together for the ceremony—a i
front—which is nice, but I just can't." I left out the obviou

"You don't have to convince me."

"Since January, I can't even leave the house without my parents flipping out. They're even debating whether they'll let me leave for college in the fall."

"No way. And you didn't tell me?"

"Telling you makes it real. I don't want any of this to be real. Except for Jude, my entire senior year has been a bust."

Hannah gave me an irritated look.

"I shouldn't have to mention you, Han." I rolled my eyes. "Nothing compares to you."

"I should hope so."

I grabbed Hannah's hand as we were swept into the crowd. No longer shielded by the tallest guys in our class, Sylvie had a clear view of me as I rounded the corner. The bodies around me spilled into the atrium—a two-story, octagonal space, fed by four main hallways that resembled spokes on a bicycle wheel. The bodies stalled out a few rows in front of Sylvie. She raised her eyebrows, her lips moving, as she waved me toward her. I put my hand to my ear to let her know I hadn't heard a thing she'd said, and twirled, riding a well-timed surge of classmates away from her.

"Sylvie's in full-blown tracking mode." Hannah had to shout to be heard over the chatter.

"I know," I shouted back. Ignoring Sylvie was mean, but I didn't care. I needed some space from her and from everything she represented.

"She looks like she's about to explode," Hannah said. "All that Type-A energy can be combustible, you know?"

"She wants us to stand together for the ceremony—a united front—which is nice, but I just can't." I left out the obvious fact that being part of the notorious Bakersville Dozen had ruined my life.

Hannah said something else, but her words were lost in the roar of the crowd. I pulled her along, past the main office, noting the two police officers standing in the doorway. Their presence only made me walk faster. I'd talked to the police too many times in the last few months, answering enough questions to last me the rest of my life. There was no way I would let them steal my Last Day Ceremony.

Elbows and shoulders jabbed us as we made our way toward the center of the atrium. All I wanted was a few minutes of normalcy. A few seconds where the weight of the missing girls wasn't pressing me into the ground.

And then, just like that, my wish was granted. I heard him before I could see him—the chanting of his words twining through the current of bodies—the perfect distraction.

"We made it, freaks, geeks, and Barbie dolls!" His voice pinged off the angled brick walls. "It's the *last*, the *final*, the *closing* day for seeeeen-yours!"

He stepped up on a platform that had been planted in the center of the atrium, and I could finally see him—gorgeous him—a ripple of silky brown hair falling across his left eye as he turned in a circle, one hand pumping the air, the other holding a microphone up to a pair of lips that I knew, firsthand, often tasted like spearmint.

"Juuuuude," someone called, voice deep and drawn out. Others joined in. From his spot on the stage, Jude smiled. To most of the crowd he was leader of the spirit committee, honorary host of the Last Day Ceremony, or maybe party boy with a wicked sense of humor that could liven up any situation. To me, he was so much more—kind and patient and supportive—he represented everything right in my world.

"Are. You. Read-yyyyy?" His voice was deep and gravelly. He thrust one fist into the air, his tanned arm tight, showing each muscled line.

The seniors shouted, pressing together, their arms raised and waving, like strands of wild grass thrashing in a salty, mid-summer storm. Above, more people leaned over the glass railing that ran along the atrium's second-floor balcony, cheering down at the rest of us.

"Jude is insane!" Hannah shouted into my ear.

I smiled, tugging her farther toward the center. Looking around, I took in the faces of people I'd known all my life. People I would never again see on a daily basis. It felt sad, but not all the way. Real sadness was reserved for thoughts that could shatter. Like learning that one of my friends had disappeared. Then another. And knowing that I might be next.

I squeezed my eyes shut, trying to push it all away, not for a week or even a day, just long enough to enjoy the last few minutes of high school.

My eyes fluttered open when the music began, a mash-up of songs compiled years ago and passed down from one graduating class to the next for the Last Day Ceremony—"School's Out" by Alice Cooper, "Fight for Your Right" by the Beastie Boys, "We're Not Gonna Take It" by Twisted Sister.

The deep tone of multiple drums echoed through the space, a steady beat that pulsed through my entire body. Slowly, the crowd parted, allowing the BHS drumline to march in, twelve guys, all funk-dancing, their instruments harnessed to their chests. The cheerleaders came next, pompoms whipping wildly as they leapt into the air.

"I can't believe it's finally our turn!" Hannah shouted, her eyes glowing as she twisted her mass of long brown hair into one thick strand and threw it over her shoulder. "Last Day Ceremony rocks!"

Jude found me in the crowd and our eyes locked. He winked. I scrunched my nose up and blew him a kiss, feeling lucky to have him to keep me grounded, to remind me that everything in my life wasn't a crazy mess.

Jude began to clap to the beat of the drums. Of course, everyone followed along. It was like that for Jude. Always had been.

But that made me think of Leena "I Like it Hard" Grabman, cheer queen who'd reigned as captain of the varsity squad, a legend for radiating that same kind of magnetism. JJ "Juicy Fruit" Hamilton, too, with her vocal and guitar skills; she'd led her band from a high school talent show win straight to a recording deal in Cincinnati. And Suze "I'm Sexy and I Know It" Moore, who exuded effortlessness, the kind of girl who had always been totally sure of herself, sure enough to risk everything to follow her dream of becoming a fashion designer.

As the lyrics pulsated from the speakers overhead, washing over us as we spent our last moments together as a class, I tried to push thoughts of the girls away—the five who had gone missing and the others from the video. As my classmates danced, I tried to forget everything that had happened over the past nine months. But it didn't work.

Hannah bumped into me and I lost my balance, falling into the guy who had sat behind me in pre-calc last year and, from what I could tell, was *always* wearing a hoodie. Hoodie Guy pumped his hand in the air, shouting another drawn out, "Juuuuude." Something felt off, almost like he was mocking the entire scene, but he was lost in the shuffle of the crowd before I could figure out why.

It was like the music and the energy were enough to sweep away everyone else's troubles. I stood in the middle of the joyful chaos, but the whole thing felt forced, strangely surreal.

The ceremony seemed to last forever, but somehow it also passed in the blink of an eye. I felt defeated as the final song faded, like I'd lost my last chance. As the drumline hit their finale, Jude caught my attention, mouthing a quick, *You okay?* I smiled and nodded, but that did nothing to erase the concern in his eyes.

Jude drew the mic to his lips and gave a discreet reminder about continuing the celebration. Everyone cheered. News had traveled far and wide about the party at Jonesy's farm the next night. Jonesy's two older brothers had spent years in college mastering the art of partying, and their farm was infamous for killer events. The ten-acre property featured a fire pit, a pole barn, fully stocked bar, and shooting range. The guest list would include people from the current graduating class and those from the last four years—friends of Jonesy's brothers home from college.

I stood there in the middle of my classmates, resentment washing through my entire body. Life was going on all around me. But it was a life I couldn't live.

I expected Jude to close the ceremony by wishing us all good luck, or maybe with a joke about how Kyle Jenkins (dork of the century) had free reign to leave his job at The Flying Pizza and put us all to shame by making millions with the latest high-tech invention. Instead, Jude sighed, his eyes meeting mine for a beat as he surveyed the crowd.

"Before we leave, I think it's only fitting to offer a moment of silence in honor of those classmates who cannot be with us today."

The entire crowd got quiet. No one moved. The joyful energy of the celebration evaporated. I looked around, my eyes locking on the two officers. One was checking his phone. The other gazed out over the crowd, a smirk playing on his lips. His name was Tiny Simmons—a Bakersville graduate who had not so long ago celebrated his own Last Day Ceremony. I wondered if he was reliving some moments from his glory days.

"Emily Simms, Leena Grabman, JJ Hamilton, Becca Hillyer, and Suze Moore should be with us today, tomorrow, and this summer as we celebrate graduation. But they are not." Jude turned, facing a display case recessed into the wall at the back of the atrium. The entire crowd turned, too.

Together, we stared at the memorial—the collection of items meant to represent each girl: Emily's team jersey, a volley ball, a stack of yearbooks, and an assortment of pictures she'd taken; Leena's red-and-black pompoms propped in front of the trophy the varsity cheerleaders had won at Nationals, and the sparkling tiara representing her reign as BHS prom queen; one of JJ's acoustic guitars, a microphone, and a CD from her band's first studio session; a spread of playbills featuring Becca as the lead, fanned out across her favorite Juilliard hoodie; a jacket, off-the-shoulder T-shirt, flared skirt, clutch, and jewelry, all created by Suze, who had been thrilled when she announced she'd been accepted into Parson's School for Design in New York City.

Sylvie said that the items were supposed to keep the girls in everyone's thoughts so that we'd never stop searching. I thought she was crazy—no one would ever forget. Every single girl had hit the prime of her life the month before the kidnappings began, from college acceptance letters to team championships, these girls had it all. It was no wonder the police had struggled to find my place in the mix. I was nothing if not ordinary.

There were pictures, too, candid moment of each girl's high school life, blown up and hanging from the ceiling by fishing line. The display was framed with a cluster of notes, song lyrics, poems, and pictures, taped around the glass front of the case. I knew every detail because, under the expert direction of Sylvie Warner, along with the remaining *Bakersville Dozen* girls, I'd helped put the display together.

The way I looked at it, the entire thing was just a reminder of what had been lost. I wasn't stupid. I knew the statistics. Those girls . . . they had to be dead.

"We will never forget you," Jude said, his voice wavering. "We will never stop searching for you or hoping for your safe return."

My eyes started to sting. As I squeezed them tight, each girl flashed like a slideshow on the backs of my eyelids.

"Bailey," Hannah whispered, her hand gripping my wrist. "Are you okay?"

I opened my eyes, finding Hannah's face inches from my own, the smell of her strawberry bubblegum breath washing over me.

"I'm fine." I pulled away, backing into Hoodie Guy, who was suddenly there again.

"Hey, Like a Virgin," he said with a wink. I shoved past him, weaving through the crowd. Jude caught me as I moved toward the edge of the atrium, his eyes clouded with concern. I gave him a little wave and mouthed the two words once again. *I'm fine.* The refrain echoed through my head as I pushed through the crowd toward my locker.

I took a deep breath, and then another, reminding myself again and again that I *was* fine. That I would *stay* fine. That I would *not* end up like those girls.

By the time I was halfway down the hall, I'd shaken off my panic. As much as I could anyway. I felt better—more steady—as I reached my locker. Behind me, the hall rumbled with oncoming traffic as the crowd in the atrium broke apart.

With no time to prepare, I wasn't ready when she glided up to my side. I startled like a scared animal, and instantly hated myself for not being able to control my reaction.

"What's up?" Sylvie asked. "Did you not get my text? I wanted us all to stand together for the ceremony?"

"I got it," I said, with a shrug. "Just wanted to hang with Hannah. I've lost a lot of time with her this year. It hit me today and I just needed to—"

"You know how important it is for all of us to stick together. When people see us, they see the others, and that might prompt someone to join a search team or just pay more attention at a crucial moment. It could make all the difference in finding the other girls and bringing them home. Or finding the kidnapper so no one else goes missing."

"I get it." I sighed and leaned back against my locker. "But it's the last day of high school, Sylvie. Don't you ever want to just feel normal?"

Sylvie narrowed her eyes. "We aren't normal, Bailey."

"Doesn't that part ever piss you off?"

"That would be a waste of energy. We need to stay focused on what's most important—we cannot forget the girls."

"God, Sylvie." I pushed off the locker with more force than I'd intended. "You really think—"

"Bailey, don't—"

I leaned in, my voice shaking as I reached out and gripped Sylvie's hands. "No one wants to say it—the truth—but we're all thinking it."

"Don't." Sylvie yanked her hands from mine, pressing her arms to her sides.

"I have to bail on the thing at your house tomorrow night."

"But we have to stick together. If we're together—"

"—we'll be safe," I said, rolling my eyes. "I've heard it a hundred times. I'm not buying it anymore."

"If you pull away from the rest of us, you might as well call the media and tell them you're next."

"Seriously?"

"There'll be police surveillance at my party." Sylvie widened her eyes. "No one will be able to get to us. If you go off on your own, you're easy bait."

"Last time I checked, I'm not the one they call *easy*."

Sylvie gave me a disgusted little grunt, then turned and walked away, her hands balled in tight fists.

I turned to my locker, feeling a little bad for throwing a line from the video in her face, but she kind of deserved it. Besides, lashing out had taken a little of the pressure off. I might not be able to do everything I wanted, but I sure as hell didn't have to follow all of Sylvie Warner's rules.

I spun the dial on the circular lock. The metal groaned as I yanked the door open onto five spiral notebooks and the yearbook

I'd picked up at lunch. I shoved the yearbook into my backpack first. As I reached to grab the notebooks, I glanced at the collage of photographs I'd spent four years plastering to the inside of my locker door.

That's when I saw it.

A dark red envelope with my name—BAILEY HOLZMAN—printed across the front in caps.

A little thrill rippled through me. The message was from Jude, no doubt. He was known for leaving me notes in random places—tucked into pockets of my jacket, jeans, and purse, slid between the pages of my textbooks, folded under my pillow, hidden in a pair of my fuzzy winter gloves. This was totally his style. And it was exactly what I needed.

Dropping my notebooks, I ripped the envelope from the door, and slipped my finger under the flap, drawing out a thick square of cream-colored cardstock, the font on the outside a perfect match.

I turned, leaning against the bank of lockers, and bowed my head, biting my lip to keep from smiling as I read the words at the top of the card:

THE SCAVENGER HUNT

THOUGHT YOU MIGHT NEED
A DISTRACTION,
SO I PLANNED A LITTLE GAME.

THE OBJECTIVE IS SIMPLE:
YOU HAVE FOUR DAYS
TO LOCATE FIVE TREASURED TROPHIES.

EACH CLUE WILL GUIDE YOU
TO WHERE AND WHEN

YOU CAN FIND THE NEXT.
THE MOST IMPORTANT RULE FOR NOW:
PLAY THROUGH TO THE END.
QUIT AND YOU'LL FACE A SERIOUS PENALTY.

READY? SET . . .

GO DIRECTLY TO YOUR SUMMER'S MOST CHERISHED SPOT.
CLIMB UP HIGH SO YOU CAN SEARCH DOWN LOW.
WHAT YOU SEEK IS HIDING IN A SEA OF TALL GRASS.

HAPPY HUNTING!

CHAPTER 2

2:57 PM

"A scavenger hunt?" Hannah asked, steering her silver Escape off the curved, back-country road that ran along the outskirts of our little Ohio farm town. The car swayed, its tires unsteady on the gravel-lined drive that led to my house. She'd seemed preoccupied for most of the ride, worried even, so I'd thrown out the news about the hunt to bring her focus back to the present. "Jude has got to be the most romantic guy in the entire world."

"I know." I closed my eyes and turned my face toward the open passenger window letting the warm breeze toss my hair as I breathed in the scent of freshly-cut grass.

"Seriously. You and your whole 'Cutest Couple' thing make me sick." Hannah snorted as she steered the car between my house and the Greens', the only neighbors within a mile. My eyes were still closed, but I knew exactly where we were as the car dipped around a curve.

"I can't wait to see what he has planned." My eyes fluttered open as Hannah pulled the car to a stop at the end of the drive. While she checked her phone, I lost myself in the line of trees swaying a hundred feet in front of us, the northern border leading to a complex web of wooded trails that spiraled out for miles. Hannah sighed with what sounded like relief, but I didn't get the chance to ask why before she slipped her phone in the side pocket of her purse and launched us back into the discussion of the hunt.

"Okay, so, your summer's most treasured spot? It's obvious where you need to go."

"I think that was the point."

"Want me to come with?"

"Nah," I said. "I'm good."

"You're sure?" Hannah asked, narrowing her eyes.

"It's just a little walk. I'll be fine."

"Right. But you're *sure* this is Jude? I mean, what if—"

"I already thought of that, okay? I'm not stupid."

"That's not what I meant, and you know it."

"It's Jude's thing. He's been leaving me random notes since the day we started dating."

Hannah shrugged. "I'm just spooked with everything going on. Not to mention the police presence during Last Day Ceremony. I don't love the idea of you going off on your own."

"It's not like you have a choice," I said. "It's the first fun thing I've had to look forward to in a long time. I'm sick of not being able to do anything. My parents have been hovering over me for the last five months, afraid I'm going to disappear in front of their eyes. I feel like I've been trapped, living in a cage since the day Leena went missing—one of those see-through deals they have at the zoo. I swear, I know how those poor gorillas feel, Han. It's not pretty."

Hannah glanced back toward the pair of houses sitting behind us, biting her bottom lip. "Fine. I'll go in. Say hey to your brother and see if he can score us some beverages for tomorrow night. But I'll time you. Send in reinforcements if you take longer than fifteen minutes. Or if you fail to reply to any of my check-in texts, which you'll receive roughly every three minutes. No arguments. Capiche?"

"Sounds like a plan," I said, opening the door of the Escape. "I won't be too long."

As soon as my sandals crunched on the gravel, I heard it. The high-pitched wail of the Greens' screen door, opening and then slamming closed. I swiveled toward the back barn, looking up at the peeling paint on the tree house my father had built with Mr. Green when I was seven.

"Ladies," a deep voice said. "Been a long time."

I let my breath flow slowly from my lips as I turned around. I could do this—had to do this—no matter what.

"Wes!" Hannah called, rushing the tall, solid figure walking toward us, arms outstretched as she leaped to pull him into a hug.

"Hannah Banana."

"You know I hate that name." She smacked his shoulder as she pulled away from him, then made a show of looking him up and down. "Freshman year was good to you. You're looking hotter than ever."

"As are you," he said, giving Hannah a wink. He grabbed her hand and twirled her in a circle, her dress fanning up as his eyes found mine. The deep green went dark with an emotion I'd never be able to decipher. Wes Green had always been the most confusing thing in my world. He nodded to me as Hannah stopped twirling, then stepped back. "Hey, Bailey."

It was the first thing he'd said to me in five months.

"Hey," I said, taking in all the ways that he'd changed. His hair was longer, his shoulders broader beneath his plain white T-shirt, his cargo shorts slung a little lower on his hips. "How was the drive home?"

He shrugged and ran a hand through his hair, so blond in the sun it looked like gold set on fire. "Mind-numbing, as always. But your brother blasted some new indie bands the entire way back, so it went fast enough."

"You get in today?" Hannah tossed her hair across one spaghetti-strapped shoulder.

"Nah. Late last night." Wes was still looking directly at me.

I shrugged, like I couldn't have cared less. But I knew exactly when they'd pulled into the drive—2:17 AM. I'd waited up, my room washed in darkness as I leaned against the walls of my cushioned window seat, so I could have one glance with no one else watching. I thought it might ground me, but when I watched Wes step out of my brother's Jeep and stretch his arms over his head, panic had set in. After everything, I was going to have to face him.

But not like this. I refused for it to go like this.

"Look," I said, worried that Hannah would pick up on the awkward vibe, "it's good to see you, but I gotta go."

Wes cocked his head to the side, his eyes going dark again.

"She's on a mission," Hannah said.

Wes gave me a forced half-smile. "Sounds mysterious."

"No." The word came out harsher than I'd intended. "It's not."

"Go," Hannah said, looping her arm in Wes's. "We'll hang with Tripp. We can chat party details until you're back."

"I was actually leaving," Wes said. "I have this thing with—"

"Not anymore," Hannah said, tugging Wes a few steps toward my house. "I want a full update of your college experience, minus the more *private* moments."

"Nothing to tell." Wes shook his head, a smile playing on his lips. "Honest."

"Shut it, Wes," Hannah said. "I know you. Once a player, always a player. You can tell me how many hearts you broke while we wait."

"He has plans," I said, standing a little taller. "Just let him go, Han."

"It's not a big deal," Wes said. "I can reschedule."

"Perfect," I said. Except the entire situation was anything but.

CHAPTER 3

3:06 PM

As my feet hit the trail, the earthy scent of early-June air rushed into my lungs. Trees rose from the ground on both sides of me, closing in the farther I walked into the woods. I took the first trail on my right and followed the curve down a small hill until I hit a fork, one path leading to the back of Sydney Village, a ritzy development that had gone up when I was in middle school, and the other to the first location in Jude's scavenger hunt.

It had been months since I'd been in the woods. Five months and one day, I realized. The last time I'd been out on these trails, it had been winter, and snow had crunched beneath my feet.

Turning left, I walked toward an opening along one side of the trail and saw it—my summer's most treasured spot—the large pond that connected our property with several others.

I walked along the edge of the pond, watching the sunlight flicker across its surface. When I reached a tree on the opposite side, I stopped, placing my hand on a wooden plank hammered into the trunk—the bottom of the makeshift ladder Tripp and Wes had made over a decade ago. A knotted rope still hung from the thick branch that extended over the water. Chickens swung in. The bravest climbed up to that limb and made the twenty-foot leap into the water below. I'd been nine when I graduated from Chicken Little to Bailey the Brave.

Turning in a slow circle, I squinted, trying to find a clue in the tall grass that grew between the tree and the line of woods. There was nothing but a tangle of greens and browns, not even the slightest sliver of color to guide me. I planted my foot on the bottom rung of the ladder, hoping it would still hold me, and grabbed for the fourth plank with one hand. The motion was still so familiar to my body, hand over hand, reaching, grasping, my toes balancing on each rickety step.

When I got to the top, I swiveled and leaned against the twisting limb that stretched over the water, surveying the scene beneath me. The brush looked the same from up here, just more snarled. Skimming my eyes across the grass, I noticed a trampled patch. That's when I saw it—a bright pop of yellow against the greens and browns. It felt like a small triumph. In that moment, I was so excited to find out what Jude had left for me I almost forgot everything that had gone wrong since the reveal of that awful video.

But that excitement was cut off by the sound of a deep voice that was all too familiar.

"You gonna jump, Chicken Little?"

My entire body spasmed with a jerky startled reflex. I hated myself for the reaction so much that I didn't turn around. "Go away, Wes. Leave me alone."

"I'm not the one who called this meeting, Bailey." His voice was closer now.

As soon as his frame crossed into my line of vision, I turned, facing the tree again. "I didn't call any meeting. This has nothing to do with us."

I heard footsteps, the whisper of his gym shoes in the silky grass. Slowly, I climbed down.

"You expect me to believe you decided to walk out here—directly to *our* spot—the moment you saw me, and it has nothing to do with us?"

"This isn't *our* spot," I said, as my feet stretched from the bottom rung to the soft ground at the base of the tree. "There is no *us*, Wes. Not anymore. I have nothing to say to you."

I didn't want to turn. Didn't want to face him. But I didn't have any other choice. I swiveled quickly, catching him off guard, and tried to step around him, but his hand shot out, gripping my right arm so tightly I could feel each fingertip pressing into my skin.

"I don't believe you."

Avoiding his eyes, I looked toward the pond, the sparkling water, the dense cover of the trees. As much as I wanted to avoid the memories, they came in short bursts, hitting me from all sides—Wes's smooth skin reflecting the moonlight, his satiny lips touching mine, his hands tugging through tangles in my wet hair.

"I don't care what you believe," I said, feeling his grip tighten around my arm. "I just need you to leave. Now."

"I don't think so." His voice rippled like the surface of the water.

I pulled away from him in one swift movement. "You're hurting me, Wes."

His hand slipped away in an instant, his feet shuffling as he stepped back, offering me a clear path to the thicket of grass. I took it.

"Before I go," he said, "we have a few things to sort out."

"What *things*?" I asked, parting the grasses with my arms, feeling the itch of their spiky edges.

"I feel like this deserves your full attention," he said, following me.

Taking one step, two, and then three, the grasses swallowed me whole. But not fast enough. Wes was there, right behind me, the heat of him blazing against my skin.

"Like I gave you every day last summer?" I asked.

"Let's not talk about last summer."

"The whole thing was doomed from the start. Your plan was flawed."

"It was a master plan." Wes's voice was soft, so familiar it hurt. "And you know it."

"It was a mistake." I whipped my hair over my shoulder, taking a few steps to my right, going deeper, closer to the trampled patch that I'd seen from up above. I caught a fleck of yellow. Then, with each step closer, more yellow, until my eyes put the puzzle together and I understood it was the edge of a blanket. Jude had probably planned something romantic, which meant that Wes was the last person I needed by my side.

Wes grabbed my elbow, spinning me around, forcing me to face him. I was too tired to resist. And I saw him—really saw him for the first time in what felt like forever. His freckled nose, the sharp line of his jaw, the nearly invisible scar where he'd pierced his ear in middle school and then changed his mind.

"What?" I asked, my voice cracking.

Wes's eyes searched mine. For a moment, it felt like nothing had changed. It was just us, here, together, like before. Like it had been for most of our lives.

"What do you want me to say?" I backed toward the blanket, ready to find whatever treasure was waiting for me and to grab my next clue. Then I'd just dodge around Wes and run, as fast and as far as I could.

His gaze flicked over the top of my head, and he sucked in a deep breath, pulling me to his side, then twisting me around until I was behind him, one of his arms wrapped around my waist, pressing me up against his back.

"What the fuck, B?" he asked, his voice high-pitched, shaking, his free arm reaching out and spreading the final grass curtain wide open. "What the fuck is that?"

I stood on my tiptoes, peering around his shoulder.

And then I saw her.

The whole world tilted as my eyes took in the scene.

She was lying in the grass, a fuzzy yellow blanket spread beneath her.

My lungs tightened, unable to take in enough air.

Her hair was fanned out, her legs crossed at the ankles, and her lips were painted a shiny red, screaming out against the pale white of her skin.

My vision blurred, pinprick lights distorting the image before me.

Her hands were perched on her chest, her fingers clutched tightly around the edges of an envelope.

A red envelope.

With two words emblazoned across its front.

BAILEY HOLZMAN.

CHAPTER 4

3:31 PM

"Holy shit," I said, grabbing the waistband of Wes's shorts to keep myself upright. I wanted to run, needed to run, but my legs wouldn't move. Instead, I tipped sideways, throwing up, the splatter of my sickness splashing across my ankles, and I knew for sure the whole scene was real.

"That's a dead body, Bailey." Wes whipped around so fast I lost my hold on him and almost plunged to the ground. "That's a dead fucking body and you were just—"

"Wes," I said, my voice as thin as a sliver of glass. "What's going on?"

"You're asking me?" His eyes were wild.

I swiveled, seeing her once more—recognition hitting me. The echo of her name tripping through my mind before I had a chance to shoveshoveshove it away. I bent at the waist, vomiting again because I *knew* her, could see her sitting on the couch in Sylvie Warner's basement, the center of our group of thirteen, her laughter ringing through the room as Sylvie tried to take control, telling us to *focus* and consider *all possible suspects* behind

The Bakersville Dozen. Leena Grabman was always laughing—even about the stupid tagline attached to the footage of her on that video: I LIKE IT HARD.

But then I remembered a time when she wasn't laughing; she'd been crying, swollen tears sliding down her cheeks as she gripped my hand, her fingernails digging into my skin. That was the day we'd found out Emily Simms had disappeared. The day the video went from an obnoxious prank to something way more sinister.

"That's Leena Grabman," Wes said, his voice shaking. "Leena Fucking Grabman is lying right there, Bailey. *Dead.*"

I didn't say anything. I couldn't. Leena and I hadn't been close before the video, but since the fall she'd become like family. The thirteen of us had little in common, but we'd spent countless hours together trying to find answers about why we'd been chosen and who was behind the video. As each girl vanished, the group had pulled together more tightly. Even though I hated the reason I was connected with the girls, I loved them all. Seeing Leena like this, it made me feel detached from my body, like nothing was real anymore.

"Why are you out here, Bailey?" Wes asked. "Why are you searching through the same patch of weeds where Leena Grabman is lying, dead?"

My phone vibrated in my pocket. I knew it was important, yet I had no idea why. Nothing felt more important than the way Leena's feet were crossed, so casually. She was so still.

But then I saw the red envelope clutched in her hands. "It was the clue. It led me out here and—"

"Clue?" Wes's hands gripped my shoulders, pulling me upright so he could look into my eyes. "What are you talking about?"

"A scavenger hunt. The first clue was in my locker. It led me out here. I thought it was a game, a surprise from Jude."

Wes winced. Then he shook his head. "*Jude* did this?"

"What? No! I—"

"Jude left you the clue?"

"I thought so, but . . . this obviously isn't him."

Wes reached into the pocket of his cargo shorts and pulled out his phone.

"What are you doing?" I asked, my hand reaching out for his.

His eyes met mine, his breath coming in short, billowy gasps. "I'm calling the police. There are five missing girls, B. One of them is officially dead. And you're in the middle of this whole thing. We have to call the cops, or else—"

"But there's a rule," I said, panic rising in my chest. "The first clue warned me. I have to play this out to the end."

"Bailey, no. You can't—"

"She's *dead*, Wes." I pointed toward Leena without looking at her. "I do not want to face that kind of penalty."

"Maybe the penalty happens no matter what. Maybe this whole thing means you're the next missing girl, B. Ever think of that?" Wes held his phone up between us. "We have to call the cops. It's *their* job to figure this out."

"Let me think for a minute," I said, looking at the red envelope, everything inside me screaming that the game had begun and that ignoring the clues would be dangerous. "There's another clue. Whoever did this, they're expecting me to—"

"You're not suggesting we read it," Wes said. "Please tell me you're not suggesting—"

"Not *we*. Me. And I don't want to, but what happens if I don't?" I knew I sounded hysterical—the alarmed look on Wes's face told me more than the tremble in my voice—but I couldn't help it.

Wes turned facing Leena who was lying so very still on the buttercup-colored blanket. He ran his hand through his hair, the stubble on his chin glinting in the sunlight.

"The cops sure as hell won't let us see it," he said, more to himself than me. "Not if we call them before we take a look. Maybe you're right. It's not like we can help her. To keep you safe, we need to know as much as possible. Okay, we read the clue. Then we go back to the house and figure out what to do. And by that, I mean we're calling the cops."

The words pounded through my head as Wes stepped toward the blanket. I followed, my hands pressed against his back, feeling like my connection to him was the only thing real about the moment.

He bent forward, one hand outstretched, grabbing the envelope with two fingers and yanking it free. Jerking back, he bumped into me, and we fell in a heap at Leena's feet, jostling her so roughly that her ankles uncrossed, the top leg slipping away from the bottom. Time stopped, flies buzzing all around us, and my eyes took in every detail, searing a snapshot of her into my brain.

"Shit!" Wes said, jerking away from the blanket, pulling me with him. The last thing I saw was her legs, the skin tinted gray with death, dark blue-black splotches pooling along the underside of each calf.

Leena would die if she could see herself now, I thought, the words firing through my mind before I understood their irony. It felt out-of-this-world crazy to think that the Leena I had known since elementary school—girly and popular and untouchably gorgeous—was the same Leena who had been left in the woods, the same Leena who was lying in front of me. Dead.

Wes pushed me away from the body toward the tree and the water's edge, toward everything I had considered safe that would now forever be haunted.

I pulled ahead of him, my phone buzzing again as I broke free of the itchy prison. My mind was working more clearly by then, and I remembered Hannah and her check-in texts. I pulled my phone free and typed a quick reply so she wouldn't charge into the woods with reinforcements. Wes pushed his way into the clearing a minute later. His hands shook as he held out the red envelope so that my name was facing me, but upside down.

"You sure you wanna read it?" he asked.

"I don't think I have a choice." I grabbed the envelope, my fingers fumbling under the flap, and tore it open before I had the chance to talk myself out of facing whatever might come next.

Wes reached my side as I pulled the cream-colored cardstock free and the envelope fell to the ground.

IT'S OFFICIAL.

THE GAME

IS

ON.

I'M GUESSING YOU'RE A BIT SHOCKED,

SO LET ME REMIND YOU

TO OBEY THE RULES.

RULE # 1 REMAINS THE SAME.

FOLLOW EACH CLUE

UNTIL YOU'VE
PLAYED THROUGH TO THE END.

RULE #2 SHOULD BE OBVIOUS.
NO COPS.
CALL THEM AND I'LL KNOW.
TRUST ME. DON'T TEST ME.

FIND YOUR NEXT CLUE
IN THE HAYLOFT AT THE JONES'S FARM.
TOMORROW NIGHT.
10PM.

FOLLOW THE INSTRUCTIONS PRECISELY,
AND YOU'LL HAVE THE CHANCE TO
SAVE
ONE OF YOUR GIRLS.

BREAK A RULE,
I'LL PICK OFF
THE WHOLE BAKERSVILLE DOZEN,
ONE BY ONE.

HAPPY HUNTING!

"Bailey," Wes said, his breath grazing my cheek, "this is fucking crazy. We need to call the cops. We can't just blindly follow—"

"Fine," I said.

"Wait. Just, fine? You'll let me call them?"

My fingers gripped the cardstock tighter, crinkling it in my hand. "If we have a chance to save one of the girls, we have to get this right."

Wes leaned down and plucked the envelope from the ground, then tugged the card from my hands, stuffing it back into hiding. He grabbed my shoulders and pulled me in, his arms wrapping around me and holding tight. "We'll figure this out. Okay?"

"Not here," I said, my voice a whisper. "We have to go back to my house. In case someone's watching."

I closed my eyes and pressed my face against his chest, the familiar scent invading me, giving me a sense of security that I knew was dangerous, but that I was grateful for, nonetheless.

I nodded, suddenly glad to have him there—listening and feeling and caring—to find the two of us connected again after so much time.

CHAPTER 5
3:49 PM

Stepping into my airy kitchen, I felt like I was floating—a prickly, unsteady kind of floating that made the entire scene seem unreal. I jumped when the screen door slammed behind me, steadying again only when Wes's hand pressed against my back, his body sliding up to mine in a way that I wouldn't have allowed a half hour before.

"Jesus, B. I was starting to get worried." Hannah was sitting at the butcher-block table, her chair turned toward the television in the adjoining family room. She aimed the remote at the screen, lowering the volume until the sound of agitated newscasters faded to nothing. "What the hell took so long?"

Tripp swiveled toward us, the old Led Zeppelin T-shirt he was wearing blocking my view of the TV. "I can't believe you had something more important to do than welcome me home. And Wes, I thought you were just going next door to get that CD."

Tripp glanced at me, then Wes, and then back to me in a flash. I looked past him to the sliver of TV screen beyond his right shoulder, focused on the fragments flickering by, willing myself to act normal.

"I'm just glad you're back," Hannah said. "Wait'll you hear the latest news. Totally crazy, and I think—"

"Shut up, Han," Tripp said, walking around the side of the table, his gaze fixed on me. "What's wrong, Bailey?"

I looked down at his bare feet. I couldn't say a word. If I did, he'd know something was really wrong. And I couldn't tell him. He'd try to take over, and then he'd be at risk, too.

Hannah stood, pushing her chair back with a long scraping sound. "Shit, B. You're white as death. What happened out there?"

I grabbed for the table, curling my fingers around the edge. "Nothing. I just . . . got a little dizzy. Wes found me on the trail and helped me back to the house."

"Have you eaten?" Tripp asked, moving toward the refrigerator and pulling the door open. "Are you sick?"

"No." My mouth still tasted like bile.

"Maybe a little water." Wes pulled a chair out and pressed my shoulders until I sat.

"So?" Hannah asked, leaning her hip against the table, narrowing her eyes at me. "What'd you find?"

"Nothing," I said, a little too fast and way too loud.

"Nothing?" Hannah crossed her arms over her chest and looked from me to Wes.

I hated her for knowing me too well, and I hoped she wasn't going to push. When Hannah pushed, she wouldn't let up until she had exactly what she wanted. And I could not let her get involved. The situation was too dangerous. Leena was proof of that.

"Drink," Tripp said, placing an open bottle of water in front of me.

I tipped the bottle to my lips, swishing the cool water around my mouth before swallowing. But then I thought of Leena, of how she would never swallow a drink of cold water again, and I almost threw up right there on the table.

Hannah swiveled her chair back to the table so she was facing me. "For the record, I don't believe you, but if you're not gonna spill, you're gonna listen." I could have kissed her for letting me off the hook. "I was talking to Tripp about beverages for tonight when he got a call. So it was just me sitting here, flipping through channels while I waited for you, right? I hit the string of obnoxious news channels, which are always, like, my least favorite because they're a freaking horror show, but they totally suck me in at the same time. Anyway—"

"Hannah," Wes said, "I'm not sure now's the best—"

"I'm getting to the good part, I swear. Bailey's gonna want to hear this." She slid the remote across the tabletop and started spinning it in circles. I wondered if Wes and I should have gone to his house instead of mine. Calling the police without Hannah and Tripp finding out about Leena was going to be tricky, but it felt important to keep them in the dark as long as possible. "As I'm sure we all know, the reporters are gearing up for more news in *The Bakersville Dozen* story. Again, sick and twisted, but whatever. I thought they were just doing a standard recap and terror drill—the kind where they make sure we all know about the pattern and how someone else could go missing within the next five days, seven hours, thirty-three minutes, and twelve seconds. You know some blog actually posted a countdown clock? It's insanity."

I tried to look past her to the TV screen, but couldn't make out anything. My eyes wouldn't focus. All I could see was Leena lying on that blanket—the details washing over me again—a butterfly ring on the middle finger of her left hand, dirt and blood caked under her broken fingernails, the splotchy purple marks on her ankles.

"Bailey?" Hannah's voice snapped me back to attention and the images on the screen swam apart, forming five distinct faces. Yearbook photos from last year, one of each missing girl. I locked on Leena. Her sky-blue eyes, which would never again see. Her perfectly pink lips, which would never again smile. "What the hell? Are you even listening to me?"

"Yeah," I said, before taking another sip of water. "The reporters are doing their terrorize the public thing. I'm with you."

"Well, that's what I thought at first. But then I heard them saying stuff about Roger Turley."

"Suspect zero," I said, my voice a whisper, as I pictured the balding man who, in addition to being the first suspect, was also Emily Simms's step-father. Emily had been the first from *The Bakersville Dozen* to go missing, and the police had flagged Roger Turley from day one. The media had stalked him, blasting the airwaves with footage of things being confiscated as the police searched his home—a laptop, a few boxes of files, a bag of something that looked like clothing or blankets, a pair of tennis shoes—items that supposedly supported the rumors that Mr. Turley had sexually abused Emily. The list of evidence had included a diary with information on each girl in the video, proof, according to some pundits. Roger Turley had been escorted to the police station three times for questioning, but had never actually been charged. "I thought he'd been cleared."

"Not officially," Hannah said. "And today, the man is in even deeper."

"Why?" I asked, my heart leaping with the hope that this whole thing was about to end, that there was some way I could ease out of this insane scavenger hunt before I ever began playing. "Did they find evidence?"

"No."

"So why's Roger Turley in trouble?" I asked.

"Dumbass was busted for being on school grounds."

"After everything," Tripp said. "The guy's got balls."

"He was at the high school?" Wes asked. "Today?"

Hannah nodded, turning to face the television just as a clip of Roger Turley flashed on the screen. The footage showed him walking from his car to the front door of his house—Emily's house—his jaw set, his eyes dark and filled with anger.

"He was there with Emily's mother," Hannah said. "Apparently they went to pick up Emily's diploma."

"Didn't the class officers plan some memorial thing at the graduation next week?" I asked. "I thought they were going to honor each of the five girls and then hand their families the diplomas."

"They are," Hannah said. "But the principal told Emily's mother that he thought it would be best if her husband wasn't present, so now she's not going because she wants to show the world that she supports him."

"So he went to the school?" Wes asked. "Today?"

"Yeah," Hannah said, her fingers tapping the table, the glitter in her pink nail polish sparking in the kitchen light. "Which is apparently why the police were stationed by the office. The whole thing was planned. Mindee Selby is an office aid seventh period and she overheard the whole thing. Mr. Turley had permission to stop in for the diploma, but he wasn't supposed to wander beyond the main office. Somehow, the cops lost him when he said he had to use the restroom. Worst part? Totally creep-city, by the way—I saw him."

"At school?" I leaned forward until my chest hit the edge of the table. "Today?"

"Yup."

"Where?" Wes asked.

"Athletic wing. Stalking the girls' locker room."

"You cannot be serious," Wes said.

Hannah nodded, her eyes going wide. "I went to say goodbye to Coach Stevens after the Last Day Ceremony. Might be kinda cheesy, but she totally rocks and I wanted her to be the last teacher I saw before walking out forever, you know? Anyway, the hall leading to the parking lot was crazy, people shouting and practically jumping over each other to get outside. I waited until I'd pushed through the doors to the athletic hallway to text you, B, to let you know I might be a few minutes late and that you should wait for me at the car. Since I was texting, I didn't really look around, just kind of kept walking because no one was in my way. Until there was someone. Right there, in front of the doors leading to the girls' locker room."

"And it was him?" I asked. "Roger Turley?"

"Yeah. He grabbed my shoulders to keep me from falling. My phone dropped to the floor and after I bent down to pick it up, I was so freaked I just pushed through the locker room doors and ran toward Coach's office. But her door was closed and there was a sign on the window that said she'd be back in ten minutes. That's when my brain kicked in and I realized that a pair of stupid doors that said GIRLS wouldn't keep Roger Turley from following me if he wanted to, so I raced toward the back exit."

"Why the *hell* didn't you tell me any of this in the car on the way home from school?" I asked.

"At first, I didn't want to freak you out." Hannah bit her lip. "And then I didn't want to ruin your moment. You were so excited about that scavenger hunt."

My stomach lurched at the mention of the game. "Just tell us what happened. Did he follow you in?"

"I've never felt so alone in my entire life. And I was—*totally* alone, even with all those people just outside the athletic wing. Then, when I was about halfway to the back doors, I heard a locker slam. It scared the shit out of me, but I realized the sound had come from the direction I was heading, so it couldn't have been Mr. Turley. Unless he turned himself invisible and flew over my head. I called out like a loser from some horror movie, *Is anybody there?* and sure enough, someone was."

"Who?" I asked. "Who was it?"

"This is where it gets really freaky."

"We weren't already at really freaky?"

Hannah shook her head. "It was Sylvie Stalk-You-Long-Time Warner."

"In the girls' locker room?"

"By herself."

"Holy shit," I said. "What if he was there to take her?"

"Exactly what I was thinking." Hannah sucked in a shaky breath. "She was checking on the status of the volleyball scholarship that's being offered in Emily's name. Something about needing current information for the speech she's giving at graduation. Anyway, she flipped when I told her who was outside."

"Obviously."

"And then we ran out the back exit, around the outside of the gym, and straight to the parking lot."

"End of story?" Wes asked.

Hannah nodded.

"And now the guy's all over the news," Tripp said. "Coach Roberts found him just outside the athletic wing and called the main office. The police were already there to monitor his visit with Emily's mom, so it wasn't long before he was escorted off school grounds."

"Which I saw when I checked my phone after we got here," Hannah said, looking at me with her eyes wide. "For the record, with the way he was stalking Sylvie, I never would have allowed you to go out in those woods alone if I didn't know he was in custody. He's got to be the kidnapper, right? I mean, who else would—"

"You never know," Wes said. "Ask me, you can't be too careful."

I looked at the TV screen again. A reporter stood in front of the school reporting away while a banner scrolled across the bottom of the screen.

"It looks like our little Hannah is a hero," Tripp said, ruffling her hair.

Hannah swatted his hand away. "Don't touch. And I'm not a hero."

"You saved Sylvie Warner," Tripp said.

"Jesus," Wes said from behind me. "You really think he was there to get her?"

"What other explanation is there?" Hannah replied. "Tripp and I were about to call the cops, so I could tell them everything that happened."

"We were about to do the same thing," I said, thinking of Leena, all alone, lying out there in the grass.

"You were?" Tripp asked. "Why?"

I shook my head, pressing my fingers to my eyes. I didn't want to say it. The words would make Leena's death all-the-way real. Not to mention, this day was supposed to be the start of something new. It was officially summer break, and summer equals freedom. Instead, the Bakersville Dozen had taken the destruction of my life to a whole new level.

"It's kind of a long story," I said, looking at Wes.

"If Roger Turley is the one behind everything, maybe what happened today will give the cops enough reason to arrest him or hold him for more questioning or something." Hannah jiggled one of her feet. I could practically see the adrenaline surging through her veins.

"Yeah, and if they keep him off the streets, maybe no one else will end up missing." Tripp walked to the counter and grabbed the phone, stopping at the refrigerator where my mother had listed all of Bakersville's emergency numbers years ago. The contact info for the detective leading the investigation of the Bakersville Dozen was written in bold Sharpie on a Post-It just below.

I turned, looking over my shoulder. Wes was still there, gazing down at me, his eyebrows raised in question. When I looked back to my brother, I found him staring directly at me, the phone forgotten in his hand, hovering near his left ear.

"Somebody better tell me what the hell is going on here," he said, "or I swear to God, I'm gonna call Mom and Dad and tell them to ditch work and get their asses home."

Tripp leaned against the countertop. I stood, meeting his eyes as I crossed the room, closing the space between us in a few short strides. I reached for the phone, tugging it away from his face. "We found something—*someone*—out in the woods."

A look of confusion clouded his eyes. His face went white as his fingers loosened their grip on the phone.

I heard a deep voice reach through the line. "Detective Holly, here."

Tripp's hand released the phone. I pressed it to my ear, feeling oddly detached as I spoke into the receiver, my voice clearer and more determined than I would have ever thought possible.

"It's Bailey Holzman. I need to report evidence in the Bakersville Dozen case." I couldn't say it, the part about the body. And I couldn't say Leena's name and the word *dead* in the same sentence. Not yet. The police would know soon enough. For now, I had a little more time before my freedom slipped away forever.

CHAPTER 6

3:57 PM

"You guys found a dead body?" Hannah asked. "A *real live* dead body?"

"Most dead bodies aren't live, genius," Tripp said, dropping into the chair next to her, disbelief clouding his features. It reminded me of the way he'd looked the day we found out Grandma Holzman had died.

"Was it one of them?" Hannah looked at me, then Wes, her eyes wide. "Holy shit, it was, wasn't it?"

"Yes," I said. "But I don't really think we should—"

"Which one? Wait. Lemme guess."

"Hannah," I said, "this is not one of your slasher shows."

"Duh," she said with a weak smile. "But I've learned a lot from watching them. It was Emily Simms, right? Missing girl numero uno?"

I shook my head.

"Suze Moore, then?" Hannah's eyebrows lifted toward the ceiling. "The very last one he took?"

"No," I said. "Leena Grabman. Number two."

"Really?" Hannah started twirling her hair around one finger. "That's odd."

"You think?" Tripp asked, his words heavy with sarcasm.

"I'm not talking about the obvious," Hannah said. "I mean the pattern. Whoever did this is deviating from the pattern of the last five months. Instead of kidnapping a new girl, he's leaving a body behind for the first time. Unless he's left another body that just hasn't been found yet, but I doubt that with all the search teams still going out. He's switching up the order he started with. I don't get the point."

"Oh, there's a point," Wes said. "The killer wants to play a game. With Bailey."

"Holy. Shit." Hannah leaned forward, her elbows sliding across the table. "This is the scavenger hunt? Leena was the first treasure?"

"Yeah," I said. "I guess you could look at it that way. But I was going to leave that out."

Wes swiveled in his seat, his knees bumping my leg. "You really think we were going to get away with just telling them the part of the story where there's a dead body?"

"I don't know," I said. "I'm still figuring this out. I just want to keep everyone safe."

"What do you mean?" Tripp asked. "*You're* the one we need to keep safe."

"Just knowing about it puts you at risk, right?" I said.

"A scavenger hunt to find dead bodies," Hannah said. "Oh my God, B. That's awful. Even if Leena was the biggest bitch at BHS."

"Leena is—*was*—not a bitch," I said. "I told you to stop calling her that."

"Hey, I'm entitled to my own opinion."

"Hannah." Tripp put his hand on the top of her head. "Stop. Talking."

"Fine." Hannah gave a little snort and sat back in her chair. "For the record, I care, okay? These last five months have been awful and creepy and totally fucked up."

"I know you care," I said. "I saw your face every time we learned a new girl went missing, even when it was Leena. I saw you there every time the girls and I went out with a search party or put up posters or stood at one of those candlelight vigils."

"It's just so real," Hannah said, her eyes tearing up. "It's *too* real when I let myself think about it. Especially considering how that stupid video mixes you up in the whole thing."

"We need to focus," Tripp said. "Tell us more about this hunt."

"I don't want any of you involved," I said, shaking my head. "Wes kind of stumbled into this out there by the pond—"

"Yeah, *literally*," Wes said.

"But you guys have to keep your distance." I looked at the three of them, knowing this was the right decision, hating it because I needed help, but not at the expense of their safety. "You should all leave before the detective gets here. Let me handle this on my own."

"No way," Wes said.

Hannah nodded her agreement. "There's not a chance in hell we're leaving your side, B."

Tripp balled his hands into tight fists on the tabletop. "Someone's messing with my sister, they're gonna have to go through me first. You said that detective would be here in an hour?"

"They told me he's dealing with a pressing matter."

"I bet that pressing matter has a name." Hannah snorted. "Roger. Turley."

"That gives us time." Tripp leaned forward, his chest bumping the edge of the table. "Now, spill."

"I can't." I sighed. "It's too dangerous for you guys to be involv—"

"The first clue said she had to find five trophies over the next four days." Hannah said, tipping her head to one side with an I-dare-you-to-stop-me look in her eyes.

"Five girls are missing," I whispered. "I officially hate the number five."

"There are rules, too," Hannah said. "She has to follow the directions exactly, she has to see this thorough to the end, that kind of thing."

"I'm not supposed to call the cops," I added. "And if I break a rule or fail to follow a clue, I'll face a penalty."

"A penalty?" Tripp asked.

I nodded. "It pretty much said I'd be responsible for more girls going missing. And dying. But if I play along, I have the chance to save them."

"Incredible bait," Tripp said. "Enough to control every move you make."

"I cannot believe Leena Grabman is lying out there, dead," Hannah said, her eyes shifting from me to Wes to Tripp, her voice strengthening with every word. "And this guy is threatening Bailey? No fucking way. We have to go out there."

"Seriously, Hannah," Wes said. "You don't want to see her. Not even if she was the biggest bitch at BHS."

"The bitch part is a simple fact. And I'm not saying I *want* to see her," Hannah said. "But it's the best way to get more information. If we know how she died, or can get clues from her body, then—"

"No!" I shoved my chair away from the table and stood, glaring down at all of them. "You're not playing detective, Hannah. We are not going back out there."

"I don't think we have a choice, Bailey."

I glanced toward the television, the footage of an angry Roger Turley walking from his car to his front door, looping again and again and again.

"None of us are going out there," I said, looking first at Hannah, then Tripp, and finally at Wes. "Okay?"

Hannah nodded, but she wouldn't look me in the eye. I knew she wasn't going to let this go.

"Hannah," I said, "Leena is dead. *Dead.* Do you hear me? We can't do anything now except—"

A screeching sound ripped through the kitchen, freezing us for a moment before time felt like it raced forward again. We all swiveled toward the screen door.

At first, all I could see was a dark shadow standing in the doorway, blocking out the sun. My skin prickled, and my entire body screamed for me to run. I thought it was him—whoever was behind the missing girls, the scavenger hunt, and Leena lying there dead. I thought he'd come to get me.

But then I saw Jude.

In three steps, I'd leaped into his arms, burying my face between his shoulder and neck, drinking in his solid heat and the steady pressure of his hands folding against my back.

CHAPTER 7

4:14 PM

Jude picked me up and twirled me in a circle. "You should always be this glad to see me. What's up, B? You seem upset."

I couldn't think of a thing to say. At least, nothing that I could say to Jude. As much as I wanted to tell him about what had happened, I couldn't pull him into the mess, too. There was too much at risk.

But Jude was looking at me, his eyes wide, waiting for an answer.

"It's the news," Hannah said from behind me. "This whole thing with Roger Turley being at school."

"Yeah," I said, turning to Hannah and mouthing, *Thank you*.

But then I saw them—the two red envelopes with my name in bold print. Standing on my tiptoes, I bumped my nose against Jude's, trying to block his view of the table. "I might just need some fresh air. Can we go outside?"

"Sure," he said, his mouth crinkling up for a moment. "But I'm not actually here to see you."

"Oh," I said, confused.

"Shit, man!" Tripp said. "I was supposed to meet you."

"No worries." Jude grabbed my hand and spun me toward the door. "Follow us out?"

I stepped through the doorway and into the blinding light of the early-June day. Jude was there, his hand gripping mine, keeping me steady without even knowing it as I moved across the deck and down the five steps that led to a shady patch of grass.

"Been a long time, bro," Tripp said when we were all standing together in the shade. "How are things?"

I noticed the front of Jude's truck peeking from the space between our house and Wes's, and wondered why he hadn't parked at the end of the drive, next to Hannah's Escape.

"Couldn't be better." Jude squeezed my hand. "Last day of high school. Graduation's next week. We've got the whole summer ahead of us."

"I'm with you." Tripp offered a half-smile. "Exams are over. I passed freshman year. I'm officially finished with dorm life."

"Tomorrow night's party is going to rock the start of summer." Jude laughed, holding a fist out to Wes. "Good to see you again, man."

"Always," Wes said as he bumped Jude's fist with his own. Guilt exploded through my chest, watching the two of them together. But then I reminded myself that Wes and I were the only ones who had any idea of our history. All I had to do was keep it that way and no one would get hurt.

Jude stepped back until he was by my side again, the motion so natural it gave me a boost of strength. Jude's arm glided around my waist, pulling me tight. I leaned into his body, tilting my head onto his shoulder.

"You guys still going to get those fireworks tonight?" I asked, wishing he could stay, knowing he couldn't because I needed to keep him safe, too.

"Yeah," he said. "Sucks that we have to truck it all the way to Kentucky for the big ones, but it'll be worth it tomorrow night when we're watching the show."

"The cash is inside." Tripp turned, taking the steps two at a time. "After you texted me, I hit up all the BHS grads I saw during exam week—every single one of them was planning to come. This is going to be a huge-ass party, you know?"

"You got that," Jude said, his fingers twisting the braided belt looped through my capris. "Jonesy's parties always are."

"His parents are okay with the crowd?" Hannah asked, her bare feet swimming in the grass, toenails glistening with the same glittery pink polish she'd used on her fingernails.

"They're out of town," a voice said from behind Jude and me. I turned and found Jonesy walking toward us, the line of woods a shadow behind him, his trademark, one-dimpled grin lighting up his face. "Annual trip out west to a bunch of wineries with their dinner group. Won't be home until the day before graduation."

Lane was a few steps behind Jonesy, his eyes shaded by the brim of a Bakersville High School baseball cap. "His safety has been entrusted to his two older brothers. Like that should be some kind of relief."

"We're expecting a few hundred, minimum," Jonesy said. "My brothers mowed the back field yesterday so there'll be enough room for everyone to camp out."

"Standard rules apply." Lane wrapped an arm around Jonesy's neck as they stepped into our circle—it was a cross between a hug and some awkward wrestling move. "Most importantly, no one drives off the property until morning. Last thing we need's a five-oh alert for this one."

From inside the kitchen, Tripp kicked the screen door open and stepped down to the grass. "Here you go, man. It's—" Tripp stopped mid-sentence, noticing Jonesy and Lane. "Hey. Where'd you two come from?"

"I was about to ask the same thing," Hannah said, her eyes darting from the tree line to Jude's friends.

"Woods." Jonesy threw his thumb over his shoulder. "We walked from my place. Jude told us to meet him here so we could collect the rest of the cash before we head out."

"This is almost two hundred," Tripp said, handing a wad of cash to Jude. "Sorry, again, that I didn't meet you after school. My mom left a list of shit for me to do this morning, and I kinda passed out on the couch after I finished."

"No big deal." Jude squeezed me against him. "Bailey made it worth the trip."

"Ugh." Hannah rolled her eyes. "Stop. You were already voted Cutest Couple. Had pictures taken for the yearbook and everything. No need to shove all that sickening happiness in our faces."

"Agreed," Jonesy said.

"Jealous much?" Jude laughed and nuzzled his face in my neck, planting a string of kisses from my ear to my collarbone. I looked at Wes as Jude's lips touched my skin—I couldn't help it—and the guilt sizzled to life again. I didn't deserve Jude. I hadn't for months now. But when I noticed the look in Wes's eyes, the guilt was burned away by a new feeling. Confusion. Wes didn't look angry or irritated or even bored. He looked hurt.

"So, Bailey," Jonesy said, "you coming to the party?"

"Dude," Jude said, "I told you not to mention that."

"Sorry, man, I was just thinking if we all talk to her, let her know we'll watch out for her, that maybe—"

"She's not going," Tripp said.

"Yeah." I swept a strand of hair behind one ear. "But I totally understand Jude's commitment to help, so no worries."

"I heard all of *The Bakersville Dozen* girls are too scared to camp at the farm, so they're heading to Warner's house for a slumber party."

"Dude," Lane said. "Terrified girls dressed in nighties? We should hit that."

Hannah smacked Lane on the shoulder. "Have some respect."

"Fair warning," I said. "Cops are staking out Sylvie's to make sure everyone's safe. I'd steer clear."

"Maybe they're using you as bait," Jonsey said with a laugh. "All of you in one place? Makes it easier to figure out where the next girl'll go missing." He paused then, looking around, his laughter faded away. "That was insensitive, yeah? I'm sorry. I didn't mean to—"

"Well, it doesn't matter, because Bailey isn't going," Hannah said. "It's a girls' night for us."

"Wait, you're staying here?" Jude asked. "Isn't that going to piss Sylvie off?"

I shrugged. "I don't really care. All I want to do is hang out with Hannah. And maybe, just maybe, if we get bored, we might swing by the farm."

"You're kidding," Jude said, pulling me tighter, a grin spreading across his face.

"Yeah," Tripp said. "She is. Because she's not going to any party tomorrow night. She's staying right here."

"Lighten up, Tripp. I could go for a few. Just to feel normal. I deserve that much, don't I?"

I did. I knew I did. Normal was something I needed. But that wasn't the only reason I was thinking about the party. The latest clue had directed me to Jonesy's farm. If I had the chance to save someone, I had to do everything in my power to try. Once I told the detective about the clues, I'd convince him to let me go to Jonesy's. I might be able to help them catch whoever was behind this.

Tripp shook his head. "Right now, it's not about what you deserve, B. It's about keeping you safe."

"You guys should get going." Hannah grabbed my hand and spun me away from Jude. "Whether we're there or not, fireworks are important for tomorrow night."

Jude reached out and snagged my wrist, pulling me back to his side. I wanted to melt into him, but I couldn't. I had to face this scavenger hunt on my own. He kissed me, the action so natural it didn't matter that we were standing in front of everyone. Until I thought of the look I'd seen in Wes's eyes, and, for a flash, all of my guilt blossomed again.

"I'll call you when we get back," Jude whispered into my ear. "I want to see you later tonight, okay?"

I closed my eyes, feeling Jude's voice wash over me. Then his hand slipped free from mine, and they were walking away—Jude, Jonesy, and Lane—side-by-side, toward the red Ford pickup Jude had bought from his grandfather the year before.

"You think he heard anything?" Hannah asked as they hopped into the cab, both doors slamming as the engine roared to life. "Before he came into the kitchen, we were talking about her."

"You're asking if he heard us talking about a dead chick out at the pond, and then played it off for the next ten minutes?" Tripp's voice was soft, like he was afraid someone was listening in.

"Stupid question?" Hannah asked.

"Yeah," Tripp said. "Very."

"He didn't hear anything." I watched as Jude pulled forward, circling the end of the driveway and heading back the way he'd come, waving just before he disappeared between the two houses. "If he thought something was up, he never would have left my side."

CHAPTER 8

4:33 PM

"Unless, of course, he's in on it," Wes said, his eyes locking on mine.

"What?" I asked.

Hannah snorted. "Seriously?"

"Guys who look like saints? They usually aren't." Wes clenched his teeth, his jaw tight.

"You're just jealous," Hannah said. "You couldn't be committed to a ham sandwich for more than ten minutes."

"No offense or anything, B," Wes said with a shake of his head, "but Jude could never compare to me."

As I stood there in the grass by the deck, I felt like my heart was going to break open. Part of me—a part that I would never give into again—believed him. But that was nothing more than a momentary lapse—reflex. Which is exactly what had happened five months ago, the night Wes's family hosted their annual Christmas party. I loved Jude. And that was all that mattered.

"If you're crazy enough to bring up Jude, you might as well throw Jonesy and Lane into the mix," Hannah said. "I mean, they both just waltzed out of the woods."

"Point taken." Wes shrugged. "It's worth considering all three."

"Well, it isn't Jude," I said. "My boyfriend is not a killer."

"Why are we even talking about any of those guys?" Hannah asked. "May I remind you that Roger Turley was at the high school today?"

"He could have put the clue in my locker. Combinations are still listed on the homeroom class lists, and those are always at the attendance desk."

"I'm all for creating a list of suspects," Tripp said. "But first, we have to consider our options."

"What options?" I asked, my mind spinning as it returned to the memory of Leena's body, lying there, so very still.

"Option one," Tripp said, "we wait for the cops."

"I thought that's what we were doing," I said.

"Yeah, but they won't be here for a while yet. We need to consider the clues, right? Try to figure out the identity of—"

"*No,*" I said. "I've already broken one rule. I'm worried enough about the penalty for that."

"How in the hell would a kidnapper-slash-killer have insider information?" Tripp asked. "It's an obvious bluff to scare you into silence."

"But what if it's not," Hannah said. "What if the killer has a way to keep track of Bailey's movements?"

"You're creeping me out," I said, taking a deep breath.

Tripp backed toward the deck and sat on one of the wooden steps. "Option two: We do whatever this freak says—with the police as back-up, of course—follow the clues and don't mess around."

"Not a good idea," Wes said. "The killer would be in control of everything then. Us. The girls who are missing. And the police."

"What if we turn it around on him?" Hannah looked at me, her eyes glistening with a crazy scheme. "We all know who the most likely suspect is. Since I saw Turley at school, we have something to go on. It's a way to spin this whole thing so we can track him down and—"

"How do you suggest we do that?" I asked. "Seeing Roger Turley in the athletic wing is way different than seeing him in front of my open locker with a red envelope in his hand. And tracking him down once he's released? If he's the killer, that's beyond dangerous."

"Look," Hannah said with an exaggerated sigh. "I don't know, okay? But we have to try something here. Something that'll trip him up. Whoever this is, he's messing with all of us now. And if we have the chance to save those girls, we can't fuck it up."

"Just because Roger Turley looks guilty doesn't mean it's him." Wes backed his way to the porch railing, crossing one foot over the other as he leaned against it. "The only thing we know for sure is that whoever it is, he's close enough to you to know details about your life, where you live, that the pond is one of your favorite places, and—"

"If you look at it that way," Tripp said, "we have a lot more to go on than a few random clues and a dead body."

"Yeah," Hannah said. "If we list all the little things, we might just be able to make some progress."

"Maybe we can nail down a few more suspects," Tripp said. "Wes and I can watch them at the party tomorrow night. Mr. Turley or not, the killer has to slip up at some point. We can help catch him."

"Jude's at the top of my list," Wes said.

Hannah laughed, like Wes had made a hilarious of joke. Tripp just shook his head. I almost told Wes to drop the jealous act—*he* was the player extraordinaire—but I couldn't say anything, not with Tripp and Hannah standing right there.

He wouldn't pull me in. Not this way. Not any way. It was exactly what he wanted.

"Whatever," I said. "You go right ahead and keep an eye on Jude . . . Hannah and I can watch everyone else."

"No way," Tripp said. "Wes and I will cover the party. Mom and Dad would kill me if anything—"

"I have to go," I insisted. "I'm sure the cops'll agree. After all these months, I'm the only person who's had contact with the killer. They can set up some kind of surveillance or wire me or—"

"Forget the cops," Hannah said. "Forget the party and the next clue. We have to act now. You guys already know what I think we should do next."

"No way," Wes said. "We are not going back to the pond, Han. Trust me. You don't want to see the body. Besides that, we're waiting for the detective."

"We have time." Hannah pulled her phone from the pocket in her sundress. "About a half hour. It's the best way to gather more information."

"No." Wes uncrossed his ankles and took a step forward.

He kept talking, but the sudden rushing in my head blocked out his voice. All I could see were his ankles. Crossed and uncrossed, one slipping off of the other. My eyes blurred until Wes's ankles were no longer his, but different, pale and dainty. The image of Leena lying at the pond leaped to my mind. I had missed something. Something so obvious.

Leena had been placed there on that blanket. Her hair was spread around her head and shoulders like she was floating in water. Her arms had been propped on her chest like she was sleeping. Her legs, gray and waxy, were crossed delicately at the ankle.

"He posed her," I said, interrupting Wes. "Leena. He posed her body."

"He did?" Hannah looked from me to Wes, and back again, her eyes wide. "How could you leave that out? It changes everything."

"There's more," I said.

"I don't want to hear it." Hannah stood, her sundress swooshing around her legs. "We have to go out there. I need to see her."

"She moved." My voice was so soft, I could hardly hear my own words. I cleared my throat and I said them again. "Leena moved."

"I'm confused," Tripp said. "Leena moved? As in, she's not really dead?"

"Trust me, dude," Wes said, "that chick is completely and totally, all the way dead."

"But she moved." I looked at Wes. "When you grabbed the clue, her legs were crossed at the ankle. And when we fell, we bumped her and the top leg slipped off. Aren't dead bodies supposed to be as hard as stone?"

"Holy shit." Hannah tipped her head, checking her phone for a moment before she answered. "Rigor mortis."

"Yeah," I said. "That."

Hannah's fingers danced across the screen, her eyes squinting in the sunlight. "According to Wikipedia, rigor mortis starts three to four hours after death, reaching maximum—eew—*stiffness* after twelve hours, and gradually dissipates until approximately forty-eight to sixty hours later."

"So," Tripp said, "she either died sometime this afternoon, maybe even late morning, or it was a few days ago."

"It's the first week of June. Sunny and eighty degrees with humidity," Hannah said. "Was she showing any signs of decomposition?"

"What, exactly, does that look like?" Wes asked.

"I'm not sure," Hannah said, her nose crinkling, "but I think you'd pretty much know."

"She was gray. And the bottoms of her legs were kind of black and splotchy."

"Blood starts pooling to the lowest part of the body right after death," Hannah told us. "Do you guys realize what this means?"

"You watch *way* too many crime dramas?" Tripp asked.

"No, genius. It means that she's been alive all this time." Hannah's words were punchy and forceful. "Leena's been alive since the guy took her that first week of February."

"That means the others could be, too!" I felt a new surge of hope.

"And if they are, we have the chance to save them," Hannah said. "But only if we gather evidence before the cops come in and shut us out of the investigation. Even if they use Bailey for the clues, they won't tell us a thing."

I looked at Hannah, Tripp, and Wes; they'd all gone silent. My mind replayed a million little moments that had passed since Emily Simms went missing in January—tying yellow ribbons to the trees in the center of town, their forked tails whipping in the breeze of an approaching storm; listening to the press conferences where each set of parents pleaded for the return of their daughter; avoiding the news vans and reporters lined up at the front of the high school, throwing facts around like they didn't affect real people. The details shuffled through my mind. If we played our hand right, we might be able to return four girls to their grieving families. We had the chance to take the tragedy that had brought our entire town to its knees and turn the whole thing into a miracle.

Hannah started walking then, away from the house and the sweet gum and the three of us, her arms swinging, her sundress swishing back and forth with each determined step.

"Where the hell are you going?" Tripp asked.

"To see Leena," Hannah called over her shoulder. "You guys coming or not?"

CHAPTER 9

4:47 PM

"You're really just going to stand there?" Hannah asked, hugging herself. Behind her, the tall grass leaped toward the sky, as if each blade wanted to flee from Leena's body as much as I did. Tripp was there, too, looking smaller somehow, and pale.

"Yes, I'm going to stand right here," I said, leaning against the old tree at the water's edge. My capris caught on a rusted nail poking out from one of the ladder rungs I'd climbed earlier. "I saw her already. The image is burned on the inside of my eyelids, so if you need my input on anything, I'll just refer to my mental files."

"Fine." Hannah sighed. "Wesley?"

"I'm going to stick with B," he said.

Hannah turned and placed a hand on Tripp's back. "At least you're not a total wuss. Lead the way?"

"This was your idea," he said, his feet shuffling on the soft ground. "Shouldn't you go first?"

"Pathetic," Hannah said, then snorted. She reached out with both hands and parted the grass, stepping through the screen it created. After a few seconds of mental preparation, Tripp followed her. The grass swooshed back into place, serrated edges linking together. In just a few steps, every trace of Hannah and Tripp had disappeared.

I swiveled toward the pond watching the late-afternoon sunlight filter through the trees to dance on the surface of the water.

From the corner of my eye, I saw Wes squat and pick up a rock; then he stood and tossed it across the water's surface. It skipped five times. *Not bad.* But it didn't beat his record.

"I don't get why you're so pissed," he said. "That night at the Christmas party, after . . . you said you couldn't talk to me anymore. I did what you wanted, so why—"

"I'm not pissed." Guilt washed through me for Wes again, instead of Jude. Which was ridiculous. It's not like I'd broken the heart of the biggest player I'd ever known.

"If you're not pissed"—Wes's voice was a gravelly whisper—"why is it so hard for you to look at me?"

My eyes snapped to his, a lifetime of memories fluttering through my mind like the pages of a flip-book. Us out here as kids, Tripp by our sides, the three of us racing circles around the pond, fishing, playing hide and seek in the woods. Us as teens, me harboring a secret crush, watching Wes bring home one pretty girl after another, sure that he'd never see me. And then, last summer, the moment he finally did; how I'd pressed myself against his body, hoping to make sure he'd never again see anyone else.

"Just let it go." I twisted away from him, the tree's rough bark biting into my arm and shoulder as I tried to push away the memory of his smooth skin burning against mine, the need I had felt as I lay wrapped in his arms.

Wes tossed another rock. I closed my eyes, pushing him out. Wes didn't matter anymore. What we'd had was over before it even began. I had Jude now. He wasn't afraid to show the world that he loved me.

But no matter how hard I tried, I couldn't block the memory of the night things between Wes and me had changed forever. The night this whole crazy thing had begun.

He'd come home late—the middle of a night when sleep had totally escaped me—windows down, music blaring, baseball cap backward as he slipped out of his truck and slammed the door shut. One chance glance and he started walking my way, flipping his keys around his thumb and catching them in the palm of his hand. *Ca-chunk, ca-chunk, ca-chunk.* I was on the hammock, one leg trailing to the ground, toes curled into the cool dirt beneath me, pushing myself slowly back and forth as I gazed through the canopy of leaves to the stars filling the blue-black sky.

He motioned for me to scoot over. As he slipped onto the canvas, I turned onto my side and rested my cheek on his arm. He twisted, facing me, his eyes locked on mine. His breath smelled like beer, pot, and bubblegum. His eyelashes swept up and down, his chest rising and falling, breaths shaky and tense.

I wondered if he wanted me. I hoped so.

Tilting my chin up slightly—very slightly—I closed the inches separating us, and did the thing I'd spent years imagining.

He froze when my lips met his. I wondered if he could hear my heart crashing against my ribs, but then his hand slid down my side, grabbing my waist and pulling me closer. With the hammock swaying us from side to side, the heat of his skin and silky feel of his lips lit me on fire.

He'd swept a strand of hair from my eye, his thumb tracing the outline of my jaw. "This has to be our secret, B. I don't know how people would feel—your parents, Tripp. This has to be just for us."

"I can keep a secret," I'd said with a smile. "As long as we keep doing this." I kissed him again, harder, arching my body toward his as his fingertips teased their way beneath the hem of my tank top.

Pulling myself back to the pond, I opened my eyes, looking right at him. "I kissed you," I said. "I'm the one who started it. I should have known better."

"Yeah," Wes said. "I guess you should have."

"Especially after you came up with that plan," I said. "One night a week, just us and the stars, right here at the pond. Our secret."

"It wasn't like I—"

"Please, don't, okay? It was stupid. I knew it would never last. And now it's over."

"But—"

"Wes, I just can't. Especially now. With this scavenger hunt and Leena and the rest of those gir—"

"Bailey, I'm sorry." Wes walked toward me, the fabric of his cargo shorts rustling with each step. He grabbed both of my hands, pulling them to his chest. My body soaked up his heat, his energy, every piece of me vibrating with the nearness of him.

"I am so sorry for the way that I let you call things off when I left for school last fall. That I didn't fight harder. But I didn't know how I would feel. Not until I left and—"

"Stop." My eyes started to sting and tears spilled down my cheeks. I almost told him the one thing I'd always regretted keeping to myself. "Please, just stop."

But I heard Hannah's voice—shrill, staccato—and Tripp's—deep, shaky. Yanking away from Wes, I swiped the tears from my cheeks and shoved my hands in my pockets. My fingers grazed a folded slip of paper, which felt like a touchstone bringing me back to reality. I squeezed my eyes tight, feeling like the worst person in the world, and pulled the paper free.

> I CAN'T WAIT TO SPEND THE SUMMER WITH YOU. THIS IS OUR TIME, B. I WON'T LET ANYONE TAKE IT AWAY.
>
> —JUDE

So I wasn't just the worst person in the world. I was the worst person in the entire universe. I crinkled the note in my hand, ducking toward the big tree just as the curtain of grass parted with a slithery rustle.

"She's wearing her tiara," Hannah said, her words sharp and sure as she marched toward us. "You guys failed to mention that little detail."

"What the hell are you talking about?" Wes asked.

"I'm talking about Miss Leena Grabman, the only chick in America who could pull off a landslide win for prom queen without even being near the school the entire quarter before the vote. The tiara she should have been crowned with, but couldn't be, seeing as she'd been missing for three months? *It's on her head.*"

"No way." I pictured Leena lying there on that blanket, the cascade of her so-blonde-it's-almost-white hair rippling around her head and shoulders. "There was no tiara. Not when we saw her."

"Bailey's right," Wes said. "I don't remember any tiara."

"Maybe you just missed it," Tripp said. "It is a pretty gruesome scene. An awful lot to process when you're taken by surprise like that."

"Give me some credit," I said. "I'm telling you, she didn't have a tiara on her head."

"Well, there's one there now," Tripp said.

"And it's the same one from prom," Hannah said. "I'd know it anywhere. Three rows of tiny crystal flowers, a single black rhinestone in the center of each."

"So what?" Wes shrugged. "With everything else going on, why is some stupid tiara such a big deal?"

Hannah snorted. "First off, that tiara's supposed to be locked in a display case at the high school."

"So whoever did this has access to the school," Wes said, "and they're close enough to know that the tiara would've gone to Leena."

"Right, but there's more to it," Hannah said. "That tiara was in the display case *today*. I saw it during the Last Day Ceremony."

"I did, too," I said, remembering the spark and flare of those fake diamonds.

"So whoever killed her was in the building this afternoon," Tripp said. "Up close and personal. Stealing tiaras. Leaving notes in my sister's locker." He took a deep breath. "It was either Turley or someone who blends in, someone who didn't raise any suspicion. Guys, we gotta get back to the house. We need to tell the detective everything we know."

"Right," I said. "If we screw this up, all those girls could all end up just like Leena."

"I'm glad you're on board." Tripp grabbed my hands, squeezing hard. "All of this is too much for us to handle. If anything happened to you—"

"However you look at this, I'm at risk," I said. "Nothing's going to take that away. Which is why we have to follow the clue. It's the only way to get the answers we need. The answers the police need."

"Follow the clue?" Tripp asked, throwing his arms in the air. "Are you fucking serious right now? No way the cops are going to allow that."

"Then we convince them." I shrugged, like it would be nothing, but I knew it would be next to impossible. "If we can't, we have to follow that clue on our own."

"Okay, say we do." Tripp laughed, but the sound was distorted, half-crazy. "What comes next?"

"You guys need to stop arguing." Hannah's eyes were wide as she looked from Tripp to me. "Just *stop*."

"Bailey needs to stop," Tripp snapped. Then he looked right at me. "For one second, B, you need to think. What if by following these clues, trying to save one of those girls, you risk your own life? Or one of ours? What if we play this stupid game and one of us dies? How are you going to feel then?"

"What the hell kind of question is that?"

"One you need to think about, B. If you refuse to play, there's no game." He sighed, running a hand through his hair. "Let the cops figure this out. That's what they're trained to do. That's *if* we're right and the girls are still alive."

"Flip side, what if the cops, who've botched everything they've touched so far, still can't find whoever's behind this? It's been five months and all they've got are some suspicions about Roger Turley, which haven't led to any charges. Let's face it, they need our help. If this is someone close, we might be the best in they have."

"She's got a point," Hannah said.

"Shut up, Hannah." Tripp glared at her before turning his attention to Wes. "Little help here, bro?"

"Honestly, I can see both sides. I'm torn."

"Well, I'm not," Tripp snapped. "I don't care what any of you say. We're done with this insane debate about tracking down a killer and the girls he took who may or may not be alive. And we are most definitely not following any more stupid-ass clues."

I turned to my brother. "I'm not going to lie, I'd feel better with all of you by my side. But I'm not going to force you, so if you want out, fine." I shoved past him, moving around the edge of the pond, eyes fixed on the trailhead. "Do whatever you have to do. But you can't make me stop."

"Bailey!" Tripp called, fear tingeing the word. "Where the hell are you going?"

"Home. To talk to the detective. And then, school. I'm going to see if I can find out who stole that tiara from the display case." I let the words hang in the air between us, hoping he'd give in; I wasn't sure I could do this without him.

"What? Like someone's just going to tell you?"

"Dammit, Tripp, I don't know, okay?" I stopped, turning back to face him. He stood motionless by the tree, right where

I'd left him, his face red and splotchy. Hannah was walking away. She looked like she was about to be sick. And Wes was following ten feet behind me, his mouth set in a grim line.

"You can't," Tripp pleaded. "It's too dangerous."

"I have to. If I was missing, wouldn't you want someone to at least try?"

"She's right." Wes pressed his lips together, his eyes turning to steel. "No matter the risks, we're in. All of us. Together. Forget about the other girls if you have to. The most important thing here is Bailey. She needs us. And it's our job to help her."

Tripp closed his eyes and clenched his jaw. "If something happens, I swear to God, I'll hold you responsible, Wes."

"We're not going to let anything happen," he replied. "Not if we stick together."

"That's great in theory. But what if you're wrong?"

"We can do this," Hannah said. "This guy is close. We can help catch him."

"You three aren't going to let this go, are you?" Tripp asked.

"No," Hannah said. She walked back to Tripp, grabbed his hand, and tugged him along. He took one step, two, three, falling in behind her. "At the very least, come to the high school with us and try to find out who took the tiara. There are security cameras all over the place, right? We just have to figure out a way to watch the footage. If you want to reevaluate the situation after that when we're planning out the next step, fine."

"Don't worry, bro, we're going to keep one another safe." Wes tilted his chin, a smile lighting his face before he turned back toward me, his eyes softening. "For the record," he whispered, stepping closer to me, "I agree with Tripp. We should leave all of this to the cops."

"If that's what you think, then why are you—"

"I'm tired of fighting." Wes reached toward me, but I pulled away. "You need to know that you can count on me. This time I'm not going to let you down."

I didn't know how to respond. I wasn't even sure what I was feeling as I led the way out of the woods.

I'd been able to push thoughts of Wes out of my mind for the entire school year—minus the minor slip-up during Winter Break. But now he was back, making me question everything I thought I knew.

CHAPTER 10

5:02 PM

My thoughts were racing as we walked along the trail. I tried to remind myself that everything with Wes was too much. That the crazy way I'd always loved him might have felt better than anything, but it had ended up hurting more than anything, too. As we moved past the trees, crossing through thick shadows and streaks of light, I reminded myself that none of that mattered anymore. It never would again. Jude was my here and now, and I couldn't be luckier.

I shoved away the guilty feelings that had bubbled to the surface. After the summer Wes and I had shared, it was natural for questions to linger, I told myself. Now that he was home from college, I just needed a little time to find my balance.

"So, how are we going to get our hands on the security footage?" I asked, pushing myself to concentrate on the next major task.

"This is your brilliant idea," Tripp said. "Don't you already have a plan?"

"Drop the attitude. Really not helping."

"The administration isn't just going to welcome us in for a complimentary viewing," Hannah said. "What if we say we need footage of Last Day Ceremony to play at graduation? They're supposed to have a slideshow or video rolling as people find seats."

"Security footage at graduation?" Wes asked, reaching out to swing a low-hanging branch to the side of the path. "That'll never fly. Not with the scandal of Roger Turley being on school grounds today."

"You have any other ideas?" I asked.

"I might," Wes said, looking at me.

I ignored him and focused on Hannah, watching as she ducked under the arch of Wes's arm, disappearing behind a thick of trees as she crossed from the trailhead back into our yard.

I followed right behind her. As soon as I was out of the woods, I saw a boxy black-and-white police car parked dead-even between our house and Wes's. An officer stood on the back porch of my house, looking through the screen door into the kitchen.

"You think someone's watching right now?" I asked. "Whoever wrote those notes said they'd know if I broke a rule."

"No way anyone can watch your every move," Tripp said, his voice quiet, like he wasn't quite sure if he even believed it himself. "It's an obvious bluff to control your moves. We have to tell the cops about Leena and this scavenger hunt, B."

I yanked my phone from my pocket to check the time. "How long do you think he's been here?"

"Stop freaking out," Wes said. "Just act natural."

"That should be easy," Hannah said with a snort, picking up the pace and leading the way across the yard.

By the time we'd made it a third of the way, the cop saw us. He walked down the steps, and crossed the yard. As he got closer, I saw that it was Tiny Simmons, one of the officers who stood watch over the Last Day Ceremony. Tripp and he had played baseball together, Little Leagues and then select, all the way up until Tiny had graduated a few years ago.

"Tripp," Tiny said, giving my brother a nod, the sun glinting off the badge hanging from the front pocket of his dark blue shirt. "How you been?"

"Good, man," Tripp said. "You?"

"Just fine." Tiny hitched his pants higher on his waist.

"You're through your training?"

"Yup. Officially Officer Simmons now."

Tripp smiled. "Your old man must be proud."

Tiny shrugged, his eyes skipping from Tripp to me. He waited several beats too long before he spoke. "I hear you have some evidence in the Bakersville case?"

"Yeah," I said. "But I usually talk to Detective Holly. Is he still in charge of the case?"

Tiny's lips twitched, pulling back into an eerie smile for a moment before dropping into a straight line again. "He's working with Detective Gray, the lead from the FBI. They're a little busy this afternoon. Holly asked me to drop by and see what you had to share."

"Oh," I said, my skin crawling under Tiny's gaze. I remembered that now. He'd always had a certain creep factor. And hadn't there been something about him and the BHS computer lab and a raunchy porn site? As I stood there, I could picture Tripp in the kitchen, telling the story, laughing about how stupid Tiny had been to get caught.

"It's Roger Turley, isn't it?" Hannah said. "They're busy because he's been arrested?"

"I'm not supposed to discuss the details of—"

"Any charges filed are a public record."

Tiny shrugged. That smile surfaced on his lips again. But there was nothing friendly about it. "He hasn't been arrested. He's been taken into custody."

"Whatever. It's all over the news," Hannah said. "I was wondering if—"

"Usually, I ask the questions." His irritation was evident as he looked from Hannah to me. "I have a quick one, if you'll indulge me before we move on to whatever it is that you called about."

"Okay," I said. His eyes trailed from my face all the way down to my feet and back up again, leaving me with the distinct feeling that I had just been visually violated.

"Your label," he said. "The label given to you in the video—"

"Like a virgin," Hannah interjected, stepping closer to my side. "What about it?"

"We've been wondering what it means." Tiny cleared his throat. "The other labels are fairly clear. But yours is a bit ambiguous."

"Are you asking my sister if she's a virgin?" Tripp's words felt like a challenge.

Tiny held his hands in the air, like he was surrendering, but the look in his eyes made it clear he was enjoying himself. "We need to understand every aspect of this case. The label attached to Bailey doesn't offer enough information for us to determine—"

"I don't see how Bailey's private life is any of your business." Tripp stood tall, chest out, and took a step toward Tiny.

"Yo. Dude," Tiny said, meeting him, upping the ante with a challenge of his own. "Chill, okay. Just doing my job."

I stole a quick glance at Wes, my cheeks blazing, wanting to hide away because no one knew the truth about my virginity. No one but the two of us.

Tiny shifted his weight, looking from Tripp to me, his expression impossible to read. Something felt way off.

"Bailey called about Mr. Turley," Wes said, placing himself at an angle, so that he was partially between Tiny and me. I was startled at first, with Wes so close.

"What about Mr. Turley?" Tiny asked, his eyes narrowing.

I looked to Tripp, hoping he would take over. I wasn't prepared for the change in plans and I had no idea how we were going to get out of this without spilling the whole truth. Or even if we should. Suddenly, every way this could play out felt dangerous.

"I saw Mr. Turley," Hannah said with a shrug. "At school. By the locker room. Bailey wanted to make sure the police were aware. That was before we turned on the TV and saw that he'd been arres—Sorry. Taken into custody."

"That's all?" Tiny asked, rolling his head from side to side like he needed to crack his neck.

"It kinda felt like a big deal," Hannah said.

"I had a few questions, too," I said, jumping in. "I wanted to know if you think it's safe for me to go out this weekend. Roger Turley is otherwise occupied. It's graduation. I've just felt so trapped these last few months."

"I'm sure it's been difficult," Tiny said. The smile was back. Fake and placating.

"This whole thing has me so off balance. I want information one minute, and I'm afraid of getting it the next. But what I need, more than anything, is to feel normal again. Even if it's just for one night."

"I'm sure you've heard about Jonesy's party tomorrow," Tripp said, backing away from Tiny. He ran a hand through his hair in a casual way that didn't match the tension in his muscles. My brother was just as sketched out as I felt. So was Hannah. I could practically hear her Creeper Radar signaling a red alert. "Bailey and Hannah want to go. I'm trying to convince them to stay home."

"Turley being in custody does not mean you're home free," Tiny said. "Best idea is to lie low and let us do our job."

"Are you?" Hannah asked. She smiled then, a mirror of Tiny's expression, tipping her head to the side. "Wait, I didn't mean for that to sound so bitchy."

"Hannah meant to ask if you have any other leads," Wes said. "We all know Turley's your main suspect. But you haven't been able to nail him. I know you're not supposed to share information, but, for the sake of the girls, maybe you can tell us *something*."

"We're considering all leads and piecing together the details. So, yes," Tiny looked pointedly at Hannah, "rest assured that we *are* doing our job."

"Do you think he's going to be there?" I asked. "Whoever's behind all this?"

Tiny's expression remained flat, giving away nothing. "I didn't say that."

"Yeah, but you kind of implied it by telling us to steer clear," Hannah said. "So you must think it's someone close."

"That's not—" Tiny ground his teeth as he looked out across the yard, toward the woods. "The bottom line is that you can't trust anyone right now—not the people you think you know, or the people you definitely don't—because we haven't ruled anything out. But whoever this is, however this person is taking the girls, he's figured out a way to make them disappear."

"If you look at it that way," I said. "I'm at risk no matter where I am."

"If you have to get out," Tiny said, "head over to the event at Sylvie Warner's house. Her parents have requested police surveillance, which the chief approved, so it's your next best option. Don't go near the Jones's farm, you hear me?"

"Loud and clear," I said, feeling strange, like he had just thrown down a dare.

"Well," Hannah said with a sigh, "it's too bad you had to drive all the way out here for nothing."

"Just carrying out my duty. We're keeping a close eye on all of the girls," Tiny said with a nod and a quick glance at Hannah's cleavage. "Especially this week, given the pattern of the abductions."

"We appreciate," Tripp said.

"I do have one more question," Tiny said, jerking his chin toward the woods behind us. "What were all of you doing out there, anyway?"

We turned as one—Hannah, Tripp, Wes, and me. I could feel the tension, could almost hear our thoughts pinging through the air. Was this some kind of test?

"Just taking a walk," Hannah said, turning back to Tiny.

Tiny's eyes wrinkled in confusion. "After calling and asking for someone to stop over to file a report on evidence found?"

"Bailey said you'd be at least an hour." Wes shrugged. "It's a nice day."

Tiny narrowed his eyes again, looking us over before he held out his fist. "You guys take it easy."

My brother paused, looking Tiny in the eye before he bumped Tiny's fist with his own. "Thanks for stopping to check in."

"We'll see you around, man," Wes said with a nod.

"You bet." Tiny leaned in, pointing from me to Hannah and back again. "Be safe, girls. Make smart decisions."

"On it," I said, my skin crawling under his condescending tone.

Tiny hitched his pants up as he walked away, grabbing the radio from his waistband and saying something to the dispatcher on the other end as he moved toward his cruiser.

"Holy shit," Hannah said. "Was that creepy with a capital *C* or am I just too freaked out by what we saw at the pond to judge fairly?"

"Creepy?" Wes said, watching as Tiny reached his car and pulled the driver's side door open. "That was totally fucked up."

"I couldn't do it," I said. "I could not tell him about Leena. Something felt so—"

"Wrong?" Tripp asked.

"Yeah," Hannah said. "Like, he-could-be-the-one-behind-this-whole-thing wrong."

"Or I'm-trying-to-catch-you-breaking-my-rules wrong," I added.

"What was with him asking about your label?" Wes said.

Tripp looked over his shoulder as the cruiser's engine let out a low rumble.

"Tripp, you know the guy," Wes said. "What's his story?"

"He was always a little off. Never quite fit in. People teased him some, but not much more than anyone else. Beyond that, your guess is as good as mine. Other than a quick "Sup' at the gas station or Flying Pizza, I haven't talked to him since graduation."

"Doesn't matter," Hannah said. "You never know anyone all the way. And if you think about it, a cop would have the easiest time of all pulling off this whole sick thing."

"Jesus, guys." Tripp scraped his hands through his hair. "You *really* think he could be the killer?"

"It's a definite possibility," Wes replied. "Enough that it wasn't worth sharing what we know about Leena. Telling the wrong person would put Bailey in serious danger."

"He *was* different than I remember." Tripp drew his shoulders back. "He seemed cocky. Bold. Aggressive."

"It felt like he was playing a game," Hannah said. "Like he was saying one thing by telling Bailey to skip the party when he really meant the opposite. You think he'll be there?"

"Tiny would blend in at Jonesy's in a heartbeat," Tripp said. "He graduated with Jonesy's oldest brother, Brennan. Enough people from that class will be in town by now. They'll all show."

Hannah snapped her fingers. "During that press conference the other day, the hot detective from the FBI—Kegler or Kegan or something—said they're not sure if the kidnapper is from town and holding some grudge against the girls or if the video lured him here."

"But?" I asked, because I knew that was coming next.

"But if you think about it, the killer has to be someone from town. He knows so much about each girl. Emily disappeared somewhere between volleyball practice and home. That's, like, a seven minute drive. Then Leena vanished after work, right after two of her co-workers at the ice cream shop saw her get in her car and drive away. JJ went missing after a late-night jam session with her band, which was a typical weekly meet-up. And Becca was taken right after play practice. The person taking them knows an awful lot of details to be from out of town. Whoever this is didn't just know where they'd be; he knew their routes home."

"Yeah," I said. "All the evidence points to this being someone those girls trusted."

"Like a police officer," Wes added.

"Abductors are known for being master manipulators," Hannah said. "Some fake injuries to seem harmless, and then attack only after their victim is trapped. Others act like victims themselves. There are cases where a few dressed like cops to fake their way into a home. But actually being a member of the police force would be the best front of all."

"If we're right and it's him," I said, "this whole thing just got more extreme."

"Either way," Wes said, "we're on our own. We can't start talking when we don't know who we can trust. Protecting Bailey is the most important thing, and I'm not sure we can do that with Tiny in the mix. Even if we ask to speak to the lead detectives to try to warn them that their suspect might be a local cop, word would get back to him. If it came down to it, no cop is going to believe us over him."

"Agreed," Hannah said. "After that run-in, we have to keep the police out of the loop."

"For now." Tripp looked down at the grass, letting out a grunt of frustration. "But we have to tell them eventually."

"Obviously," Hannah said. "But not until we figure out how to keep Bailey safe. In the meantime, let's get to the school and see what we can find out about that tiara. Information will be our best defense, so let's be sure to arm ourselves with whatever we can."

CHAPTER 11

5:22 PM

"Shit!" Hannah tugged at the front doors at Bakersville High's main entrance. The teacher/visitor parking lot yawned behind us, empty except for Hannah's silver Escape, which was parked at an odd angle in the first row of spaces. "They're locked!"

"The cafeteria," I said. "We could try the delivery ramp."

"Nah." Tripp shrugged. "If the front is locked, all the other doors will be, too."

"They might have forgotten one," Hannah said hopefully.

Wes shook his head. "With Roger Turley on school grounds today, they didn't forget to lock anything."

"Wes is right," Tripp sighed. "Our only chance is the door by the custodian's office. The night shift won't remember if I'm a current or past student. If I pound long enough and give some sob story about forgetting my wallet, someone might let me in. I'll run around back and see if I have any luck."

"Go," Hannah said. "Do whatever you have to. Just get one of these freaking doors open."

"I'll do my best." Tripp dashed past two or three classrooms, disappearing around the corner.

I stepped to the middle door and pressed my forehead and nose against the sun-warmed glass, squinting my eyes to see inside. The atrium was bathed in a gold-tinted glow from the skylights above. I had a clear view of the main office—doors closed, lights off—and two of the four hallways leading away from the center of the building—the locker-lined paths a blur of deep shadow. The only thing that stood out was the display case, still illuminated from recessed lights in its ceiling.

My phone vibrated. I pulled it from the pocket of my capris, smiling at the message from Jude. He'd sent a single heart emoji. I sent one back, and swiped to my text queue, realizing I'd missed a whole string of messages from the girls.

> AMY L—4:33PM: WHAT'S THE DEAL WITH FOOD TOMORROW NIGHT?
>
> SYLVIE W— 4:33PM: MUNCHIES. EVERYONE BRING A FAVE.
>
> CARRIE H—4:37PM: I CALL BROWNIES!
>
> KELSEY H—4:38PM: THE MAGIC KIND THAT WILL MAKE ME FORGET MY TROUBLES?

The next text was a GIF from Beth, featuring a turtle wearing a rainbow party hat while eating a brownie. I laughed. Hannah looked over my shoulder. Behind her, Wes paced back and forth, scrolling through something on his phone.

"I love the turtle," Hannah said. "Is that the girls?"

"Yeah." I scrolled farther down, reading the final three messages. "They're making plans for tomorrow night."

"They know you're not going?"

"Sylvie does. But the rest?" I scrunched my nose up. "Don't think so."

BRITTANY S—4:42PM: I'LL GRAB PRETZELS AND BEER CHEESE. SOMEONE ELSE HAS TO BE IN CHARGE OF THE REAL ALCOHOL.

BETH K—4:43PM: ON IT. I CAN'T BELIEVE WE'RE ABOUT TO MISS THE BIGGEST PARTY OF OUR LIVES. SUCKS. MAJOR. SUCKAGE.

AMY L—4:43PM: DON'T REMIND ME.

KELSEY H—4:4PM: HENCE THE POT BROWNIES, PPL.

I replied, keeping my message short and sweet. GONNA HANG WITH HANNAH TOMORROW NIGHT. SORRY TO MISS, BUT I PROMISE TO BE THERE NEXT TIME.

"So, this hunt totally sucks," Hannah said, grabbing my hair and twisting it into a loose braid. "But I'm glad we're a team again."

Wes backed away, stepping out from the shadow of the overhang that covered the front entrance to the high school. I looked back through the main doors to the display case. The teardrop shaped pictures of each girl swayed slightly on thin strands of fishing line, and the items representing each stood out against the stark-white background.

"Wes," Hannah said, "what the hell are you doing?"

I looked over my shoulder and found him leaning against one of the brick pillars that framed the overhang, his cell phone pressed against his ear. He lifted a finger to his mouth, shushing Hannah.

"O'Brien!" Wes said, a smile spreading across his face. "How you been, man?"

"Oh my God," Hannah said, spinning toward me. "He's making a social call when your life is on the line? Totally not cool."

"Agreed," I said with a shrug. "But that's Wes's style: Focus for a minute. Get bored. Move on." I turned back to the window, pressing my nose against it, concentrating on Leena's picture.

"What are you doing?" Hannah asked, sliding up to my side.

Wes laughed. "Yeah," he said. "I'm back in town. And I've got a question for you."

"I'm looking at the memorial," I said, ignoring Wes as best I could, my eyes trained on the two red-and-black pom-poms spread just under Leena's picture, hearing her voice leading the ever-popular 'Go, Fight, Win!' cheer. "I want to see with my own two eyes that the tiara—*Leena's* tiara—is missing from the display. I know you said the one she was wearing at the pond looks identical, but there's only one way to be sure."

"I hate to say it, but this could easily be a trap," Hannah said. "Some wild goose chase to distract us while the killer makes his next move."

"My thoughts exactly."

"Right, man." Wes's voice was softer now. I could tell he'd turned away from us. "You're so right."

"I see the pom-poms," Hannah said.

My breath clouded the glass in front of me. I leaned back, swiping my hand across the door to clear my view.

"So, I was just checking in to make sure you still remembered that incident," Wes said. He paused. Then laughed again, way too loud. "Yes. The incident that occurred during the spring of my junior year."

Leaning forward, I narrowed my focus to those two pom-poms, to their very center, where the tiara should be perfectly perched. My vision swam under the effort to focus on something so far away.

"Do you see it?" Hannah asked.

I squinted, trying to force the tiara to be right where it belonged. But there was nothing. Not even the slightest glimmer of light splashing off rhinestones.

"Then you remember that you owe me, right?" Wes asked.

"It's gone." I turned, pressing my back against the glass doors, my heart racing with the thought that the killer had been so close to me, and all the rest of the girls, earlier today.

Wes pushed himself off the pillar. I watched as he paced in wide circles. "Yeah, I want to collect. I want to collect right now."

"What's he talking about?" I asked Hannah.

She shrugged. "I have no idea."

"I'm at the high school," Wes said, his eyes meeting mine. "Can you meet me?"

"No." I rushed to his side. "You can't just tell anyone you want about what's—"

Wes waved his hand in the air, giving me a wide-eyed look of irritation before spinning away. "Let's just say it has a little something to do with surveillance footage."

"What the hell is going on, Wes?" I asked, poking a finger into his back.

He turned then, facing me again, a huge smile spread across his face. "Really? Well, *that* is fascinating. You're still in the purple house on the corner?" Wes paused. Pressed his lips together. And then laughed. "Fine. It's gray. We'll be right over, dude."

CHAPTER 12

5:44 PM

"I don't like this," I said. The four of us were standing on the front porch of an old house in the center of town. Deep purple-gray paint peeled off the wood siding in long strips.

"You don't have to like it," Wes said. "You just have to keep your mouth shut and let me do the talking."

"Doesn't Owen O'Brien live here?" Tripp asked.

"Yup." Wes pressed the doorbell and stepped back.

"And he owes you something," Hannah said, "because of an incident that took place during your junior year?"

"Something like that." Wes leaned toward the door, peering through a pane of beveled glass that looked centuries old.

"What incident?" Tripp asked. "The night you got your truck stuck in the corn field? Was he the one who pulled your ass out?"

"No." Wes laughed. "That was Brennan Jones."

"Jonesy's older brother?" Hannah asked. "So freaking hot."

"Is this about the time you almost got busted for posting that fake Instagram page for Principal Johnson?" I asked.

"Closer," Wes said.

"The gambling ring!" Hannah started jumping up and down. "This has to be about the gambling ring you were nailed for—the underground poker tournament. You controlled that thing for months before you were caught. That was spring of your junior year."

Wes tapped his finger to his nose twice, then pointed at Hannah.

"I knew it!" she said.

"Little secret," Wes whispered. "I wasn't the mastermind behind that one."

Just then, the door swung open and Owen O'Brien was standing in front of us, his deep brown hair sticking up in little tufts. He wore a wrinkled T-shirt that was half-tucked into a pair of gym shorts.

"Wesley!" Owen held out his fist to bump with Wes's. "Been a long time, man."

"Too long," Wes said. "I appreciate your help."

"Save your thanks until we know I actually *can* help." Owen narrowed his eyes, looking us over. "I thought you were alone."

Wes shrugged. "You can trust them."

"This is my job we're talking about," Owen said. "If anyone finds out I'm sharing private footage, I'll be fired in a hot second."

Wes snorted. "You're a computer genius, Owen. I have no doubt you can cover your tracks."

Owen tipped his head to the side. I could tell he was thinking. Then he stepped aside with a jerk of his chin. "Enter."

The house was a disaster. Shoes littered the entry, at least ten different pairs, all large and worn in. Jackets meant for the coatrack had settled like limp shells at its base. The air was cool, but musty, and had a slightly smoky flavor. The steps to the second floor were strewn with books and papers. A large keg stood at the center of the hall leading to a swinging door that I assumed hid the kitchen.

"Sorry about the mess," Owen said, kicking a gray gym shoe as he stepped from the entry to an oversized living room.

We followed him, first Wes, then Hannah, me, and Tripp brought up the rear. The living room was just like the entry, a dark, dank space filled with all kinds of guy stuff. The furniture was old, ratty-looking, and the couch, pushed up against a large bay window, was dwarfed by the hulking figure of one of Owen's sleeping roommates.

"Is that Bryce Winters?" Tripp asked.

Owen nodded. "I wouldn't wake him. He's a beast if you mess with his sleep."

We kept walking, past a wooden table covered with beer cans, a few ashtrays, and a deck of cards that looked as if it had just been thrown down.

"You still playing poker, man?" Wes asked, his smirk resurfacing.

Owen shook his head. "Had my fill. You saved my life when you took the rap for that shit, man. If the administration had caught me, I never would have had a shot at head tech for the district. They're even paying my college tuition as incentive to stick around."

"No worries," Wes said. "I was glad to help. Taking the wrap for that made me a freaking legend just in time for senior year."

"And today, you collect," Owen said, leading us down a hall and into a wood-paneled room. It was dark and smelled musty like the rest of the house, but I didn't have to dodge anything as

I stepped across the carpeted floor. The desk, which sat centered in the oval space, was free of clutter. There was a dresser and a bed, too, tucked in the back corner. The bed was covered with a wrinkled mess of blankets.

"You said you can access the school's security footage from here?" Wes asked.

"I spliced the server so it links to the house. That way I can work from home if I don't feel like going in."

"Brilliant," Wes said. "As always."

"You don't have to kiss my ass." Owen walked around the desk and sat in a sleek leather chair, facing us. "I owe you. What do you need?"

"There are cameras all over the school, right?" Wes asked.

"Yes." Owen steepled his fingers under his chin. "But they're not all recording footage."

"What does that mean?" I asked.

"It means the administration would like for the student body to believe they are always being monitored, but the truth is that only two or three cameras are actually functioning at any one time."

"What about the atrium?" Wes asked.

Owen nodded. "That's one of the main cameras. The view there can sweep from the main entrance to the office, catching a good portion of two of the hallways that feed the rest of the school."

"Which means it has a view of the display case," Hannah said.

"What display case?" Owen asked.

"The one with the shrine," I said, "memorializing all the missing girls."

Owen's face went white as a sheet. His Adam's apple bobbed up and down as he swallowed a few times. Hard. "So this is about *The Bakersville Dozen?*"

"Sorry," Hannah said. "That part is strictly need-to-know."

Owen finally met my eyes, and gave me a stiff nod. "The atrium camera would have a view of the display case."

"Good." I walked around to his side of the desk. "Let's see it." Tripp dropped to the chair beside me, swinging one leg over its wooden arm.

Owen's fingers clicked across they keyboard. "I need you to be a little more specific."

"I want to see the footage from today," I said. "After school."

"Last Day Ceremony?" Owen asked, raising his eyebrows.

"You could start there." I leaned up against the desk, noticing the half-full coffee mug that said *World's Hottest Computer Whiz*. He wasn't bad, but if he was the hottest, that didn't say much for the tech world.

Owen swiveled in his chair and started typing, his fingers moving effortlessly across the keyboard. Wes paced back and forth in front of a long dresser where two laptop computers, both hooked up to chargers, displayed identical screensavers featuring half-naked swimsuit models on loop.

"Got it," Owen said, leaning back, his hands slipping from the desk and into his lap.

The flicker of a smile passed over Hannah's lips. "Nice work."

The footage was black-and-white and grainy, but it was there. As Hannah, Tripp, and Wes crowded around me, I watched my classmates streaming in from the four main hallways, the atrium going from nearly empty to full capacity in just a few moments.

"Why's it going so fast?" Tripp asked.

"Time lapse," Owen said. "It's set at double time. Makes more sense than recording in real time."

"There we are," Hannah said, one finger pointing to the screen.

I saw us, slipping away from Sylvie Warner, whose face screwed up into a mask of anger as she turned and moved toward the girls. I counted heads as she re-entered their circle—seven. I'd been the only one to ditch out on Sylvie's Last Day Ceremony plans.

"She was pissed," Hannah said.

"Not like it's the first time." I shrugged, feeling bad for leaving the rest of the girls hanging, knowing they all felt the same frustration that had taken over my life—the longing to feel normal, the overwhelming desire to move on. But none of that mattered. Not now. "Can you fast forward?"

Owen clicked on the bar at the bottom of the screen, moving the little ticker forward until the atrium was nearly empty again. The screen showed an older couple standing at the reception desk in the main office with two police officers hovering in the background, and a few straggling students racing through the atrium to catch rides home. "That better?" he asked.

"Yeah." I leaned forward. "I think that's Roger Turley. Right there in the office."

"Forget him," Hannah said, pointing to the display case. "Check this out."

I saw it then. Leena's tiara sitting on top of those two pompoms.

"Fast forward." My heart raced as I thought to myself that this could be it. I might be a few moments from seeing the kidnapper and Leena's murderer, mere seconds from learning the identity of the person who had plotted to include me in the sadistic scavenger hunt.

Owen inched the cursor along the bar. We watched a few more people walk by—their movements unnaturally fast—and then it happened. A shadow walked right up to the glass doors of the memorial, slid them open, reached inside, and slipped out of the view of the camera.

"There!" I said. "Go back. Play that at the normal speed."

We watched the shadow in reverse, returning the tiara, and walking back out of the frame. Then Owen let go of the cursor, leaning forward, his eyes squinting at the screen.

"What are you guys looking for, anyway?"

I didn't answer. I couldn't. I was frozen in place, my eyes locked on the screen as I watched the figure slip up to the display case. I knew who it was in an instant. I didn't need to see the face, the thin lips pulled into a tight line, eyes darting from one side of the atrium to the other, the hand reaching out, sliding the display case open, plucking Leena's tiara from its perch.

The hair gave her away—a white-blonde mass of curlicues, a style that only one person in my world could pull off.

"Holy shit," Hannah said, her hand gripping mine. "That's Sylvie Fucking Warner."

SATURDAY

JUNE 3

CHAPTER 13

6:04 PM

I was sitting on the couch in my basement, staring at the television screen while a reporter with big teeth directed a panel of experts discussing the most likely profile of the person behind the serial kidnappings in Bakersville. The panel members were joining via satellite; all had different backgrounds. One was a psychiatrist, another used to work for the FBI's Behavioral Science Unit, and another was a criminal prosecutor with hundreds of cases under his belt. The TV was muted, but I followed the discussion through the closed captions scrolling along the bottom of the screen.

I felt numb, inside and out. Just over twenty-four hours had passed since the scavenger hunt began, but it still didn't feel real. Leena Grabman was dead, some psycho had chosen me to play his sick game, and now it was up to me to save my friends. Then there was the little fact that for several reasons, I was officially afraid to trust the police.

My emotions flipped between fear and dread as I considered what I might face when I followed the clue to the hayloft at Jonesy's farm in just a few hours. The hardest part was not being able to tell Jude. I'd been avoiding his texts and calls since the previous night, worried that if he heard my voice he'd know something was up.

"I still don't get it," Hannah said. "What the hell would Sylvie Warner want with that tiara anyway?"

My back was turned to Hannah, but I knew she was swiveling around in the wheely chair at the desk behind me, the annoying squeal of the seat punctuating her movements—left, right, left— in tune to the beat of Adele's "Rumor Has It."

"Do you remember much from those few minutes you were in the locker room with Sylvie?" I asked, watching the prosecutor's face turn a deep red as he pointed at the guy from the FBI. The text started scrolling faster then, and I had to speed-read to keep up with what the prosecutor was saying: "Profiling the suspect as white male between the ages of twenty and forty offered the public a false sense of security. It was, maybe, even dangerous. It could have caused someone, specifically one of the remaining girls from *The Bakersville Dozen* video, to trust the wrong person." I almost laughed at that, wondering what they'd say if they could see the footage of Sylvie Warner stealing the tiara that ended up on Leena's head less than an hour later.

"I remember the part where I was freaking out because I thought Roger Turley had followed me through the doors," Hannah said.

"What about the tiara?" I asked. "Did Sylvie have it?"

Hannah stopped swiveling, the final shriek of the chair echoing through the air. "By the time I found Sylvie, I was in panic mode. I grabbed her and bolted. The only thing I can say for sure is that she wasn't wearing it."

On the TV, the FBI guy leaned back in his seat, not looking the least bit intimidated by the prosecutor, as he started in on how profiles are not meant to offer the public a sense of security, but to guide law enforcement to focus on the most likely characteristics of a suspect.

"Did she have anything with her?" I asked. "Her backpack, maybe?"

"Nope," Hannah said. "Wait. Scratch that. She had that big ass purse she's always carrying around. It bumped my thigh a few times as we raced through the rows of lockers and out the back door."

"That purse is big enough to hide Leena's tiara," I said.

"Seriously. That purse is practically big enough to hide Leena."

I laughed, the sound mingling with Adele's smoky voice as she sang the three words I wished I would never, in my entire life, hear again.

My hair whipped my shoulders as I turned to face Hannah. "Why, exactly, are you watching that stupid video again?"

"Just seeing if I catch anything new," she said with a shrug. "Not like there's anything better to do. Unless you wanna go upstairs and hang with your parents."

"Please," I said, standing up and walking to Hannah's side. "The last thing I need is another lecture on how I'm not allowed to go anywhere near Jonesy's party tonight."

"I can't believe you actually talked Tripp into letting you to go."

"After our run-in with Tiny, he understands. We need to figure out what we're dealing with and who we can trust before we try the police again."

"Have you planned our escape?" Hannah asked.

"It's a little tricky." I sighed. "I have to be at Jonesy's before ten if I'm going to follow that clue. I can't sneak out until after my parents go to bed, which won't be until at least eleven. So I came up with a lie that should ease their minds."

"Ease their minds?" Hannah asked. She paused. Then broke out into a wide grin. "Oh my God, you didn't."

"I did."

Hannah laughed. Then pressed her fingers to her lips. "You told them you're going to Sylvie's?"

"I know. It's awful. But it's my only way out of the house."

"They'd freaking lose it if they knew you were spending the night with a chick who stole a tiara that ended up on a corpse."

"*A*, I am not actually spending the night. And *B*, could you please not refer to Leena as a corpse?"

"Sorry, but she is."

The sick feeling had returned to my stomach. Twisting. Turning. Every time I heard Leena's name, I pictured her there, lying in the grass. Rotting. She was literally *rotting*. And I'd just left her there.

"Do you think she was alive?" I asked. "When that security footage was taken—while we were at the Last Day Ceremony and Sylvie was stealing the tiara? Do you think Leena was still alive?"

Hannah looked back at me. "I don't think we'll ever know the answer to that."

"She's still out there."

"Stop," Hannah said, reaching for the bag of chips next to the computer monitor and popping one into her mouth with a crunch. "Stop thinking. It's the only way to keep yourself from going crazy."

"But, Hannah"—I pointed toward the window overlooking the backyard and the maze of trails beyond—"she's all alone."

"I don't think she cares right now. What she'd want is for you to stay safe." Hannah looked me right in the eyes. I could see the little flecks of black in the chocolate brown. "Focus, Bailey. We're going to the party in a few hours to watch everyone, and take notes on everything we see to try to come up with a new lead. We can't do anything for Leena anymore, but when it's time, we might have the chance to save the next girl. The chance to end all of this."

"Thank you," I said. "That is exactly what I needed to hear."

Hannah gave me an easy smile. "I always know what you need. Which is why I'm watching the video. We might spot something new now that we know Sylvie is involved."

"Do you know how many hours I've spent talking about this video? Watching this video? Analyzing every frame of this video? The FBI, the police, the school's administration, and all of our parents have done the same. There's nothing new to catch."

"Of course I remember all of that. I especially remember those brainstorming sessions you and the rest of the girls held to figure out who recorded the footage. I can't say I was jealous, because, hello? No one wanted to be part of that. But it took you away from me. Our senior year would have been so much different without this stupid video."

"Those sessions?" I said. "They were pure torture. We always started so sure of ourselves. And then came up with nothing."

"Where did you meet?" Hannah asked.

"Sylvie's." I pictured her basement, the thirteen of us crowded into the rec room as we tried to remember some detail about the person behind the video camera. Problem was, he was smart. Each video clip was recorded during a public event, making it a nearly impossible task. Kelsey "Shaved—'nuff Said" Hathaway's dance team performing in front of a packed gymnasium at a regional competition, bikini-clad Carrie "Pants on Fire" Hixon soaping up cars during the fundraiser to resurface the school's tennis courts, Becca "Hot for Teacher" Hillyer bathed in stage lights as she presented a monologue at the community center.

"Who led the discussions?" Hannah asked. "Who wrote down the clues you guys came up with?"

"Sylvie," I said.

"Of course. Miss Type-A probably had a huge whiteboard propped somewhere in the room," Hannah said. "A flowchart of locations and possible suspects for each."

"There was a whiteboard," I said, picturing the rainbow of color-coded details written in Sylvie's looping handwriting. "It was on an easel."

Hannah laughed. "So now that we saw her stealing the tiara, doesn't that make you suspicious? Maybe she was directing those discussions *away* from the elusive videographer instead of *toward* him?"

I groaned, shoving Hannah over with my butt until we were sharing the computer chair. On the screen, Sylvie Warner looked up at us. She was sitting at a table in the atrium of the high school, her smile wide and convincing as she held out a round sticker that said I GAVE BLOOD. WILL YOU? with the American Red Cross logo centered beneath the text.

Hannah moved the cursor to the pause button and clicked. The video started again, and Sylvie began to move in slow motion, seemingly inspired by the sexy tone of Adele's voice, as she tipped her head back with a laugh.

"This video was taken at the end of the summer, right?" Hannah asked. "At that health rally?"

"Yeah. It was the Kickstart-Your-Heart rally. The school was open to the public from nine to five, and the blood drive was set up for six hours, of which Sylvie worked three, so this video could have been taken by anyone, any time during that stretch."

"But look at that smile," Hannah said, pointing to the screen as Sylvie's head tipped forward again. "Total flirty-girl. And her eyes. She's practically undressing whoever's behind the camera."

I looked at the screen. Watched as Sylvie licked her lips and leaned forward, handing the sticker to a person smart enough to keep even his hand from entering the frame. Sylvie pushed her arms against the sides of her chest then, the movement was slight, but had a big result. Her chest practically popped out of the V-neck sweater she was wearing. And then came the text, fading onto the screen in small caps:

YOU GIVE TO HER CAUSE, AND SHE'LL GIVE TO YOURS.

SURPRISED? DON'T BE. THE WHOLE THING IS EASY.

JUST LIKE SYLVIE WARNER.

Sylvie gave a little wink, then, and her portion of the video faded to black. Adele's voice rang through the room once more, "Rumor has it!" and then it was Leena's turn.

The footage focused on a pair of dancing legs, tanned, moving fast, strappy wedges fastened to her feet. The camera slowly panned up, revealing a skimpy pair of cut-off jean shorts and a silky tank top with an open back. Leena was in the middle of a crowd gathered in Jonesy's barn for a party that took place a week after the start of senior year. She was dancing to the beat of a song that had been edited out of the video's soundtrack. Her hair was tied up in a loose bun, wisps falling out and brushing against her shoulders. As she threw her hands in the air and twirled in a circle, she lost her balance, falling to the ground. She looked dazed for a moment, her unfocused eyes giving away that she'd had way too much to drink, and then she propped herself up on her elbows. Someone reached out a shadowed hand. Leena grabbed it. And then Adele's voice faded to the background as Leena's surfaced above the beat of the music.

"I fell," she said. "Hard." And then she giggled, pressing her palm to her forehead and looking directly at the camera. "Don't tell," she said with a whisper-shout, "but, I like it hard."

The video stuttered, then did this jerky motion thing that rewound the admission, and then played it back on a loop, Leena's words—"I like it hard"—repeating exactly seven times.

"Sick," I said, trying to push away from the computer. But Hannah planted her feet on the ground so the wheely chair remained in place.

"She didn't remember any part of that, I assume," Hannah said.

"No. We asked her a thousand times, but she'd apparently downed a record number of shots that night. She insisted that was what she must have been referring to when she said her infamous line—'Liquor, not man parts.'"

"Well the most important segment is next. You can't stop watching now."

I sucked in a deep breath as the image of Leena faded to black. And then I watched myself flash into view, a montage of Jude and I flitting across the screen—the two of us standing in front of my locker at school, sitting on swings at the park in my neighborhood, walking through the parking lot at the mall, sitting in the dark at a movie theater. In all of them, we looked sweet—innocent—holding hands, my head resting on his shoulder, his arm slung around my waist. There was no passion. Not a single second of the heat that had permeated Leena's dance scene. Or Sylvie's cleavage-baring shot. As a finale, my section cut to a close-up of Jude's hand holding mine, and then the text scrolled across our intertwined fingers.

> WASTE OF TIME.
>
> THERE'S NO NEED TO BOTHER.
>
> THIS ONE'S LIKE A VIRGIN.

Which was actually kind of funny if I thought about it. Jude and I had created lots of heat. We were full of passion. Just not in public. The whole virgin thing, that part was wrong, too. Which was proof that whoever was behind the video wasn't as smart as he thought.

Hannah paused the video and looked at me. "Nothing?"

I shook my head. "What are you expecting? For me to suddenly remember seeing the person sitting behind us during that movie? Or to get a flash of who was trailing us in the mall parking lot?"

"I don't know," Hannah said. "But there's got to be something in there."

"There's nothing. Trust me."

Hannah looked back to the screen, clicking play again. Suze "I'm Sexy and I Know it" Moore was next.

"Bailey?" my mother's voice called from upstairs, her footsteps clicking across the kitchen floor.

"Yeah." My voice echoed around the basement. I was glad that Hannah had muted the sound. The last thing my mom needed was to hear that song. "I'm down here."

My mother padded down the stairs, stopping three steps from the bottom. She was wearing a black dress with spaghetti straps, and had on her favorite, open-toed silver sandals.

"Your father and I have decided to go out to dinner tonight. You need to be ready in fifteen minutes."

"Mom," I said. "I'm not ten years old."

"That may be true, but you're still not allowed to be home alone with everything that's going on."

"I'm not alone," I said, tipping my head toward Hannah.

"Hi, Mrs. H." Hannah waved.

I slung an arm around Hannah's shoulders. "You can see her, right?" I asked. "I'm not imagining things."

My mom cracked a smile. "Hannah is quite visible," my mother said. "And audible. But Hannah isn't equipped to deal with a kidnapper."

"Wanna bet?" I asked, smiling.

"I know you're worried, too." My mother tipped her chin toward the computer screen. "You're still analyzing that video."

I looked over my shoulder, feigning surprise when I saw Suze "I'm Sexy and I Know It" Moore showcasing a creation from her clothing line. Her long brown hair was twisted into a braid that hung down her back, swinging with each confident step as she walked the runway last fall in the economics club's annual Homecoming fashion show.

"You have fifteen minutes," my mother said, turning and walking back up the stairs. "Your father and I are dropping you off at Sylvie's on our way to dinner."

"Holy crap," Hannah said, looking at me with wide eyes. "They're actually taking you to her house?"

"I'm screwed."

"Maybe," Hannah said with a tilt of her head. "Maybe not."

I leaned back, the chair squealing in protest, and scraped my hands though my hair. "What the hell am I going to do?"

"Flip it." Hannah snapped her fingers. "Use the opportunity to our advantage."

"Brilliant idea," I said. "But how?"

"You're smart." Hannah shrugged. "Look for clues."

"Like these *clues* are just going to be lying around her house?"

"Nothing's that easy," Hannah said. "Just start by asking a few questions. No way Sylvie's a killer, but she's involved somehow and definitely knows something. Think of this as an opportunity to get information out of her."

"Right," I said. "That should be easy."

"Just like Sylvie Warner," Hannah said with a smile, her voice sing-song sweet and full of laughter.

CHAPTER 14

7:16 PM

"What are you doing here?" Sylvie's eyes narrowed below her mass of white-blonde curls. She propped one hand on the waist of her faded denim miniskirt, blocking the entrance of the half-open front door as she stood in the foyer of her house.

"It's complicated." I held out a bag of tortilla chips and a container of gourmet guacamole, which I'd found during a three-minute search of the kitchen before we'd left. "But I brought chips and guac—your favorite."

Sylvie eyed the guacamole, her lips tight with anger. "You can't be serious."

"I am," I said, attempting nonchalance because I knew it would infuriate her.

"You expect me to just let you into my house? Do you think I forgot what you said to me after the Last Day Ceremony? No freaking way, Bailey."

"Lighten up," I said with a shrug. "It was a joke."

Sylvie closed the door, or at least she tried to, but I stuck my foot in the narrow opening just in time, pressing the toe of my sneaker against the door's brick-red paint.

"What the hell?" Sylvie swung the door open so quickly the brass knocker clanged against its base. "Why are you even here?"

"That's not what matters right now. What matters is that you're about to put a smile on your face, take this food out of my hands, and welcome me inside. Maybe even wave to my parents, who are sitting in the car parked out in the street, right behind the police cruiser."

Sylvie snorted. "Tonight's your big chance for all the normalcy you've been whining about. So why the hell are you standing on my front doorstep?"

"I need a cover story," I said with a shrug. "And you're it. My mom's probably going to call later. All you have to do is tell her that I fell asleep watching a movie."

"And why, exactly, would I do anything to help you?"

"Because," I said, leaning in for the kill, my voice a low whisper, "I know about the tiara."

Sylvie's mouth dropped open and she stumbled two steps back into the foyer.

"If you don't let me in, I'll make sure you regret it."

"You're blackmailing me?" Sylvie asked.

I shrugged. "The way I see it, blackmail isn't quite as immoral as theft."

"Fine." Sylvie stepped forward and grabbed the bag of chips and guacamole out of my hand. "You can come in."

"Perfect." I slipped past her. "I have a few questions."

I turned and waved at my parents. They waved back, sad smiles on their faces as they pulled away, weaving around the cruiser. I watched the car slip down the street, taillights burning red as they braked for a stop sign, and then they disappeared with a right turn onto Main Street.

Sylvie closed the door, pausing before turning to face me. I wanted to start at the end and ask how the tiara she'd stolen ended up on Leena's head. I wanted to find out if Sylvie had anything to do with the death of our friend. But it seemed so far-fetched, so totally off base, that I had to wonder if mentioning the fact that I'd found Leena might be a trap.

I decided to start from the beginning, instead. "Why did you steal the tiara from the display case?"

Sylvie shook her head, her shoulders slumping as she leaned back against the door. "I didn't steal it."

"Um. Yeah you did, Sylvie. I saw you."

"You're lying!" Sylvie shot away from the door, her body a tight coil of anger. "You weren't there. *No one* was there."

"I didn't say I was there." I crossed my arms over my chest and leaned against the foyer table. A vase of white daisies shuddered with the movement.

Sylvie's eyes glinted with anger. "Then how did you—"

"Ever seen the cameras they have mounted around the building? There are a ton of them. And they catch almost everything." I took a deep breath, letting the truth sink in. "I'm going to ask you one more time, why did you take Leena's tiara?"

The color drained from Sylvie's cheeks. She looked like she might be sick. And I was certain she was about to break. But a rumbling of footsteps shook the floor beneath me, a high-pitched squeal shattering the moment.

"Bailey!" Brittany "Likes to Blow" Sanford shouted, pulling me into a hug. "You showed!"

Carrie "Pants on Fire" Hixon clapped her hands. "I thought you were ditching us tonight."

"I'm just making a quick appearance," I said, "so you all know I love you."

"But you can't leave." Amy "Anything Goes" Linta said, pouting.

"Yeah," Kelsey "Shaved—'nuff Said" Hathaway added. "We've got brownies. They're not the magic kind, but they're so delish they almost qualify."

"I smuggled in some rum," whispered Beth "Squeaks, Squeals, Shrieks" Klein. "I was just coming up to grab a few cans of soda for rum and Cokes."

"She said it's just an appearance." Sylvie's voice was hard. Cold.

"You're not going to Jonesy's, are you?" asked Summer "Spicy" Jameson. "The police are right outside. We'll be safe here. At Jonesy's you're—"

"I'll be fine," I said. "There'll be people everywhere watching for anything suspicious. Besides, I'll have Jude by my side the entire night."

"If that's not a Cutest Couple statement, I don't know what is." JJ "Juicy Fruit" Hamilton rolled her eyes, but she smiled at the same time. "I still don't think it's worth the risk, B."

"I wouldn't mind taking the risk if I had Jude standing by my side," Beth said with a giggle. I looked at her and wondered for the hundredth time if the video's claim about her being so . . . *loud* was true. But then I shook that thought away, hating the way *The Bakersville Dozen* had made people see only one thing about each of us, erasing all other aspects of our personalities.

"Anyway," Sylvie said, stepping up to my side and putting her hand on my arm, "thanks for stopping by, Bailey. I hope you have a blast tonight."

"You sure you don't want to join me?" I asked, raising my eyebrows.

"Yes," Sylvie said. "Totally. But I'll walk you out. The cops aren't staked out in back yet."

Leading the way down the hall and into the kitchen, Sylvie slid the chips and guacamole onto the island that was already crowded with chips and dips, fruit and veggies, and a menu for the Flying Pizza, before making her way out the sliding glass door that led to her back deck.

"Bye, guys," I said, waving at the other girls, who were crowding around the snacks. I took a deep breath before stepping through the doorway and sliding it closed.

"I don't know what you're trying to prove with this little stunt. But the game's over, Bailey." Sylvie leaned her elbows on the deck's railing and looked out over her flat, grassy backyard.

"I'm not trying to prove anything." I stepped beside her, as a breeze washed over us. "I just want answers."

"Well, you're not going to get them." Sylvie pushed off the railing, her icy blue eyes boring into me. "So you might as well stop asking."

"Not likely. Tell me. Why did you do it?"

"Stop, Bailey!" Sylvie's voice cracked. "Just stop, or else—"

"Or else what? Help me understand." I stood there, watching the breeze tug through Sylvie's tight curls, going over everything I knew. "You took the tiara at the end of the day, after everyone had left the atrium, and the school was pretty much empty except for the people heading out to the parking lot. And then what? You went straight to the girl's locker room to get info on Emily, right? For your graduation speech?"

"How do you know about that?" Sylvie asked, her voice a whisper.

"I'm best friends with the chick who pulled you out of there. Which means I know that Roger Turley was standing right outside the locker room doors, stalking you."

I pictured the scene, Hannah swinging through the doors, Turley waiting just outside, his feet pacing the linoleum floor. Hannah's hair streaming behind her as she raced toward the back exit, her heart beating fast when she realized she wasn't alone, that she had someone to save. And then it hit me—Sylvie had more to hide than a stolen tiara.

"Why didn't you tell?" I asked.

"Drop it, Bailey. I'm warning you."

"The police busted Turley for being on school grounds, but they don't know he was following you, do they? If they knew, it would be all over the news: 'Prime suspect fails to abduct one of the remaining Bakersville Dozen.' But it's not. Because you didn't tell."

Sylvie shook her head. "I didn't want to freak my parents out, okay?"

"You're lying."

"My parents have been through enough, and the last thing they needed was—"

"But there's more to it, isn't there? You're all about honoring the girls who've gone missing. You wouldn't violate that memorial if someone offered you a million dollars, but today you stole right from the display. Someone must have put you up to it."

Sylvie's chin was trembling, her eyes glistening with tears. "Bailey, *please*—"

"Who was it, Sylvie? Tell me!"

Sylvie bent at the waist, her hands gripping her knees, and I wondered if she was about to throw up. Then I heard her voice, thin but determined.

"I can't tell you anything," she said, taking a deep breath and standing straight as she exhaled, her body tight, eyes hard. "Nothing, okay? Just leave me the fuck alone."

In that moment, I knew I had lost my chance with her. That, in fact, I'd never even had a chance, not if she was feeling the uncertainty that had begun to weigh down every one of my own thoughts.

I was dying to ask her if she'd received a note. A clue. If she'd been led to Leena's body just as I had. Maybe she'd been threatened into silence with taunts that promised more missing girls— girls who would soon turn up dead.

But there was no way to tell if I could trust Sylvie. She could be in on the entire thing.

I turned and walked down the deck's wooden steps and across the soft grass. Without looking back, I made my way to the trail where Hannah was waiting to take me to Jonesy's farm, the hay-loft, and the uncertainty of the next clue.

CHAPTER 15

7:52 PM

The light bathing the trail was darkening fast with trees blocking the rays of the setting sun. I broke out in a sweat, nervous about my unintentional trek into the woods, trying to ignore the fact that I was alone and vulnerable. But ignoring something always has a way of making it worse.

I stepped over a fallen limb, and dialed Hannah for the sixth time in the last two minutes. The line rang once, twice, then flipped to voicemail: "Hannah here. You know what to do. *Beep.*"

"Hannah! Where the hell are you? You were supposed to be waiting for me at the trailhead behind Sylvie's. I have no idea where you parked and . . . Look, just call me. Like, right now. Okay?"

Something was off. Way off. Hannah could be a little unreliable, sure, but always in a girls-just-wanna-have-fun way. Never, ever when someone was in actual need. Somewhere in the distance I heard a branch snap. The sound startled a flock of birds, all of them rising in unison.

I dialed Hannah again, listening as the line rang and voice-mail picked up again. "Please, Hannah," I said, my voice a whisper. "I'm scared."

And then I heard footsteps, slow and cautious like a predator tracking, determined to not scare off its prey. I froze, one thought pinging through my mind: *What if I am the prey?*

The crunch of a leaf startled me into action, my feet taking over, pounding the dusty path, twisting me right and then left, down one slope and up another, until I broke into the clearing at the heart of the woods where fading golden sunlight glimmered off the surface of the pond.

The pond.

I looked around instinctively, my entire body turning toward the spot where Leena lay with her legs uncrossed and that too-red lipstick staining her lips. I half-expected to see Leena rise from her grassy grave and give me props for daring to challenge Sylvie, or maybe snarl with undead anger for leaving her there to rot without telling the police where to find her. But all I saw were the grasses rippling in the wind.

I strained to hear beyond the rasp of my breathing, reassuring myself that no one was following. That I was alone with nothing to fear but my own imagination.

But the hairs on the back of my neck prickled with the feeling that I was being watched, that reassurance dying before it could fully form.

I swiveled as I caught the swish of feet moving through grass. I was ready to race for the cover of the woods, to run as fast as my legs would carry me. My phone slipped from my hand, but as soon as I registered that fact, I knew there was no time to grab it. I had to move. Fast.

I saw him a fraction of a second before we collided, a dark shadow blocking out the faded glow of the sun. He was solid and didn't budge an inch when I smacked into his chest. My heart raced and my entire body screamed at me to escape. But it was too late—his hands wrapped around my biceps and squeezed tight.

"Found you!" he said, picking me up and twirling me in a circle, before placing me back on the ground. I recognized him in bits and pieces—first the voice, clear and steady, then the eyes, a melty kind of brown. "I was worried you'd be scared out here all alone."

"I was. Totally freaked." My words came in short bursts. "Hannah was supposed to meet me, but she wasn't at the trailhead, and then I heard footsteps, but I didn't know it was you and—"

"Didn't Hannah text you?" Jude asked, his eyes crinkling together. He leaned down and grabbed my cell from the ground, placing it in my hand.

"She didn't text. And she's not answering her phone." I took a breath, willing myself to calm down. Jude was by my side, which meant everything was okay. "She was going to park near Sylvie's and wait for me in the woods so we could avoid the stakeout. I was going to surprise you once we got to Jonesy's."

"Hannah told me everything. She asked me to come and find you. Nice work using Sylvie as a cover to escape your parents." Jude smiled, giving me a little wink. "I'm stoked that you changed your mind about Jonesy's. I promise I won't let you out of my sight."

My heart was still racing, adrenaline fuzzing out his words.

"God, B, I'm sorry I freaked you out." Jude pulled me into his arms.

"If you were supposed to meet me," I said, my words muffled by his cotton T-shirt, "why weren't you there?"

"I was at the farm when Hannah called. The no-driving-off-the-property rule's already in effect, so I had to walk."

"Oh," I said, relaxing. He kissed me then, his lips soft at first, then insistent.

"I missed you," he said when he pulled away. "Hated not seeing you last night, but the fireworks run took longer than we expected. Huge accident on the way home. We were stuck in traffic for hours."

"I got your texts. What time did you get back?"

"Like two in the morning. I figured you were asleep, so I didn't call."

I wrapped my arms around his neck and squeezed, so grateful to have him—solid, easy, safe. "Thank you for coming to get me."

"Of course." Jude pulled away, his eyes meeting mine, flickers of fire from the pond catching in their deep caramel brown. "You know, we don't have to be in a rush." Jude smiled as his hands slipped inside the back of my shirt, his fingers dancing across my skin.

He leaned in again, lips brushing mine, as he guided me off the trail until my back was pressed up against a tree. The heat of his mouth warmed me, rushing through my entire body. My hands reached up, fingers tugging through his hair, and he dropped his mouth to my neck, his breath teasing my skin.

I suddenly wanted to show him how *not* "Like a Virgin" I could be. I could prove to myself that, in spite of being stuck sharing yet another secret with Wes, in spite of the scavenger hunt and the dead body lying fewer than fifty yards away, I could still feel normal.

But the timing was off. My hands were shaking, my mind spinning with thoughts of what had to be done. Not to mention the dead body lying fewer than fifty yards away. I pressed my hands to Jude's chest, and eased him away. The movement was slight, but he read my meaning perfectly, just like he always had.

"I'm sorry, B." He stood there in front of me, his breath rushed, eyes searching mine. "Are you okay?"

I leaned my head back against the tree, feeling my hair catch on the bark as I looked up at the purple-tinted sky. I wished we could disappear. That I could escape Wes, the hunt, and Leena's body.

My phone dinged; a new text had come in. I was grateful for the distraction. I couldn't risk getting lost in Jude. Not when there was a clue in play.

"It's Hannah. Finally." I swiped the screen.

HANNAH—7:59PM: HAD TO CHECK IN AT HOME BEFORE HEADING
TO FARM. MOM WANTED TO DELIVER SAFETY
LECTURE IN PERSON. JUDE'S MEETING YOU IN
THE WOODS. ON MY WAY NOW.

"We don't have to go to this party, you know," Jude said, rubbing his thumb along my jaw. "If you're too freaked out, I understand."

I shook my head, dizzy with the weight of all the secrets I was being forced to keep.

"We could go back to your house . . . Or mine. Order a pizza. Watch a movie. Maybe do a little more of—"

"No." I gave him one last kiss before slipping under his arm. "We have to go. Biggest party of our lives, right?"

Jude grabbed my hand, gently tugging me back to his side. "If you're sure."

I looked toward the swaying grasses, their quiet rustle sing-
ing out in the fading light, and pictured Leena there, the tiara's
rhinestones sparking like a beacon, the butterfly on her ring
poised to fly away, the splotchy bruises circling her ankles deep-
ening as the night's shadows swept in.

I took a deep breath.

I had to do this.

Not just for myself, but for Leena, and for all of the other
girls.

"I'm sure." I squeezed his hand, turning away from Leena
and toward the next clue. "Let's go."

CHAPTER 16

9:53 PM

People were everywhere. Cars streamed down Jonesy's quarter mile-long gravel drive, parking in surprisingly neat rows between the ancient farmhouse and the cornfields.

I stood under Japanese lanterns that were hanging from the lowest branches of an elm tree, a cup of lukewarm keg beer clutched in one hand, while a more-than-slightly-drunk Jude told the story of how he'd once found Mr. Epperson and Mrs. Hutch—teachers at the high school, both married, but not to each other—hooking up in the back of the auditorium. I knew all the raunchy details. It had been sophomore year, the auditorium was dark(ish) when Jude went in, searching for the missing science folder he thought he'd left after an assembly, and *surprise!*, found Mrs. Hutch with her skirt around her waist, straddling Mr. Epperson who was leaning back in a creaky auditorium seat.

I heard the cadence of Jude's slurred words, but I wasn't following the story. Instead, my eyes roamed the crowd until they landed on Tripp wearing a backward baseball cap, standing atop a small hill in the shadows at the edge of the property, shifting his weight from one foot to the other. I found Hannah next: she was getting up from a wooden bench by the farmhouse garden, waving goodbye as she walked away from the group she'd been sitting with. Her body was backlit by strands of white twinkle lights fixed to the frame of the farmhouse, giving the building with its peeling paint an otherworldly feel. She moved quickly, her legs sweeping across the grass, tapping her wrist with a quick nod as she came closer.

I checked my phone.

9:57.

It was time.

My heart pounded in my chest. For more than twenty-four hours, I'd known that this moment would come, yet I still wasn't ready to face it.

Jude's voice rose higher as he geared up for the climax of his story—an amplified imitation of Mrs. Hutch reaching a climax of her own. People surrounded him, as usual, hanging on his every word. He was totally in his element, which was convenient for me since I needed to slip away. Hannah wove her way through the crowd and placed a hand on my shoulder, pulling me back through three rows of bodies.

"Breathe," Hannah whispered.

"Easier said than done."

"You can do this." Hannah grabbed my hands and gave them a quick squeeze.

"*We* can do this," I said. "I'm not going up there alone."

Hannah bit her lip. "There's been a little change of plans."

"No," I said. "No one is changing plans on me now."

"Tripp found me earlier, and said he'd been here all day, help-ing to set up so he could keep watch of who was on the property.

He was trying to catch whoever is behind all of this as he was leaving the clue and . . . well, you know. Anyway, it didn't work because all kinds of people were in and out of the barn, prepping for tonight, so—"

"So, what? We're all going in. Together. I'm not going up to that hayloft by myself."

"Not by yourself. Just not with all of us."

"What the hell, Hannah? I thought you guys—"

"Look, B, there's no time. It's past ten by now. You have to get in there. Tripp's watching you from up on the hill. I'm going to keep track of Jude to make sure he doesn't follow and stumble in on you searching around."

"Thank you. I hate that you and the guys have been pulled into this and I want to keep Jude as far removed as possible. But if I'm not going alone, that leaves—"

"Wes." Hannah twisted my shoulders and gave me a swat on the butt. "He's waiting for you at the side door of the barn. Hurry."

I walked away without a word. It was too late to argue.

When I turned the corner, I saw him, the long shadow of his body stretching across the ground, melting beneath my feet.

"You're late."

"Hardly," I said. "It can't be more than three minutes after—"

"Like I said, late. But there's no time for debating. We gotta make this fast. In and out."

"Trust me," I said. "I'm down with fast."

Twisting the handle, Wes pulled open the door and disappeared into the shadows of the barn. I followed, squinting. The close air was thick with a mixture of sweet-smelling hay and motor oil. "Let there be light," he said. And then there was a beam that poured from his phone onto the hay-covered planks beneath our feet.

I grabbed onto his arm, hating myself for needing the connection, and let him pull me toward the rickety ladder.

"There's not going to be another body," I said, trying to convince myself. I was terrified of finding another one of my missing friends the same way I'd found Leena. "There's no way someone would bring a body here, to the middle of the party, right?"

Wes stopped at the base of the ladder, one foot propped on the bottom rung, and handed me his phone, aiming the light up so he could see where he was climbing. "Don't think about that," he said.

And then he was moving—up and up and up—until he reached the top, and swung his leg toward the solid floor of the hayloft.

"See anything?" I asked.

"Nothing up here," he said. "Come on, now."

I tucked the phone in the back pocket of my jeans, careful not to turn off the light, and began climbing. When I reached the top, Wes held out his hand, pulling me to his body with one swift jerk. My cheek grazed his shirt as his arm wrapped around my waist. I caught a whiff of his scent—boy and summer and beer—and felt dizzy with the weight of our past.

Wes didn't say a word as I stepped away from him, tugging his phone out. He turned and walked the length of the loft with slow, tentative footsteps. All I saw at first were bales of hay secured with thick twine, stacked high against the back wall. Then the beam from the flashlight skimmed across several brightly colored boxes of fireworks, stashed against the wall to the right of the ladder.

"What's over there?" Wes asked, pointing to a back corner that was so dark it looked like a black hole. I guided the beam toward the deep shadow, expecting the void to suck in the light. But then I saw it sitting atop a haybale—a strip of red, the shade familiar and eerie—and relief flooded my body as I realized it was just another envelope. A clue. Nothing more.

"Game on," Wes said, grabbing the phone from my hand and rushing toward the envelope.

Then I heard a creaking, shuddering sound—the barn door opening and closing—and I knew someone else was in the building with us.

"Who's up there?"

The voice was deep. Solid. And it sounded familiar. But my brain wasn't processing anything beyond the fact that the girls—Emily, JJ, Becca, Suze—still might be alive. I really might have a chance to save them.

That's when the overhead light flipped on, a bright, searing glow that burned my eyes.

"Bailey?"

Jude.

I stepped to the edge of the hayloft and looked down, meeting his eyes, which were clouding with a slow kind of confusion.

"What are you doing up there?"

My heart was beating so loudly, I wondered if he could hear it.

"I've been looking for you." Jude was at the base of the ladder, one foot on the bottom rung, his hands reaching out to grip the sides. "You shouldn't be up there."

"I'm fine." I rushed to the ladder, twisting around so I could back my way down. "Really. I am."

"Is someone up there with you?" Jude asked, shadows playing across the soft worry of his face as the single bulb swung from the ceiling above us. God, I loved the way he looked at me.

"No." My heart pounded harder, louder. I really hated lying—especially to Jude. "I'm alone. Just needed to get away for a—"

Wes's phone chimed and I froze, the uneven grain of the wooden rung scratching my skin as I dropped my forehead against it.

"Who's up there?" Jude's voice was slow, his words laced with more than a hint of impatience.

"It's me, dude." Wes looked down at us, his hair hanging into his eyes as he stood at the edge of the loft, one hand on the top of the ladder. I was directly between them, and could feel the tension.

"Oh." Jude's mouth tightened. By the time I reached the ground, his jaw was clenched.

"I asked her to help me find the fireworks." Wes swung his leg over the ladder and began climbing down. Beneath the ripple of his untucked T-shirt, I caught a glimpse of the red envelope peeking up from the waistband of his jeans. Skipping the last few rungs with one giant leap, he turned and faced Jude. "Thought it would be cool to sneak one of the bigger ones out and set it off early."

Jude narrowed his eyes and looked from Wes to me and back again. "Which one did you choose?"

"Huh?" Wes asked.

"The fireworks?" Jude raised his eyebrows, the anger in his voice clear. "Which one did you choose? To set off early?"

"Oh." Wes looked at me, pausing briefly. "I didn't. I mean, I couldn't. Bailey here wouldn't let me."

Jude looked at me suspiciously. "And you lied to me just now because . . . ?"

"You went with the guys to get them. I thought you'd be pissed." I reached out for Jude's hand, but he pulled away. Suddenly, I was afraid of losing more than just the girls.

"So you're done then?" Jude asked, swaying a bit. "We can go back to the party?"

"Not quite yet," I said, hating the waver in my voice, hating that I had to lie to Jude again. We needed enough time to read the clue and figure out our next move.

"There's an issue," Wes said. "Nothing to worry about, just something with Tripp we need to take care of."

"Right," I said with a nod. "He's acting a little off today."

"Really?" Jude asked. "I hadn't noticed."

"Wes says it's been going on for a while now, that he's been meaning to call and talk to me, maybe even warn my parents, but he didn't want to worry us or get Tripp in trouble." I tried to look concerned, which wasn't so hard. "That's why we were really up there—we had to ditch Tripp so we could talk without him eavesdropping. We just saw the fireworks and Wes got the idea to steal one. But, anyway, Wes and I, we're going to—"

"—try to get a handle on the situation," Wes finished.

"Right." I nodded. "Without my parents."

"He's in some kind of trouble?" Jude asked, concern lining his face. Here I was, lying, and he was worried about my brother? I was awful. Horrible.

I'd make it up to him. As soon as I pulled myself out of this scavenger hunt.

"He's not in any trouble." Wes said. "He's just had a rough year. The transition to college wasn't easy for him. I don't want to leave you out, but it's kind of a secret mission. The type of thing that can only include people Tripp has known his entire life."

"Please don't take that wrong," I said, "but Wes is right. This has to be Tripp's inner circle, the people he trusts the most."

"Okay." Jude shrugged, like he didn't care, but he couldn't hide the disappointment in his eyes. "You'll be back, though, right?"

"I think so," I said, even though I had no idea.

"The thing is, we need to drive. Off the property. You think that'll be a problem?" Watching Wes in action, seeing firsthand how naturally lies flowed from his lips, both scared and irritated me. There was no denying he'd had a lot of practice.

Jude ran a hand through his hair, blowing out a stream of air. His eyes were softer now. Hurt.

"I guess I could find the stash of keys. Just don't tell anyone."

I followed Jude out of the barn, watching the muscles ripple in his arm as he pulled the chain and turned off the light hanging from the rafters. I felt Wes behind me every step of the way, the weight of the two pressing against me, making me feel like I was being flattened into a paper-thin version of myself.

CHAPTER 17

10:19 PM

"Read it again," I said from the front passenger seat as Hannah steered her Escape around a curve in the road.

"It's not going to change," Wes said from the behind me.

I twisted around, reaching through the space between the front seats, and yanked the clue from his hand.

"He's right, B," Tripp said, the beams from the car behind us backlighting him through the rear window. "We picked a location. Now we have to trust our decision and just go."

"But are we sure it was the right decision?" I asked. "We have to make sure we're going the right way."

"If you want me to turn the car around, tell me now," Hannah said, her words rushed, the tone beneath them unsure.

"We have to hurry." Tripp's voice cracked. "There's a chance she's alive so we can't screw this—"

"Can everyone just *shut up* for one second?" I asked, flipping on the overhead light and reading each word again carefully.

HERE'S YOUR CLUE
TO FINDING TROPHY NUMBER TWO.
SHE WAS BREATHING WHEN I LEFT HER.

SHE'S BEEN GRETEL AND BLANCHE,
BUT NOTHING COMPARES
TO HER DEBUT AS ROBIN GOODFELLOW.

GO STRAIGHT TO HIS STAGE,
AND FIND WHAT'S WAITING FOR YOU.

SAVE HER IF YOU CAN,
BUT DON'T STOP NOW
OR ELSE——I SWEAR IT——THIS WILL GET WORSE
FOR ALL OF YOU.

HAPPY HUNTING!

"Robin Goodfellow is from *A Midsummer Night's Dream*," I said. "We read it sophomore year in English class. Becca bragged for weeks about landing the role of Puck. But the clue says we have to go to his stage. The school was renovating the auditorium that year, and—"

"The entire play takes place in the woods," Hannah said, her eyes fixed on the road. "We have to be going the right way."

"You're sure we shouldn't be heading to the community theater?"

I looked at the shadows seeping across the blacktop just ahead of the car's headlights, my eyes following the twisting pavement that led to Timber Park, the largest rec area in town. It had jogging trails, playgrounds, soccer fields—and an outdoor amphitheater right at its center.

The clock in the dashboard glowed a bright blueish-green: 10:22.

"I'm not *sure* sure," Hannah said. "I didn't go see the stupid play or anything, but—"

"Whoever's doing this isn't stupid enough to lead us to the center of town. Too much risk of exposure," I said. "We have to be right."

As the seconds passed, I tried not to worry. I tried to make myself believe that we would still be able to save Becca.

And then we were passing through the wooden arch that led into Timber Park. Hannah raced down the tree-lined road, skidding to a stop in the back lot, and we all shoved our doors open and jumped out.

We ran.

As fast was could.

Racing across the blacktop.

Leaping over parking blocks.

Plunging into the grass beyond.

"Faster," I said. "We have to go faster!"

Tripp and Wes were gaining speed, arms pumping, legs straining, pulling ahead with each step.

I dug my feet into the ground, pushing off with all the strength that I had.

My hair whipped against my back.

My heart exploded in my chest, fear and hope clashing.

We were close.

So close.

Hold on, I told her. *We're coming for you.*

Tripp and Wes dashed through the trees, shadows swallowing them whole.

As soon as they disappeared from view, I heard the rumble.

The echo of what sounded like thousands of hands.

Clapping.

And I wondered who else was here.

Then Hannah was by my side.

Right there with me.

Rounding the trees.

Dashing with me into the shadows.

My eyes darted to the domed stage.

A lattice of bluish moonlight trickled through the trees.

Another burst of applause erupted, the sound somehow frantic, wild.

I thought it was a good sign.

She wasn't alone.

But then my mind caught up.

The area in front of the stage was empty.

There was no audience tonight.

I tried to focus, each step reverberating throughout my body.

Wes leaped up, a seamless arc from the grass to the lip of the stage, his arms spread wide for balance. Tripp was right behind, his feet pummeling the stage boards, the sound echoing.

The applause came again, ripping the night open.

I kept running, leaping and catching myself on the edge of the stage before dragging myself up. Hannah was behind me. She stood and swiped her palms down the front of her shorts.

"Oh, no," she said, her voice a shaky whisper.

I tried to catch my breath as I took in the details:

Wes and Tripp kneeling.

The light shining from the phone in Wes's hand.

The girl between them, slack, lying on a sky-blue blanket.

Thick waves of red hair fanning out around her head.

Blue-black bruises ringing her ankles.

The chipped purple paint on her jagged fingernails.

And the swelling.

It distorted her entire face—lips, eyes, cheeks—running down to her neck.

Even though she looked nothing like herself, we all knew who she was. The hair—her fiery trademark on stage and off—said it all. This was triple threat Becca Hillyer. She'd won the leads in the school musical three years in a row. She'd spent her entire high school career balancing her performances with school, and earning her place as valedictorian. She'd received early acceptance to Juilliard for her mad skills on the piano. Becca Hillyer—Missing Girl Number Three—who, according to *The Bakersville Dozen*, was "Hot for Teacher." The rumor had never been proven, of course, but apparently, Mr. Epperson and Mrs. Hutch weren't the only ones to get off in the school auditorium.

"She's still breathing, right?" Hannah cried, her voice nearly hysterical. "She has to be breathing."

Tripp leaned down, his cheek inches from Becca's puffy mouth. "I don't think so."

We'd failed.

On every level.

CHAPTER 18
10:41 PM

"Focus. We have to focus." Hannah's voice changed. The emotion had hardened, solidified. "We need to be careful. None of us can get too close. The cops'll find any evidence we leave behind."

"What the hell are you talking about?" Tripp asked, one hand hovering over both of Becca's, which, like Leena's, were clasped over her chest, holding a red envelope. "I have to check for a pulse."

"You touch her and you risk leaving DNA behind." Hannah walked toward the back of the amphitheater and disappeared into the shadows. "Do I need to add that contaminating a murder scene could lead to you being *charged* with that murder?"

"What if she's still alive?" I asked, my voice growing louder to compete with another round of the applause. All at once, I remembered a thousand Becca moments: Becca directing plays during recess in middle school; Becca smiling quietly as people congratulated her on, yet again securing the lead role; Becca hunched over the keys of a grand piano, her hands flying; Becca making funny faces behind Sylvie's back as she focused on her whiteboard. The memories made my stomach churn. I thought I might throw up. "She could still be alive. We won't know unless—"

"She's not," Hannah said, her words clipped. "It was stupid for us to hope. We wouldn't be here if she was still alive. This guy's too careful. Our hope is his bait. It's why he's timing the clues. He's not going to let us save her or any of the others. If he lets them live, they could provide information that would give us an advantage."

"Hannah's right," Tripp said, as he drew his hand away from Becca's swollen neck. "No pulse. But she's still warm. So we were close."

Hannah snorted. "Way to listen to my advice. This whole thing could be a set-up. You know that, right?"

Tripp's words echoed through my thoughts: *She's still warm* . . . "I think I'm going to throw up."

"Don't," Hannah said. "That's major evidence. A treasure trove of DNA for the cops to play with."

And then there was a click so loud it practically split the night in two. The applause stopped abruptly, leaving behind a ghostly echo.

"You stopped the clapping," Wes said. "How'd you—"

"Old-school tape recorder." Hannah stepped out of the shadows with a rectangular-shaped black box in her hand. "I just pressed the little button that said STOP."

"Smartass." Tripp pointed at the tape recorder. "I thought you were worried about leaving behind evidence."

Hannah's voice was all business. "This evidence is leaving with us. Now, quick, take some pictures of her."

"What are you talking about?" Wes asked, disgusted.

"We can't stand around here all night waiting to be found with her body," Hannah said. "But we need to be able to remember exactly how she was positioned, so that we can study the details. Any clue could help us figure out who's behind all of this."

I looked at the envelope—the black ink, the precise block letters that spelled out my name—trying to push away the knowledge that Becca's body was still warm. "We need the clue," I said, my words a whisper.

"Obviously," Hannah said. "But we can't move the envelope until Wes and Tripp get a few pictures."

Tripp stood slowly and tucked his hands in the pockets of his cargo shorts. "There is no freaking way I'm taking pictures of a dead girl with my phone. Talk about evidence."

"Seriously?" Hannah asked, propping a hand on her hip. "You know your sister's life is on the line, right? This freak singled out Bailey from all the other girls to play his disgusting game, which means he has some specific interest in her. Don't you think that's strange, especially since the cops can't figure out why she was included at all?"

"What's that supposed to mean?" I asked.

Hannah's eyes went wide. "Oh, come on, you must have noticed. All the other girls have a thing that makes them stand out. Some kind of talent or—"

"You're saying I don't have any talent?"

"Not like getting in early to Julliard or Parsons. Now is not the time to be sensitive. It's a fact that sets you apart from the rest of the girls. For some reason, you not only made the cut, but you're the one the killer picked to play this game? If we don't get this right, you're probably next."

"We have to keep Bailey safe, no matter what." Tripp's voice was raw. "But we also have to protect ourselves. You're acting all worried about us *leaving evidence behind*, but in the same breath you're telling me to take pictures, to *create* evidence so I can carry it with me and implicate myself? It doesn't make any sense, Hannah!"

She glared at him. "You have to calm down."

"CALM DOWN?" Tripp yelled. "You have got to be kidding me! You want to know what I think?"

"Lemme guess." Hannah rolled her eyes. "You think we should call the cops again. You think we should take the chance and tell someone, but we can't—"

"No." He crossed his arms over his chest. "I think you just might be in on this. Maybe *you're* the one trying to set us up."

Tripp's words hung in the air, mixing with the sharp, barking call of a dog in the distance.

Hannah stood there, her lips pressed tight, twitching at the corners. She was blazing mad. Watching her reaction, I hated myself for thinking it, but couldn't she be in on this?

She knew my locker combination as well as her own. She'd been with Sylvie Warner just after Sylvie stole the tiara. Hannah was the one who had insisted that we go back to Leena's body, she'd been the one to find the tiara on Leena's head. She'd left me when she was supposed to meet me in the woods . . . which would have given her time to plant the clue in the hayloft at Jonesy's. She knew a lot about creepy crime scenes, maybe even enough to pull something like this off.

But no. *No.* It couldn't be Hannah. Even if she had all the opportunity in the world, she had absolutely no motive.

"Bailey? You're not going to defend me?" Hannah whispered, her eyes glistening with anger. "I've stood by your side from the very beginning, and you're not going to say anything after he accuses me of . . . what, Tripp? Being *in on this*?"

Tripp took a deep breath, shaking his head. "I'm sorry, Han, I just—"

"—thought you'd accuse me of somehow kidnapping five girls and holding them hostage for months? Killing two of them in two days? All while plotting and executing a twisted scavenger hunt to, what, fuck with my *best friend in the world*?"

"Look, I'm just freaked out, okay?" Tripp ran his hand through his hair, pulling his phone from the pocket of his shorts with shaky hands. "I assume that's a natural reaction after being directed to take pictures of a dead chick."

"It's not like I asked you to take the pictures for kicks," Hannah said.

Tripp grimaced. "I'm sorry. I know you're trying to help. I'll take the damn pictures."

"No," Hannah said. "Really. I wouldn't want to put you out or anything."

Tripp focused on Becca's body. The flash went off, a blinding light.

There was more barking, a string of harsh guttural sounds that drifted out from the trails behind the amphitheater.

"You guys hear that?" I asked.

"What?" Tripp aimed his camera and shot another picture of poor Becca Hillyer.

"The barking." Wes jumped up from Becca's side, jostling her body. Her hand slipped from her chest and smacked the wooden floor of the stage. "It's closer now."

Tripp squinted as he looked from Wes to me. "I don't hear any—"

Then we heard it again, this time louder, more insistent, and heading toward us.

"Take another picture," Hannah said, her voice urgent. "Make sure you get her face. The swelling, it could be some kind of reaction. We can look it up and—"

"No freaking way." Tripp shoved his phone in his pocket. "We need to get out of here. Now."

"He's right." Wes spun around, grabbing my hand and tugging me toward the edge of the stage.

Tripp leaped just before us, legs bracing as his feet hit the grass. He held his arms out, offering both hands to Hannah. I thought she was going to refuse him on principle, but she grabbed his wrists and let him swing her from the stage. They raced off toward the tree line.

"Ready?" Wes asked, grabbing my hand and squeezing once before slipping away.

And then he jumped.

I was alone on that stage with Becca Hillyer.

I felt her behind me, so I turned back. I owed her one last look.

Then I heard rustling, the snapping of a branch, someone tramping through the wooded trails, coming closer, and fast.

"Bruno!" a woman's voice called out. "Slow down!"

"Come on, B!" Wes whisper-shouted. "Jump!"

But I couldn't. My eyes were locked on the one thing we couldn't leave behind—the envelope emblazoned with my name—the red paper like spilled blood pooling in the center of Becca's chest.

Wes gripped my ankle as I stepped back, giving one swift tug and knocking me off balance until I tumbled to the stage floor.

"For fuck's sake, B. Get down here!"

"Bruno, heel!" The woman's voice was breathless, rushed, and close. Way too close. "Heel, Goddamnit!"

I crawled to the center of the stage, not trusting my shaky legs to hold me.

My fingers grazed the blue blanket. The soft cotton reminded me of my favorite T-shirt. Becca's hair rippled like silk as I grabbed the envelope and pulled it free from the hand still resting on her chest. I swiveled and crawled back to the edge of the stage, this time staying low. The dog's breath was coming in snorting grunts, his owner's feet clomping on the ground close behind.

When I got to the edge of the stage, Wes reached around my waist and pulled me down. My feet had barely grazed the ground before he was hauling me along toward the edge of the woods.

Tripp and Hannah were waiting, ghost-white faces peeking from behind a large tree.

"Shit guys," Hannah said. "I thought you were busted."

Tripp flicked me on my head. "Don't you *ever* pull something like that again!"

"I had to get the clue!" I said, holding out the envelope. "My name's on it, you guys. Talk about leaving evidence behind."

"That was too close." Wes shook his head, pulling me in until my face was tucked against his chest. His heart was beating fast, and I focused on the sound, trying to steady myself.

"Way too close," Tripp said from behind me.

Hannah was silent. She grabbed my shoulder and squeezed.

I pulled away from Wes. I had to. The whole thing—me pressed up against him, him pressed up against me, the two of us wrapped tightly around each other—it felt too familiar. Too good.

The four of us stood huddled, hair tousled, eyes frantic, shivering with adrenaline.

Then we heard the scream.

Becca Hillyer had been found.

The game had just taken a very dangerous turn.

CHAPTER 19

11:17 PM

"What the hell is going on with you and Wes?" Hannah asked. We were back in the field Jonesy was using as a parking lot.

"What are you talking about?" I ignored her stare, focusing on Wes and Tripp, who were just ahead of us. We'd agreed not to walk back together; Hannah and I would wait until the guys were in line for the keg. They'd wanted us to go first, afraid that we might disappear, but I'd said I needed a few minutes to compose myself before returning to the party.

"I'm talking about you and *Wesley Green*." Hannah sighed, twisting sideways so she was facing me. "I'm your best friend, B. And I'm not blind. You want him."

"I do not!" I whisper-shouted, smacking her arm.

Hannah laughed, her eyes going wide. "You *do*!"

"Shut up, Hannah. I'm warning you."

"Oh, come on! Admit it. You've been in love with Wes, like, your entire freaking life!"

"Please. I have not."

"Don't lie to me, Bailey Holzman."

I groaned, dropping my head in my hands. "There's nothing going on. Nothing except being stuck on this hunt with him for the next few days. And, hello? I'm dating Jude. End of story."

"Listen up, B, because I'm only going to say this once: Jude is incredible. He did the whole pine-for-you thing last fall, waiting around like you were the only girl in the world while you played the bashful, hard-to-get—"

"I wasn't acting, Han," I said, thinking of how Jude had made it his mission to win me over. "Trust me, putting Jude off had nothing to do with playing a part."

"Whatever. You decided to give him a chance and you've been inseparable since."

"It was Suze," I said, remembering how she'd stopped me in the hall, lockers slamming all around us, her eyes bright. "Suze Moore is the reason I finally decided to go out with Jude. She said he was a good guy—to the core—and that I'd be crazy not to give him a chance. So I did. And she was right. *You're* right. He is incredible, Han."

"And *that* is exactly my point. Just don't forget what Jude means to you. I'd hate for you to ruin something real for something that isn't. I mean, we're talking about Wes Green here—player of the century, heartbreaker, eternal avoider of commitment. Imagine how many girls he went through this past year, B. That alone should be enough to shut down any lingering—"

"Trust me," I said. "I'm perfectly in control of the situation."

"Are you sure?" Hannah gave me a side-glance. "Because it seems like you needed the reminder."

"Changing the subject now." I looked past Wes and Tripp at the group huddled around the bonfire, its orange-yellow flames lashing out at the dark. "I cannot believe we came back here."

"No other choice," Hannah said. "It would have looked weird if we hadn't. Especially to Jude."

I sighed, pulling my phone from my purse. "He's texted me, like, five times since we left for the park."

Hannah shook her head, twirling a brown curl around one finger. "He's on to you."

"No way he knows anything about the scavenger hunt. I've hardly seen him since I got the first clue."

Hannah untwirled her hair, then started twirling it again, giving me an annoying little shrug. "I meant Wes. Jude's not blind, either. You have to be careful."

"Shut up, Hannah!" I ducked my head and focused on the texts.

JUDE—10:27PM: WHERE ARE YOU? TEXT ME ASAP.

JUDE—10:31PM: FOR REAL. TEXT OR I'M COMING TO FIND YOU.

JUDE—10:47PM: NEED TO TALK. NOW! CALL. ME.

JUDE—10:49PM: B? PLEASE.

JUDE—10:53PM: WHERE ARE YOU?! 911.

And then there were two more, which somehow made all the others seem worse.

SYLVIE W—11:07PM: IS IT TRUE?

SYLVIE W—11:09PM: DON'T AVOID ME, B. I DESERVE AN ANSWER.

I shoved off the side of the car, worry coiling tight in my chest. Jude wasn't the clingy type. He was always cool with letting me do my own thing while he did his. But he was great at romance, coming up with the sweetest surprises like hidden notes and the candlelight picnic in the woods last month when he formally asked me to prom.

"What is it?"

"Something's wrong, I said, speeding through the rows of cars, feeling Hannah close behind me. The crackle-snap of the flames was punctuated with rushed whispers.

I saw Lane, eyes closed, face turned to the sky as he took a swig of beer.

"Where's Jude?" I asked, grabbing his shoulder.

Lane looked at me, his expression razor sharp. "Bailey? Jude's been looking for you."

"Where is he?"

"He's . . . wait. Didn't you hear?"

"Damnit, Lane! *Where is Jude?*"

Lane pointed over his shoulder toward the shadow of the barn. "Back there, but I wouldn't go charging over. He's being questioned right now."

I spun around and ran through the yard, past the tree with the Japanese lanterns, through a throng of people standing in a line fifty feet from the wooden frame of the barn.

"Bailey!" Hannah shouted from behind me. "Wait!"

But I couldn't. My heart was racing again; the lightheaded feeling of fear was back.

I shoved my way through the crowd and found him sitting on a tree stump, just in front of the barn's entrance, the double doors flung wide, a swell of light glowing from beyond, illuminating the three police officers standing around him.

Jude's head was down, his face buried in his hands, elbows resting on his knees. He was shaking, his shoulders jerking up and down.

I didn't stop to wonder what had happened.

I just ran to him, dropping to my knees at his feet.

He looked up, his eyes red and swollen, glistening in the lights.

"Bailey." His voice cracked. His hands shot out, gripping my shoulders. "Thank God, Bailey. You're okay?" He pulled me to him, burying my face against his T-shirt, and I breathed in the scent of cigarettes, deodorant, and woods.

"What's going on?" I whispered into his chest.

"I thought you were gone. I thought you'd been *taken*, and—"

"I'm right here," I said, pulling away from him, grabbing his face in my hands. "What happened? What's wrong, Ju—"

"Bailey Holzman?" The voice coming from behind Jude was gruff.

"Yes."

"You're okay?" another voice asked. Tiny Simmons. I pictured him standing in the grass in my backyard, leering, making me feel like I was on display, making me wonder if he was trying to catch me breaking the rules. The shaky fear of leaving Leena washed over me again, mixing in with the new feeling of leaving Becca behind. I could be looking their killer directly in the eyes.

Too afraid to speak, I simply nodded.

"Good," he said, his lips turning up at the corners in the same fake half smile he'd used back at my house. "We've been concerned. We were going to call your parents as soon as we secured the scene."

"Scene?" I asked. "What scene?"

"I wasn't sure where you went." Jude sniffed loudly, rubbing his nose with the back of his hand. "I've been totally freaked."

"Did you leave the farm?" Tiny asked, raising his eyebrows, the tone of his voice sounding more eager than it should for an officer questioning a potential victim. "Jude said he texted you several times, but you didn't reply."

I opened my mouth, but had no idea how to respond. There was no way I could tell a trio of police officers that I'd just been at the Timber Park amphitheater where Becca Hillyer's body was lying center stage. Especially if Tiny Simmons was the one behind the threats. This entire thing could be a horrific test, and if I failed, I would be putting the lives of seven other girls at risk.

"We went back home." The lie slid from my lips without hesitation. I looked over my shoulder and found Wes standing with his shoulders pulled back, chest tight, like he was ready for a fight. Tripp and Hannah were on either side of him. "Forgot something. No big deal."

"So you were right." Tiny looked down at Jude.

"What's he talking about?" I whispered.

Jude shook his head, dropping his eyes to the ground. "I didn't like it—you leaving the party—it felt strange and I thought you seemed nervous, like maybe you didn't really want to go. So I went looking for you. I thought if I walked through the woods, I'd be able to catch up and maybe snag a ride back here with you guys."

"You went to my house?" I asked, my stomach twisting. I'd just told Jude and three police officers that we'd gone home. If Jude did anything to ruin that story, we were screwed. Like, taken to the station, locked in an interrogation room, *Did you happen to find a dead body at Timber Park?* screwed.

Jude shook his head.

"I'm confused," I said, placing a finger under his chin and tipping his face up so he had to look at me. "You didn't go to my house?"

"I didn't make it that far." His voice was a choked whisper.

"Okay, well where did you go?"

"The pond."

I felt my entire body stiffen. Tiny caught the reaction—I could feel his eyes on me.

"I followed the trail to the pond and was heading to your house, but I had to take a piss."

I pictured her then, Leena, lying still in her grassy grave . . .

"I walked around that big tree with the rope swing and the rotting step ladder, and went straight into the grasses off to the side."

. . . her hands tucked neatly together in the center of her chest . . .

"I was a little stumbly and went farther in than I'd planned."

. . . her blood red lips shining in the bright light of the moon.

"And I saw something glowing on the ground. I figured it was someone's phone. Maybe someone else who'd had to piss in the woods like me." Jude gasped for air.

I wondered if Leena had gasped, too.

"But it wasn't a phone," he said. "It was a tiara, the fake diamonds catching the moonlight and—"

Jude looked right at me, then squeezed his eyes tight. Tears leaked down his cheeks.

"I found her," Jude said. "I found Leena."

I didn't move.

Stayed solid as stone.

And I waited.

Because I knew he wasn't finished.

"She's dead, B. Leena's dead."

Jude leaned forward, hiding his face in the slope of my neck, and he began to sob.

SUNDAY
JUNE 4

CHAPTER 20

1:23 AM

I couldn't sleep. I was lying on my stomach on top of my bed with my feet kicked up in the air, the ominous red envelope caught in a beam of moonlight streaming in from my window. My phone buzzed, offering a much needed distraction.

> SYLVIE W—1:24AM: WORD'S OUT. HAD TO TELL THE GIRLS.
>
> AMY L—1:24AM: OHMYGOD, B. ARE YOU OK?
>
> SUMMER J—1:26AM: PLEASE COME BACK. WE NEED YOU HERE.
>
> BETH K—1:28AM: IS JUDE A WRECK? WHAT DID HE TELL YOU?
>
> KELSEY H—1:29AM: IS IT REALLY TRUE?

I couldn't deal with them. Not now. I powered off my phone and turned it facedown on my bedspread. And that just brought me back around to the envelope. My name stared up at me, taunting me. I sighed, weighing my options. I wished I could just tuck the envelope into the inside pocket of my purse, along with the others, and forget everything.

But I knew that wouldn't work.

I slipped my finger under the open flap and tugged the card free for what felt like the hundredth time.

The words were the same, not that I had expected them to change since I'd first read the note in the front seat of Hannah's Escape as she'd driven us from the park back to the party. While the police shut down the festivities at Jonesy's farm, I'd debated handing the clue over, just ending the whole hunt right then and there, but fear stopped me. Fear that if I gave up, I'd face an even worse situation, fear that if Tiny was the killer, we'd lose even more girls and all because I didn't follow a rule.

The knowing look Tiny had given me as Jude pulled himself together had convinced me I was making the right decision back at the party. But as I re-read the latest clue, I wasn't sure that *right* decisions existed anymore.

DID YOU LIKE IT,

BAILEY?

HER STANDING OVATION?

A FINAL PERFORMANCE DESERVES ONE!

HERE'S HOPING SHE HEARD THE ROARING APPLAUSE . . .

AS SHE DRIFTED AWAY.

AND NOW IT'S TIME

TO KEEP

MOVING FORWARD.

THE NEXT TASK IS A BREEZE:

SIMPLY PONDER WHICH TOPPINGS

YOU WILL CHOOSE AT THE FLYING PIZZA.

TOMORROW NIGHT.
10PM.

ORDER FIRST,
THEN SIT AND WAIT.
YOUR NEXT CLUE COME BY SPECIAL DELIVERY.

HAPPY HUNTING!

My mind was spinning. The Flying Pizza sits in the center of town. Like, dead center. The kidnapper was daring to take this hunt public. So many things could go wrong. I felt trapped, my only choice to follow the clue and wait for whatever came next.

Anger spread through me. For the girls—all of them, but especially Leena and Becca—and for myself.

No one had the right to do this to us.

I realized as I lay there in the purplish glow of the moon that I had lost all feeling of control. I'd thrown it away as soon as I'd found Leena by the pond.

But that was over.

It was time for me to figure a way out of this mess.

I had to formulate a plan.

I flipped over onto my back, eyes closed as I let this new determination wash over me.

But my resolve was shattered by the *clickety-clack* of something hitting my window.

I bolted upright, my bare feet sweeping to the floor, and stepped silently across my room. It was instinctive, I realized—an automatic reaction. My body tingled as I parted the curtains. I expected to find Wes, his face turned up to me, glowing in the light of the moon, just like so many nights from last summer.

When I realized I was wrong, the guilt flooded in. Jude was standing below my window, offering a sad smile as he waved for me to come meet him.

I held a finger in the air, then took a deep breath, reminding myself as I swept down the back staircase and through the kitchen that I had nothing to feel mixed up about. The past was just that: the past.

"I had to see you," Jude said. He stood there, his hands tucked into the front pockets of his jeans, swaying back and forth. Exactly how much had he had to drink?

"Are you okay?" I asked.

Jude shrugged.

"How did you get here?"

"Walked," he said. "From Jonesy's. The police took me to the station for questioning, then called my parents. They obviously freaked, but I talked them into letting me stay at Jonesy's anyway."

"And then you walked over here?"

"I couldn't sleep. Lane's already passed out in his tent, snoring. Jonesy and his brothers are on clean-up crew."

"You came through the woods?" I asked, though I knew the answer from the thistles clinging to the legs of his jeans.

"Yeah, but I—" Jude's voice cracked. He cleared his throat. "I had to take the long way. The pond is swarming with cops. They're looking for evidence."

I stiffened. Evidence.

Wes and I had been at the scene a little more than twenty-four hours ago; we'd fallen right on that blanket, and I'd thrown up on the ground next to Leena's body. Then we'd taken Tripp and Hannah to see what we had found. I wondered what we'd left behind that we didn't even know about.

"Should we walk?" I asked, suddenly wanting to go directly to the pond, where I could hide in deep shadows and watch the police.

"Nah." Jude turned and stumbled toward the hammock, collapsing onto the canvas.

He held a hand out to me, and I felt a surge of relief as he wrapped his arm around my waist and pulled me down. I snuggled up to his side, breathing him in, feeling the heat of him melt away all my fears.

Jude was safe, and he was mine. He knew me better than anyone. It's like the scavenger hunt—being forced to follow the clues with Wes at my side distracting me—had made me forget the facts, but lying there next to Jude brought them all rushing back.

I had this sudden urge to spill everything: the clues and the threats and how I had been the first to find Leena. That I'd left her there. And then done the same to Becca.

"I have something to tell you," I said slowly.

"Me, too. Can I go first?"

I closed my eyes, pressing my cheek to his chest, feeling the vibration of his voice run down the length of my body until it hit my toes.

"Of course." I was sure he had a lot to unload. He probably wanted to tell me all about what he'd seen when he'd found Leena.

"I'm worried about you," Jude said, his words heavy.

"What's new?" I asked. "People have been worrying about me—about all of the girls from *The Bakersville Dozen*—for months now."

"It's more than that," Jude said, his voice slow, cautious.

I met his eyes. "What's up?"

"I don't want to piss you off."

"What's going to piss me off?"

"It has to do with Wes. I know he's like a brother to you. That you're protective of him. But—"

"I'm hardly protective," I said, rolling my eyes. "He can handle himself."

"Okay," Jude said. "That's good."

"What is it?"

"I don't trust him."

"With what?"

"You."

I wasn't sure what to say next. I pressed my lips together, waiting. Jude took a deep breath. "It's not like I'm spending time with him," I said. "I mean, he just got home from college, like, forty-eight hours ago."

"Yeah, but he's been back before now." Jude dropped a foot to the ground and started slowly swinging the hammock. "I've seen him around a few times."

"When?" I asked, trying to sound casual. As far as I knew, Wes hadn't been home since Winter Break.

"I saw him driving through town a few months ago. Then again on one of the back roads last month."

I shrugged, but that odd feeling of fear and doubt and not knowing who to trust, started creeping back in, spreading to places I'd never expected it to reach.

"So?"

"I don't know," Jude said. "It's not something I can put my finger on, okay? But he's never serious, so all of his pranks and plots seem shady. I never know what he's thinking. It's like he has something to hide."

"Jude," I said, "Wes is the last thing you need to be—"

"Take the last day of school. I saw Wes in the hall, and he just breezed past me, like he'd never seen me before."

"Wes was at school yesterday?" I asked, trying to sound nonchalant when I felt exactly the opposite. Wes hadn't said a thing, not even when our attempts to find out about the stolen tiara had taken us right to the school's main doors.

"Yeah. It was right after the final bell. I thought it was fate that the host of last year's Last Day Ceremony walked past me right before we started. I tried to stop him so I could ask a few questions about how he introduced the music, but he just blew me off."

My skin broke out in a cold sweat. If Wes was hiding a trip to school, what else was he hiding? And why?

"Anyway, he was headed toward the student lot—seemed to be in a big hurry. But that's not what really bothered me. Tonight was just weird. The way he dragged you away from the party."

"It wasn't like that. I told you, I had to go with him."

"Right," Jude said. "Because of something he told you about your brother. Who seems totally fine to me, by the way. I mean, I know you trust Wes, but I don't. He's shifty. Pulling you all the way up to the hayloft to talk to you about your brother? What was that about?"

I shrugged. "He wanted to talk in private."

"There are lots of other private places on the farm."

My mind raced with all of this new information, my doubt about Wes growing by the second.

"Look." Jude ran his thumb along my jaw. "I trust you, okay? And I'm not trying to be all paranoid or overprotective, but I don't trust that guy. He's either in love with you and trying to stir up something—"

"Jude, that's crazy." I twisted away from him, trying to slip out of the hammock, but he caught my wrist, his fingers squeezing tight.

"That leaves another option," Jude said. "If his whole cloak-and-dagger thing doesn't have to do with you, it might be about something else. *The Bakersville Dozen.* The missing girls."

"Wes doesn't have anything to do with any of that," I said. But as the words slipped out of my mouth, I knew that I could be wrong. The truth was, the killer could be anyone.

"You never know," Jude said.

I slid out of the hammock, feeling it bump against my side as I stepped away. "I'm tired, Jude. I'd better go in."

"I love you," he said, looking up at me. "Bailey, I need you to promise me one thing."

"What?"

He slipped out of the hammock, wavering a little as he stood. He grabbed both of my hands and squeezed them tightly. "Don't be alone with Wes. Not until the police figure out who's behind this whole thing and it's over for good."

I looked Jude in the eyes—he was afraid, but not for himself.

"Okay," I said. "I promise."

Jude sighed, then pulled me to him. "Thank you. You have no idea how much better that makes me feel."

I propped my chin on his shoulder and wrapped my arms around his neck, feeling my feet lift off the ground as he spun me in a slow circle. When my toes hit the grass again, I was facing the shadow of the Greens' house. I glanced up instinctively, my eyes locking on the window of Wes's bedroom.

And I saw him.

He was standing in a ray of moonlight, just beyond the window frame.

Staring out at us.

CHAPTER 21

10:27 AM

"Did you see the press conference?" Hannah asked. I'd called her as I left my house, just like I'd promised. She was driving; the steady sound of wind and music streamed from her end of the line to mine.

"Yeah." I twisted my way down the trail that led away from my house. "When my parents learned about the bodies, they lost it."

"I'm surprised they let you leave the house."

"That's not exactly how it happened," I said. "They flipped into hover mode, but I faked a headache and said I needed to rest. It was easy to sneak out—they were fully engrossed in the media frenzy." Watching my dad comfort my mom as they stared at the TV, tears streaming down their cheeks, made the situation feel terrifyingly real, but sneaking away was a risk I had to take if I ever wanted to find a way out of this mess.

"You're as slick as Wes," Hannah said. "You must have picked up some of his tricks along the way."

"Shut it," I said. "There's no time to talk about Wes. The cops are searching both locations. You think we need to be worried?"

Hannah laughed.

I stopped walking, turning my face to the sun as I leaned against the tree that marked a fork in the trail. "There's nothing funny about any of this."

"That laugh was one of supreme sarcasm. Don't you know me well enough to translate the tone of my—"

"We don't have time for this," I said. "We need a plan, Hannah."

"We *have* a plan," she said. "That's why you're walking out to the pond while I head to the amphitheater."

"Sit-Watch-Wait won't work. We need to get ahead of this guy."

"What are you suggesting? We plant hidden cameras at The Flying Pizza to catch him?"

My stomach churned as I pictured us sitting at a table covered with a red and white checkered tablecloth later that evening, the scent of baking pizza spiraling through the air as we waited for the next clue to be delivered to us.

"Actually," I said, "that's kind of a brilliant idea."

"I was kidding. Where the hell are we supposed to pick up cameras, let alone hide them?"

"I don't know. But if we could, we might actually learn something new."

"*If*s are not something we can work with. So let's get serious. We need to talk suspects."

"I thought we were meeting up with Tripp and Wes to do that later."

"Well, I thought maybe we should chat a little on our own first."

"You have a reason?" I asked, shifting my weight so the tree's bark scraped my back through my T-shirt.

"Kind of."

I sighed.

"I have a few ideas that I might keep to myself when we meet up with them," Hannah said. "I'd like to see what the guys come up with on their own."

"You're testing them?"

"Something like that." I heard a car door click open and slam closed.

"Are you at Timber Park?" I asked.

"Just got here. Parking lot's pretty full. You remember Becca's bumper sticker?"

"The one that says THESPIANS DO IT ON STAGE. WANNA WATCH?"

"That's the one. I'm counting eleven cars with the same sticker. Which means there are lots of mourning thespians here. Should be *dramatic*."

"Hannah," I said with a groan, looking down at the batch of daisies and Queen Anne's lace I'd cut from my mother's garden. The yellow satin ribbon tying them together stirred in the breeze.

"Sorry. I had to," Hannah said. "Okay, aside from the creep factor of Tiny Simmons, we have Roger Turley."

"Both obvious possibilities," I agreed.

"If the rumors are true that Turley was forcing himself on Emily, then he could be the one."

"So why take the other girls?" I asked.

"Diversion. Pulls the focus away from him when the others go missing. And, if he's twisted enough to get it on with his step-daughter, he might actually enjoy a little time with the others."

"Eww," I said. "But you have a point. Plus, he was at school Friday. I'm sure it wouldn't have been hard to find out which locker was mine so he could plant the first clue. And, thanks to you, we already know he was near the locker room where you found Sylvie."

"Which leads us to suspect number three," Hannah said.

"Sylvie Warner." I shook my head, thinking of how solid her voice had been after I'd confronted her about stealing the tiara, her eyes locked on mine as she told me to leave her the fuck alone.

"She's a freak of nature," Hannah said. "Totally type A—high-strung, obsessive and controlling to the extreme. Something just might have set her off, you know? Put her in a place where she thought she needed to teach some people a few lessons."

"She hated Leena," I said. "It was obvious whenever we'd meet to try to figure out who was behind the video. Sylvie was all business, and Leena was always laughing at her. But Sylvie's not strong enough to drag bodies through the woods."

"Maybe she didn't," Hannah said. "Maybe she walked them to the spot where she wanted them found, and then killed them."

"Oh, God, Han, I hadn't thought of that."

"You've gotta think of everything, B. Even your brother's totally effed up suggestion that I might be behind all of this."

"He's an idiot. He didn't mean it," I said, but my heart lurched a little, all the same.

"There's Jude, too," Hannah said. "I hate to add him in, but he actually found Leena's body, which could be suspicious, depending on which way you look at things."

"No way, Hannah. *I* found Leena's body *before* Jude. Does that make me a suspect, too?"

"I wasn't going to go there," Hannah said. "But the cops definitely will if they figure out you were at both scenes. Speaking of, *are* you at the pond yet?"

"No," I said. "I stopped walking. Thought it might look disrespectful if I was on the phone when I got there."

"You're chickening out?"

"Of course not." I pushed away from the tree and started walking down the trail again, my feet carrying me to the last place I wanted to be. "But I'm still not convinced this is a good idea."

"It's perfect," Hannah said. "Everyone's meeting up at one place or the other, though Leena's bound to draw a bigger crowd. Chances are, the person we're looking for will be at one of the scenes. Take notes. Get a video if you can do it without anyone noticing."

"We're done with the suspect list?" I asked.

"Not quite," Hannah said. "I'm throwing Wes's name on it."

"Why Wes?" I asked, trying to keep all emotion out of my voice.

"He followed you out to the pond, Bailey. He put himself there, at the scene, in the exact moment that you found Leena's body. I can't explain how he would be able to take all the girls or put the first note in your locker. Or how he'd have slipped the tiara on Leena's head. But him appearing right by your side when you found Leena would be a genius way to join in on the scavenger hunt so he'd be able to ensure that you'd trust him, all while watching every move you make. It's strange enough to make him a suspect."

With everything Jude had told me, I couldn't help but wonder if she could be right. And then my mind tripped back to Friday afternoon, the moment Wes and I had found Leena lying on that yellow blanket.

"It's not Wes," I said, suddenly sure. "You should have seen him when we found Leena. His face, his voice. He was horrified. And you saw how frantic he was when we were racing to the amphitheater to find Becca. No one could fake that."

"All right," she said. "I was just throwing it out there. It was a longshot, I know. I mean, it's not like you left him alone with Leena. Right?"

"What, so I could go take a dip in the pond or something? Why are you asking me that?"

"The tiara." Hannah said. "If he was with you the entire time, there's no way he could have slipped that tiara on Leena's head after you saw her without it. Which would make him innocent."

And then I remembered texting Hannah just after exiting the grass, standing there after hitting SEND, waiting for Wes to emerge behind me. I'd been entirely focused on trying to forget what I'd seen. How much time had passed between me sending that text and Wes breaking his way into the clearing? A minute? Two? It would have been long enough for him to grab the tiara from where he'd hidden it and plant it on Leena's head.

"I'm almost to the amphitheater," Hannah said. "But there's something else we need to consider."

I couldn't speak. I was too busy trying to come up with a reason—any reason—why Wes had taken a minute or more in

the clearing alone before he'd followed me. A reason that didn't involve him tucking a tiara into Leena's hair.

"The timing of this is important, Bailey. We have to go back to the beginning."

I made the final turn onto the trail leading to the pond, hearing a rush of voices just ahead. Taking a deep breath, I tried to prepare myself.

"Hannah, back to the beginning means the video. All of this started with that stupid video."

"I've been thinking, analyzing every angle, and I'm not sure that's right," Hannah said. "The video was out for more than three months before Emily went missing. That's a lot of time between the two events. Something else—something closer on the timeline—might have triggered the kidnappings."

"But the video is the root of everything."

"It may look that way, but I think there's a lot more going on here. Which might be why the cops are having so much trouble cracking the case."

"Hannah, the girls who have gone missing, they're *all* in the video."

"Right. But we still don't have any motive to connect the video to the disappearances. Or the murders. Think of what we said about Roger Turley. If he's the guy, then all of this loops back to Emily. Maybe he accidentally killed Emily and then took the others to throw the cops off track and the whole thing spiraled out of control."

"So you *do* think it's Turley?"

"I don't know. With so many people involved, there are a thousand scenarios. My point is, we have to stop focusing all of our attention on the video and start to look at the timing of the disappearances."

"Emily went missing January second," I said, my words mingling with the drone of voices drifting from the pond.

"Exactly. So we need to look back to December. What was going on with each of the suspects during Winter Break? There has to be some kind of emotional turmoil—a failure or loss or rejection—that set events in motion."

I stopped suddenly, my feet planted on the trail in a cloud of dust. I'd escaped down this very trail in the dead of winter, powdery white snow kicking up with each of my rushed footsteps, a heavy sense of guilt weighing me down. It had been just a few days after the Christmas party, a few days after my final moments with Wes. He'd essentially hidden from me the rest of his time home, leaving for school without so much as a goodbye. That week had been tumultuous for both of us. There was a definite sense of failure and loss. I wondered if Wes had felt rejected.

"B? Are you still there?"

"Yeah," I whispered. "I'll think, okay? About Winter Break. About stuff that might have triggered the kidnapping. But I'm at the pond now. Call you later."

I shoved my phone into the back pocket of my shorts. Then I bent over, propping my hands on my knees as I tried to catch my breath and push away the memories.

Memories of my black wedge heels sinking into plush carpet as I climbed the Greens' back staircase; the pine-scented garland wrapped around the banister, lit by a string of white twinkle lights; the sound of chatter below, mingling with the clinking of silver on china; the wobble of my body as I hit the top step and turned right, following behind an unsteady Wes as he navigated the dark hallway; the soft giggle that I couldn't quite hold back as we stepped into his bedroom and he closed the door behind us, one finger pressed to his lips.

"I missed you," he'd said, his apple-cinnamon words coating my entire body.

"I didn't miss you," I replied, the smirk on my lips feeling numb after three glasses of spiked apple cider.

"Liar." His eyes twinkled with mischief.

I tipped my head to the side, ignoring the wild beat of my heart. "I have a boyfriend now."

"Jude?"

I nodded. "I think I love him."

Wes's eyes had gone dark for a fraction of a second. But then he'd smiled. "You up for one more night?"

"Our secret?" I'd whispered, enjoying the comfort of old patterns.

"Always." He'd leaned in, waiting for me to meet him halfway.

I did.

With Wes, I always did.

Even when I knew it would hurt in the end.

Because, with Wes, the pain was worth it.

The thing was, I had no idea that night would hurt anyone besides me.

CHAPTER 22

10:43 AM

As I rounded the final bend, I saw him, my eyes locking on his profile. It was like my body had some kind of super-powered Wes radar. From his spot in the crowd, he glanced at me before I could look away, tilting his chin up in a quick hello. I ignored him, avoiding his eyes specifically, because that type of contact would cloud my thinking. If he was somehow involved in this mess, I must have played a part in sending him over the edge. But that was ridiculous. Wes had never cared that much about anything.

A throng of cheerleaders—freshman through varsity—stood near the edge of the pond where the yellow POLICE LINE—DO NOT CROSS tape began. The cordon line snaked through the grasses, offering a wide perimeter around the spot where Leena's body had been, and wound its way to the opposite side of the jumping tree, stopping there where the water began. The rope hanging from the tree swayed slightly in the breeze, and I wondered if a ghostly version of Leena was hanging on, watching over all of us.

All of Leena's cheer sisters looked uncharacteristically swollen and soggy, leaning against at least a dozen of the varsity footballers. Behind them stood social mid-listers, people Leena had probably never spoken to in her life, but who felt as if they actually had known her. Behind them were the gawkers, standing on tippy-toe, trying to get glimpse of the final resting spot of the most popular girl in school. Almost everyone was holding some sort of offering—flowers, notes, pictures—waiting to add their gift to the pile forming near the base of a tree.

From my position near the trailhead, off to the side of the group, I had the perfect view. Most faces were angled toward me, so I could at least get a profile shot of the crowd. Pulling my phone from my pocket, I held it low so it wasn't completely obvious, and pressed the camera app. I was about to select VIDEO when I heard movement close by.

"Hey," came a voice from behind me, so soft I almost didn't recognize the sound.

I turned, feeling at ease for the first time all day.

"Jude," I said. "I tried to call you but—"

"I'm sorry." Jude's hair fell forward, curtaining his face as he looked at the ground. "I couldn't talk. I'm still—I can't stop thinking about her. It was just so awful and I'm not sure how to . . ."

As he trailed off, I was finally able to focus. Jude was a mess, totally out of character, and looked nothing like himself: eyes swollen and red; skin one shade away from I'm-going-to-throw-up; the same clothes from last night, wrinkled and dirty.

"Are you okay?" I asked, my hand gripping his wrist.

"I wasn't sure if I could come today. But then I wandered the woods and kind of ended up here without thinking." He shrugged, tugging free before reaching up with both hands and scraping his fingers through his hair. "This whole thing is crazy.

I can't get her out of my head, you know? The way she was lying there, so freaking still. It was horrible, but the worst part is how I can't stop thinking that it could have been you." Jude paused, his eyes going wide. "Sorry. I didn't mean for it to come out that way. That's gotta be the worst thing I could have said."

"It's okay. Trust me, it's not like I haven't already thought the same thing. My parents did, too. It's natural, right?" I took a deep breath and let it stream slowly from my lips. Jude needed me, which was going to make it impossible to shoot video of the mourners. I took his hand and led him a little closer to the crowd.

"The cheerleaders just sang a song," Jude whispered. "They finished a few minutes before you got here. Something about making this place her home."

"Yeah?" I asked. "That's nice."

"It was," Jude said, his voice shaking. "I just can't believe she's gone. I mean, just *gone*."

I leaned my head on his shoulder, hoping it would keep him from noticing me watching the crowd. My eyes were drawn to Wes again. His posture was stiff. He'd crossed his arms over his chest like he was angry. Tripp was standing next to him, head bowed eyes closed. Beside him, I was surprised to find Owen O'Brien. There were other former grads around, too. Most had younger siblings in our graduating class, people who had known Leena growing up together in Bakersville.

Skipping forward a few rows, I found the girls from *The Bakersville Dozen*, all seven of them huddled in a circle near the front of the pack. Sylvie had texted earlier about paying our respects as a group—they were starting here at the pond, and heading to Timber Park next. I could practically feel the fear streaming from them. I was pretty sure their thoughts were an exact echo of my own—*It could have been me. It could have been me. Holy fucking shit, it could have been me.* I felt it then, my responsibility to keep them safe weighing heavier than ever. If I didn't figure this out, any one of us could be next. I focused on Sylvie, who was standing in the center of the pack, her blonde curls quivering as tears rolled down her cheek.

She turned, slowly, her eyes roaming the crowd until they locked on the group of former grads. Curiosity overtaking my fear, I wondered if she was staring at Wes. Then I was sure her gaze was fixed on Tripp. Her eyes narrowed, her lips pressing together in a tight line. Without looking away, she leaned in and whispered something to Kelsey "Shaved—'nuff Said" Hathaway, who was standing right next to her, and then inched her way through the crowd. She stopped near Tripp, and whispered something to Owen O'Brien.

His eyes crinkled, and I wondered if he was confused or angry. Sylvie slipped away then, pushing past dorky Kyle Jenkins, to where Hoodie Guy from my pre-calc class stood on the outskirts of the gathering. As Sylvie passed him, he gave her a quick nod before she ducked into the shadows of the trees.

I tried to remember his name, but it was just out of reach. And then I forgot all about him, because Owen O'Brien was following Sylvie down the trail she'd chosen.

No one but me seemed to notice. Their attention was drawn to the near-hysterical break-down taking place directly outside the band of yellow tape.

"She can't be dead!" a voice shouted. It was Ava Ginger, who, up until February first, had served as co-captain of the varsity squad with Leena. "It's a *lie*! Do you hear me? It can't be real!"

"I can't take this," I whispered, pulling away from Jude. "I gotta get out of here."

"I'm not sure I can." Jude turned, facing me, pain flashing through his eyes. "I need to be here. To be part of this. Will you please stay?"

I chewed my bottom lip for a moment before looking him in the eye. "I just need a minute."

"But you shouldn't be out there alone," Jude said.

"I won't be long. I promise." I felt awful leaving him when I knew he needed me most, but I didn't have a choice. I sighed, taking a few slow backward steps. "I just need a break, okay?"

"There are pieces of fabric and some pens in a basket up there." He pointed toward a tree with yellow tape wrapped around its trunk. "We're supposed to write our names. We can add a note, too. Or song lyrics. The cheerleaders are making a blanket for Leena's family. I figured you'd want in on it considering how close you guys have become since—"

"Yeah," I said, leaning in and giving him a kiss, lingering over the taste of spearmint and tears. "Promise."

And then I pushed my way through the crowd, taking one last quick glance at Hoodie Guy, before darting down the trail Sylvie and Owen had taken.

It was one of the least used trails in these woods, narrow with branches crisscrossing the path. I raced around twists and turns, trying to remember where the trail led, and remembering too late that it simply dead-ended. The trees were thicker, their canopies letting little light through.

As I stood there, wondering where Sylvie and Owen might have gone, I heard the silver ring of Sylvie's laughter followed by the sound of a deeper voice.

Walking slowly, I moved off the trail and between trees, my feet crunching leaves from the previous fall.

I saw the rock wall first, trees growing sideways from the steep slope. I remembered trying to scale the wall as a child, the taunts of Tripp and Wes calling from overhead as I slid down each time I tried to chase them to the top.

And then I saw Owen, his back pressed against the barrier, eyes rolling toward the sky, a pair of khaki shorts pooled around his ankles.

Sylvie was there too, kneeling between his feet, her head ducked down, each and every one of her curls shivering as Owen snaked his fingers through her hair.

CHAPTER 23

10:07 PM

"So, you didn't see anything suspicious at Timber Park?" I asked, taking a sip of soda.

Hannah shrugged, folding her paper napkin into a triangle. "There were more people than I expected, mostly sitting on the grass in the audience section, just staring up at the empty stage. I heard a lot about how Becca was heading to Juilliard in the fall, how she dreamed of making her debut on Broadway. But nothing that would add anyone to our suspect list."

"What about the cassette tape?" I asked, the chatter of pizza-goers drifting around the filled-to-capacity restaurant. "Did you listen to it yet?"

"Yeah," Hannah said. "The recorder is from the Bakersville library, old-school, and the tape has nothing on it but a few minutes of applause, looped over and over again."

"Well, that was a bust," Wes said. "Whoever's behind all this has been covering his tracks."

"What about the pictures of Becca," Hannah asked. "You look at them yet, Tripp?"

He groaned. "Yeah. Other than the swelling, there was nothing much to see besides the thick band of bruises around her ankles."

"Just like Leena," I said.

The pizza arrived then. Kyle Jenkins slid the silver pan onto the stand on the middle of the table. The pizza steamed, piping the scent of pepperoni, onions, and green pepper into the air.

"You guys talking about the missing girls?" Kyle asked, swiping his hands down the front of the sauce-stained apron tied around his waist. No one replied, but that had never stopped Kyle. He was one of those brilliant types who was completely socially awkward. "The police are bombing this entire case. Figuring out who made the video should've been a piece of cake. They've had five months to find these girls, and they've come up with nothing."

Hannah looked up at him. "They only had five months if the girls were kept alive the entire time. The clock stopped ticking as soon as they were killed. And nobody knows when that may have been."

"Leena hadn't been dead for long," Kyle said. "She only showed the initial stages of decomposition. And Becca, she was still warm when they found her. The responding officers thought she was alive at first."

"How do you know that?" I asked, alarm bells going off as I added Kyle to the ever-growing suspect list.

Kyle shrugged. "It's not so hard to find the police radio transmissions frequency."

"Is that what you do in your spare time?" Hannah asked.

Kyle shrugged. "When I'm bored."

"What else did you hear?" Hannah asked.

"They're doing an autopsy on both girls, obviously. They're not sure how Leena was killed"—Kyle glanced toward the kitchen, then back toward us—"but they think Becca died of anaphylactic shock. Some kind of allergic reaction."

"Oh my God, yes," I said. "She had one of those needles. We were in the same class in fifth grade, and I remember Mrs. Waggoner making her take it to the office to store in the clinic."

"An EpiPen?" Hannah asked. "How in the hell do you remember that?"

"The thing was huge." I shrugged. "It completely freaked me out."

"Do you remember what was she allergic to?" Tripp asked.

"Peanuts," I said, picturing her face, swollen beyond recognition, wondering if her last minutes struggling for air had felt like drowning. "She even had to sit at the nut-free table for lunch."

Wes slid the spatula under a slice of pizza and transferred it to my plate. "Busy night tonight," he said.

"Yeah," Kyle agreed. "We're on summer hours now, eleven to eleven every day of the week."

"You notice anything suspicious?" Tripp asked, tugging a piece of pizza from the tray as Wes served Hannah, and then himself. "Anyone acting strange?"

Kyle laughed. "Yeah, try everyone. This whole town is buzzing since Leena and Becca were found. Reporters have been flocking in all day. And then there are the weird out-of-towners who're delusional enough to feel like they're part of the girls' families because they've been obsessing over all the media reports for the last five months. Only show they've had so far was earlier. A guy walked in and tried to get a table, but he was so wasted, he could hardly keep himself upright."

"You're kidding." Wes gave a little snort.

"My boss kicked him out before he could vomit all over the floor," Kyle said. "Bonus for me, because I'da been the one cleaning it up. Aside from that, nothing unusual other than Tiny Simmons out in the parking lot earlier, taking down license plate numbers from out-of-state cars. Total waste of time, if you ask me."

"Tiny Simmons?" I asked, my heart rate speeding up.

"Yeah. As if someone as green as him is going to come up with the one piece of evidence that's going to blow this case wide open and make his entire career."

"You never know. He just might be the hero." Hannah kicked me under the table. In one sentence, Kyle Jenkins had wrapped Tiny's possible motive up in a neat little package.

"Not likely," Kyle said.

"Then what's your theory?" Hannah asked, taking a bite and wiping her mouth with her triangle-shaped napkin. "If you think the cops are wasting time with out-of-towners, who do you think is really behind all of this?"

I looked down at the slice cooling on my plate, but couldn't bring myself to eat.

"My theory is simple," Kyle said. "The person behind this is holding a grudge against each of the missing girls. Whoever this is wants revenge. It's not some pedophile who watched the video a thousand times sitting in front of his computer in dirty underwear, then decided to rent a room in Bakersville so he could pick the girls off one by one."

"Agreed," Hannah said with a nod. "That theory doesn't make any sense."

"As for who it might be, take your pick. There are tons of assholes in this town. Trust me, I know. And they don't exactly need a logical reason for their behavior."

"Kyle!" a man with a round belly and thick brown hair called from behind the counter. "Pie for table twelve is up. Move it, already."

Kyle looked directly at me before he backed away. "You wanna stay safe, Bailey, try to think of someone who has a grudge against you. And when you come up with that person, keep your distance."

From his seat beside me, I felt Wes stiffen. Was he holding a grudge because of the way we had ended things at Christmastime? Or maybe because I was dating Jude? Across from us, Tripp and Hannah didn't seem to notice the sudden tension. They were staring at something just behind me, eyes narrowed.

I turned, wanting to see what had caught their attention, and my eyes locked on a red envelope with BAILEY HOLZMAN scrawled across the front.

"Bailey, right?" The voice was deep. But I couldn't take my eyes off the envelope. All I knew about the guy in front of me was that he had a habit of chewing his nails.

"Yes," Hannah said. "That's Bailey."

I looked up then, finding a face framed by the soft fabric of a dark gray hoodie.

"This is for you." He dropped the envelope, then turned and started walking away.

"Wait!" Hannah and Tripp called at exactly the same time. Hannah shot up from her seat and grabbed Hoodie Guy by the shoulder.

"Hey!" Hoodie Guy said, jerking himself out of her grasp. "Watch it!"

She held her hands up in the air and took a small step back. "Sorry," she said. "It's just . . . we need to know how you got that. Who gave it to you?"

Hoodie Guy shrugged. "Some guy. Said he'd pay me to sit here and wait for you."

"*Some guy?*" Wes asked, his jaw clenched tight. "Can you give us a clearer description?"

"He was older, you know, kinda balding on top. And he smelled pretty bad."

"Smelled like what?" Hannah asked. "Like he just worked out or like he'd been dumpster diving for meals?"

"Neither. He smelled like a freaking distillery. Anyway, that big dude behind the counter was kicking him out when I got here a few hours ago. Guy could hardly stand up, so they wouldn't serve him. That's when he said he'd pay me to sit here and wait for you."

"He knows me?" I asked, my words catching in my throat.

"Nah, I don't think so." Hoodie Guy glanced out the window that looked out onto the parking lot in front of The Flying Pizza. "He had a picture of you, though. A printout from that, uh, video. He said all I had to do was sit and wait for you to get here and order. Once your pizza arrived, I was supposed to give you the envelope, and then my job was done. So I'm going."

"No way, man," Tripp said. "You're going to tell us every single detail you can remember. You hear me?"

"Dude," Hoodie Guy said, leaning in, "I don't know what this is, but I am not about to get sucked into it."

"Wait. Just *wait*," I said. "What's that supposed to mean?"

Hoodie Guy sighed and lifted his face to the ceiling for a moment before he looked at me. "I'm not stupid. I know who you are. What you're mixed up in. Two girls are dead. I don't want any part of this besides the cash I earned for sitting in a booth and waiting for you."

"Fine," Tripp said. "One last thing—where'd he go after he gave you the envelope?"

"I don't know," Hoodie Guy said. "Look, this guy was pathetic, boozed up and desperate. I just wanted to get away from him, so I promised I'd do what he asked, took the money, and walked inside. I didn't watch him leave."

"You're Chris, right?" I asked, the name that I'd struggled to find coming to me in a flash.

Hoodie Guy nodded. "Chris Beekman. We had pre-calc together."

"I remember," I said.

"I swear," Chris said. "I told you everything I know."

"Are you stupid or something?" Tripp hissed, his face turning a deep shade of red. "With five girls missing, you just took this guy's money and didn't think to call the cops?"

"No, I'm not stupid." Chris narrowed his eyes at my brother. "I'm a fan of self-preservation. Whatever this is, I have no intention of getting involved. I only took the envelope because the guy was begging me, okay?"

"Fine," I said, shrugging, like the whole thing was over. "We get it. No big deal."

"Look, I'm sorry." Chris pulled the hoodie from his head and ran a hand through his dull brown hair. "Maybe I should have paid more attention. But the guy was making a full-on scene and all I could think about was getting away."

"Right," Wes said. "We get it. You can go now. Preserve yourself, why don't you?"

Chris grunted, turned, and walked away.

"You think he knows more than he's saying?" Hannah asked, watching him slip out the front door and walk to a black SUV parked in the front of the lot.

"I don't know," Wes said. "It sounds like our killer spooked the town drunk into bringing the clue here, and when he couldn't get a table he pulled Chris into the mix."

"That'd be my guess," Tripp said.

Wes pointed at the envelope. "Open that and see what it says."

I leaned over the table, my body shielding the words on the cream-colored cardstock as I quietly read them the clue.

TO FIND
THE NEXT TREASURE,
YOU WON'T HAVE TO GO FAR.

HEAD TO SYDNEY VILLAGE,
AND TWIST
'ROUND THE BEND

'TIL YOU FIND
THE ROAD'S
SHADOWED DEAD END.

FROM THERE
TAKE THE TRAIL
'TIL YOU HIT A SMALL CAVE.

DUCK THROUGH THE ARCHWAY
AND WAIT
FOR THE SHOW TO BEGIN.

HAPPY HUNTING!

"I don't like the sound of this one," I said.

"I don't like the sound of any of them." Hannah plucked the clue from my hand and read it over.

"No time for feelings," Wes said, pulling his wallet from his back pocket and throwing a twenty on the table. "We're on."

"Let's hit it," Tripp said, pushing his chair back as he grabbed a slice of pizza.

"You've got this, B." Hannah looked at me, sliding my phone off the table and gripping it with both hands. "You are a force to be reckoned with, you hear me? This sucks, but you'll get to the other side."

"Promise?" I asked. Because I felt positively forceless.

Hannah crossed a finger over her heart. "I swear it."

I felt better having Hannah by my side as we walked out of the restaurant and slipped into Tripp's Jeep. She'd said exactly what I needed to hear.

My mind raced with one daring thought: Two might be dead, but there were three left to save. And maybe, just maybe, we could bring them home, and stop the killer.

We pulled up to a red light just a few blocks from the pizzeria. Music from O'Leary's Pub and Grub drifted in through the open window. My gaze shifted toward the front of the bar, resting on a man leaning against one of the pillars framing the front patio.

He was wearing jeans and a T-shirt, and he simmered with anger.

"Shit," Hannah said. "There's Roger Turley."

I sat there, refusing to look away, determination coursing through my body.

Roger locked eyes with mine, then raised a glass full of amber-colored liquid, tipping it toward me before taking a long swig. Above him, the smoke from his cigarette curled toward the night sky like a ladder for the dead.

CHAPTER 24
10:57 PM

"I swear," Tripp said, "it's right over here." He was navigating the narrow trail I'd taken just that morning as people crowded around the police tape blocking off where Leena had been found.

"You're sure something's out here?" Hannah asked, her arms spread wide, keeping branches from lashing her as we followed behind him.

There was something quite *surprising out here this morning*, I wanted to say, but I kept it to myself. Owen leaning against the steep rock slope, Sylvie kneeling in front of him, the two oblivious as I watched until understanding swept in and I turned, slipping away.

"You're sure this is the right trail?" Wes asked from behind me.

"Yeah," Tripp said, his breath coming in huffs as he led us deeper into the woods.

"It's been about a million years since we've hiked to this cave, bro."

"I know."

Moonlight trickled through the leaves. My body was numb, shaky with fear of what was ahead.

"Hey, Han. What's that thing you always say about expectation?" I asked. "When you're about to do something really horrible and all you want is to be through with it?"

"Your expectation is always worse than the real thing, so it's a waste to get all stressed out?"

"Yeah, that. It usually makes me feel better."

"Well"—Hannah made a little grunting sound—"it only works for stuff like going to the dentist or having to give a speech in English class. What we're about to do is going to be way worse than we expect."

"You usually know the right thing to say, but that right there was a pretty sucky attempt."

"Anything else would be a lie." Hannah looked over her shoulder, her eyes flashing. "I would never lie to you."

But *someone* was lying to me. Someone close. Someone I thought I could trust.

"Here!" Tripp said from just ahead, making me jump. "Right here. Just like I said."

Tripp veered off the trail a few feet away from where I'd been that morning. He reached out a hand, running his fingers across the stone face. Dirt and pebbles cascaded to the ground.

He stopped walking. Hannah bumped into his side as he turned and faced the wall, staring at a bruised-looking space before us. I stared, too, squinting into the darkness, my eyes struggling to focus.

"It's smaller than I remember," Tripp said, holding his phone in the air like a flashlight.

"That's the entrance?" I asked, feeling as if I was about to disappear like the rest of the girls.

Wes stepped up behind me, the heat from his body radiating against my back. I needed to escape his orbit; I couldn't risk being sucked in by whatever force had pulled me to him nearly all of my life. Wes might be dangerous to more than my relationship with Jude. He had secrets. He might be a danger to me.

I walked through the archway, attempting to put even more space between us. Just inside, I heard trickling water as a wave of cool, dank air swept across my face. Before we were all the way in, light from Tripp's phone dimmed and then died out.

"My phone's dead," he whispered. "Someone, give us a little light."

The darkness felt solid. I shuffled my feet along the ground, afraid of falling. Suddenly, I felt pressure on the front of my ankles. I froze, throwing my arms out to keep anyone from walking past me. It didn't work. I wasn't fast enough. Hannah got tripped up by whatever was lying across the path. She fell with a loud grunt, her voice bouncing off the walls, echoing through a space that suddenly felt even smaller.

And then the light started flashing—a bright white that set the entire cave ablaze for one moment before winking out again. The strobe effect flared through the cave again and again and again, in time with the echoing *snap-click*. At first, the light was blinding, and between flashes all I could see were stars. But then my vision adjusted to the pulsing beam.

As I pulled a shaky Hannah from the ground, I noticed the wire, thin and clear, and totally out of place there in the middle of the woods. The line stretched across the cave's entrance, like it had been set up just for us.

We'd tripped it.

That scared me more than the woods or the dark. Whoever had set this up had planned it as a trap, and we'd fallen right into it.

The *snap-click* continued to echo.

First, I saw Hannah, her eyes wide as she gripped my arms, her fingernails digging into my skin.

Everything went black.

When I saw her again, her face was turned toward the center of the cave, hair in her eyes, her mouth hanging open.

Everything went black.

I turned to see what she was staring at.

The light flashed again, and I saw them.

The girls—*two* of them—propped in portable beach chairs, facing each other with their legs stretched out, ankles crossed.

They looked stiff, ashen, their heads hanging down, chins on their chests, hair falling across the once soft skin of their cheeks.

In the span of a second, the scene was seared to my memory.

"Jesus," Tripp said from behind me, his voice a thin whisper. "Two?"

"That's Suze," Hannah said, pointing. "See her bracelets? She made them last year and sold them at lunch. Remember?"

I saw them in the next flash. The *snap-click*s seemed to get louder, coming faster. Both of Suze's forearms sparkled with the beadwork she'd spent hours on. I saw her fingers, too, curled into fists. Those hands would never design another accessory or piece of clothing again.

"The other one's Emily, right?" Wes asked. "She was the first girl to go missing?"

"Yeah," I said, my voice muffled by another jolting *snap-click*. I could not believe this was them—girls I had laughed with and cried with as we'd attempted to uncover the secrets behind *The Bakersville Dozen*—and that they were actually dead.

Emily was wearing her volleyball jersey—the one that had been missing from the athletic bag the police had found sitting wide open on the passenger seat of her car the day she disappeared. The rust-colored stains that streaked the front of the jersey made my stomach churn. There was so much blood. Which meant that whatever she had been through had *hurt*.

"What is this?" I asked, my stomach heaving as I fought the stream of images spiraling through my mind—all of the girls, facing and trying to fight off some attacker. An attacker who was now using them as bait.

"I don't know," Wes said. "But we can't just stand here and stare all night."

"He's right," Hannah said, her hand slipping from my arm. "We have to move. But stay away from the bodies, okay? And shuffle, so you don't leave any footprints."

Eyes down, Hannah followed the white wire that stretched from the entrance of the cave, circling around Suze's chair.

"We're supposed to have the chance to save them," I said. "The only reason I'm doing this is because the clue said I could—"

"Stop," Hannah said. "This is not the time. Just look for the clue and we'll deal with the rest later."

I scanned the scene, searching for the red envelope.

"It's a camera," Hannah said when she'd reached the back of the cave. "It's propped on a stepladder and hooked to some sort of device attached to that wire."

"It's taking pictures?" Wes asked. "Of us?"

"I think so," Hannah replied. "This is bad, guys."

"So we take it," Wes said. "Like you did with the tape recorder."

"We can't keep this up," Tripp said from the cave's entrance, his voice echoing through the space. "We need to call the police and tell them everything."

"What if Tiny really is behind this whole thing?" Wes asked, his face hard, illuminated suddenly by another brilliant flash. "He was just at the scene where we found the latest clue."

"We already talked about turning him in," Hannah said. "They'd never believe us over him. Even worse? If it *is* Tiny, he has evidence. He could plant it. He could set one or all of us up to take the fall. That would leave Bailey on her own."

"You trust Tiny with your sister's life?" Wes asked. "Because I sure as hell don't. We have to finish this. We can't risk it, Tripp."

"I'm unhooking this thing," Hannah said. "We'll need light, so get on it."

I listened to the *pop-snap* of wires being unhooked, unsure of the next best move.

"Where's the envelope?" Wes asked, light from his phone suddenly illuminating the scene before us. "Do you see it?"

"Guys," Tripp said from the mouth of the cave. "I think I hear something."

"Then help," Hannah said, tucking the camera under her arm as she circled back to me. "Help us find the damn clue."

"Got it," Wes said, scrambling across the dirt floor and ripping the envelope from the front pocket of one of Suze's signature over-the-shoulder purses. The light from his phone bounced wildly off the rock walls surrounding us.

"Do you hear that?" Tripp's back was to us, his words so quiet they were nearly lost in the vacuum of the cave.

"Jesus, Wes," Hannah said. "Focus that light. I can't see where I'm going."

"I've got you," I said, stepping around Emily and holding my hand out to Hannah as Wes trained the light on the ground near our feet. "Grab my hand and we can—"

"You guys, we've got to get the hell out of here." Tripp swiveled, backlight from Wes's phone highlighting the fear on his face in an eerie way.

The next few seconds were a blur of motion and sound and intuition as Hannah and I made our way toward the mouth of the cave. I was leading, my hand gripping Hannah's like my life depended on my connection to her, but I stumbled as my toe caught in a loop of the wire somewhere near Emily's chair. Instead of hitting the ground, my hands landed squarely on Wes's chest, the summery scent that had always surrounded him washing over me. He steadied me, drawing me forward until I stumbled from the black-hole darkness of the cave and into the glow of the moon.

Tripp was there, waiting. When he saw me, he grabbed hold of my shoulders and looked me right in the eye. "Run. Straight home. Don't stop for anything."

"Tripp, I can't." And I meant it. My legs felt like they were about to collapse beneath me.

"I hear it now." Wes gripped my hand and started walking through the trees, forcing me to work the numbing panic from my legs. "It's definitely music. But where's it coming from?"

"The pond, I think." Tripp was behind me, guiding Hannah. "But it's getting closer."

Wes slowed his pace, stopping as we broke from the trees and stepped onto a narrow trail. "We've got to create a diversion."

"We could head to the pond," Tripp said, everything about him taut and alert. "Just you and me. If we face this head on, we'll make sure the girls have a chance to get out of here and, at the same time, maybe nail this bastard."

Hannah stepped to my side, the camera she'd taken pressing against my arm. Standing there, with everyone still, I finally heard what had the guys in a panic: the steady beat of drums, Adele's smoky voice, and the words—*Rumor has it!*

"You can't go to the pond," I said. "You'd be walking into a trap. There's too much that could go wrong."

"There's no time to argue," Wes said. "We can't just walk away. We have a chance to end this."

"He's right," Tripp said. "All you guys have to do is run through the trails until you get home."

The music was getting louder, pressing in from all sides.

Hannah's eyes locked on mine, her hair swinging wildly in her face. "What are we waiting for?"

"You have to go," Wes said, pressing the familiar square envelope into my hands. "Take this. *Don't* lose it." His lips turned down at the corners and his eyes darted from me to the woods. The moonlight added a silver sheen to his skin, reminding me of every night we had spent together last summer.

"Wes, I—"

"Go!" he shouted, his hands pressing against my back. "Now."

I did. I ran with all the strength I had inside of me.

Hannah followed close behind.

Our feet pounded the ground.

Branches stretched across the path like switches, stinging my skin as I raced on.

All the while, the eerie tune twined through the trees, following our steps, a clear reminder of the person threatening to take away everything I had ever loved.

CHAPTER 25

11:32 PM

I sprinted around the final bend, bursting through the trees and into my backyard, my hand gripping the red envelope tightly. Hannah's Escape was parked at the end of the drive, glistening in the light of the moon. Struggling to suck in enough air, I turned just as Hannah emerged from the darkness of the wooded trail.

"We did it," I said, breathless as I folded the envelope and tucked it into my back pocket.

Hannah bent at the waist, placing the camera on the ground and bracing herself with her hands on her knees as she gasped for air.

"You okay?" I asked.

"I really have no idea anymore," Hannah said. "That scene back there at the cave? It did not feel real, B."

"I know. I wish it wasn't, but we can't do anything about that right now. The guys are still out there. We have to help."

"Help?" Hannah asked, the buzzy vibration of an incoming message fuzzing out the word. She pulled her phone from her pocket and glanced down at the screen. "How are we supposed to—Ugh. It's my mom. I missed her check-in call and she's freaking out."

"How did you miss a check-in?" I asked. "Check-ins are the ticket to what little freedom we have left."

"It wasn't scheduled, okay? I talked to her before we ordered the pizza and she was fine. Besides that, I was in a cave with two dead bodies when she called. I felt my phone vibrating, but I didn't think it was her. I gotta hit it, like, right now."

"You can't," I said. "We need to find the guys. We need to get them out of there."

"And how do you suggest we do that?" Hannah asked, tucking her phone away and reaching down for the camera. "Going back out there could put us in the direct line of the killer."

"What about them?" I asked, terrified by the thought of something happening to either of them. "We're talking about my brother and Wes. We have to drive to the trailhead closest to the pond. If we park where Tripp did and head in, it'll take us directly to the pond."

"No way. They're out there because they wanted to give us the chance to escape. If the killer didn't kill you for going back out there, they would." Hannah handed me the camera and started to back-step away, her feet swishing in the silver-tinted grass. "I'm sorry. I love you, but I can't."

I watched her go, feeling lost and abandoned as she pulled her driver's side door open and slipped into her car. The engine surged to life and the Escape began to roll, tires crunching and spitting up gravel as Hannah disappeared between my house and Wes's.

I looked down at the camera, my finger grazing the power button as I stepped away from the trailhead. And then I heard the unmistakable sound of footsteps and the snapping of brittle twigs.

My mouth went dry.

A cold sweat slicked my skin.

I wanted to run, but I saw movement through the trees, a flicker of white darting from the left side of the trail to the right. I almost called out for help, but the footsteps pounded toward me, so I pressed myself into the shadows against the rough bark of the nearest tree.

He sprinted past me a moment later, straight into my back-yard. I didn't get more than a glance, but I knew who it was. I always did when it came to him. But why was he here instead of back at the pond with Tripp?

"Bailey!" he shouted, his voice shaking. He glided through the rustling grass as if he were skating on silver ice, speeding across the yard. "Bailey? Where are you?"

As he leaped up the steps to the back deck, my eyes darted to the light in the kitchen window. I thought of my parents, tucked into their bed, sleeping peacefully after I replied to my latest check-in. They were ignorant of the dangerous game I'd been playing. But they would know everything if I didn't stop Wes. Then they'd try to stop us. And someone else might die.

"Wes!" I shouted.

He swiveled, his hand raised, ready to pound on the back door.

I was halfway across the lawn by then, the camera clutched in my hands, my hair streaming behind me. "Stop! I'm right here!"

His shoulders sank, and I could hear the rasp in his voice as he called out, "You're supposed to be inside. Why the hell aren't you—"

"Hannah just left."

"Like, *left* left?" Wes jumped from the deck into the grass, grabbing my hand and pulling me into the shadow of the sweet gum tree.

"She missed a check-in. Her mom was freaking out."

"But she's safe, right?"

I nodded.

"Listen Tripp's on his way back. After we circled the pond the music stopped. We didn't find anything, so we split up; he went to his car, and I came on foot to be sure you and Hannah weren't still in the woods. He should be here in a few."

"Good," I said. "I want us all home. I want this night to be over."

"Before he gets back, we need to talk." Wes pulled the camera from my hands and settled it in the grass, next to the tree.

"About what?" I asked. "We don't have any secrets from Tripp anymore."

"We need to talk about us."

I shook my head. "The thing between us is over."

Wes ran a hand through his hair. "What if it shouldn't be?"

"Because you're back in town again and want a little action?" I stepped farther into the shelter of the tree, closer to him, even though everything inside of me was screaming to pull away. "Just like winter break, right? News Flash: I'm not your toy, Wes."

"I could never think of you like—"

"Really?" I stepped closer. "Then why didn't you want to tell anyone about last summer?"

"Because I didn't want to deal with everything that would have come with us being together. We would have had my parents and your parents and Tripp all butting in. Not to mention

Hannah. Who the hell knows what would have happened if everyone had gotten involved? Last summer was for us. *Just* us."

My mind was working too fast, tripping forward and backward and sideways, considering all the information I'd pulled together from the start of this hunt. "That sounds good," I said. "Rational, even. But every time I think I can trust you, Wes, you do something to destroy that trust."

"You asked me to leave you alone after the Christmas party. I listened. I respected the fact that you were with Jude. That has to count for something."

"Were you angry? "

"It didn't feel good. But, even worse, I didn't get to tell you how I felt. That I—" Wes's eyes narrowed. "Wait. Do you think this is me? Do you actually think I could do this to them? To *you*?"

"You've had opportunity," I said.

Wes leaned back against the body of the sweet gum, tucking his thumbs into the front pockets of his jeans. He looked me in the eye and tilted his head to the side, waiting.

"You were at school," I said. "Right before the Last Day Ceremony. You could have put the first clue in my locker. You could have taken that tiara."

"I was there picking up transcripts for an internship." Wes raised his eyebrows. "But let's say I did those things. When, exactly, would I have had time to put the tiara on Leena's head?"

"If you hid it in the woods before you followed me," I said with a shrug, "you could have put it on her head after we found her and grabbed that second clue. You were at least a minute behind me when we made our way back to the pond."

Wes snorted. "I thought I heard something in the woods that day. *Someone*, actually. I didn't want to scare you, so I never said anything, but I stayed behind because I thought we were being watched. I thought, if I had the chance, that I might be able to stop the whole thing. Catch the freak who killed Leena and keep you safe."

"But you didn't catch anyone, did you?" I asked. "And you didn't keep me safe."

"No," Wes said. "I didn't."

"I don't know about anyone else, but I know about you. You were *right* there, when I found Leena. If you're behind this, that's almost as good as an alibi. You put yourself in the center of the hunt from the very start. You made sure I'd need to rely on you."

"Fine," Wes said with a shrug. "I'll keep playing along. If I did that—set everything up so you'd find the clue and go running to the pond, and then chased after you, telling you I'd followed because I thought you were finally ready to talk—"

"Finally ready? Wes, what is there to say after—"

"*If* I did all of that, it means I also kidnapped five girls and hid them away for five months. Please share how you think I pulled that off."

"I know you came back to town a few times after Winter Break." I was working to keep my voice steady. "It wouldn't have been hard, really. They all know you. And you have a way of charming everyone you meet. You could have taken them."

"For the record, I stayed away from you when I came back to town because after the Christmas party, you made it clear that you wanted nothing to do with me." Wes shook his head. "As for the girls you think I kidnapped, where do you think I stashed them? My dorm room?"

"No idea. But everyone knows you pull off the impossible. Planning the most intricate schemes and—"

Wes leaned forward. "Have you asked yourself why? What on earth would I have to gain from plotting something this twisted? From targeting *you*, of all people?"

"Revenge?" I shrugged. "You've spent the last nine months partying your way through your freshman year. That counts as moving on. That's exactly what I did with Jude. But you didn't like that very much, did you? You thought I'd be waiting for you when you came home, ready to pick up where we'd left off."

"To be clear, I hardly *moved on*. I spent most of the time feeling awkward at parties because all I could do was compare every girl I met to you. And none of them measured up. Your visions of me screwing my way through the freshman class didn't happen. But let's keep going, because I'm curious about something. Say I was jealous enough to want revenge. How, exactly, does that lead to me plotting some scheme that involves you searching for a string of dead bodies?"

"You hate that I chose Jude over you," I said, feeling distracted. Suddenly, nothing about this conversation felt right. He had compared other girls to me, and none of them measured up?

Wes bit his lip for a moment, looking at the ground. "I hate that you're with Jude, sure. I can admit that."

"You hate it so much, you tried to ruin my relationship with him," I said, my voice low, nearly a whisper. "The night of your parents' Christmas party. You took me to your room because you knew I wouldn't be able to resist. That I can never resist you. And then you had something to hold over my head."

"If I needed something to hold over your head, why haven't I used it?" Wes asked, stepping forward, his eyes locked on mine.

"You were angry after I left you. Angry enough to do a lot more than use me cheating against Jude to break up our relationship." I shrugged. "You decided to do this instead."

Wes laughed. "That's ridiculous and you know it. Taking you up to my room had nothing to do with blackmail. I pulled you away from everyone else because I missed you."

Wes closed the space between us in an instant, his hands gripping mine, his heat rippling through me, washing away all the anger and uncertainty. For a moment, it was just us, standing there looking right at each other, the sea green of his eyes pouring into me. And as many times as I'd sworn to myself that it would never happen again, all the old feelings came rushing back.

"And if you're serious about any of this—if you think I'm capable of kidnapping and killing multiple girls—why are you standing out here with me? Shouldn't you be afraid?"

I looked at him, the sadness in his eyes making me regret every accusation I had made.

"You're not afraid, B," Wes said. "Because you know I would never hurt you. Ever."

I closed my eyes. Breathed him in. "But you did, Wes. You already did."

"I was going to explain," Wes whispered. "The night of the Christmas party, I'd planned to tell you breaking up was a mistake. But we got caught up in each other first. I thought I had time, but then you told me it was over. You were gone before I had a chance."

He shifted, moving closer. I wanted him even closer. Desperately.

Which is exactly why I pulled away.

I slipped my hands from his, twisting away so he couldn't read the desire on my face.

He sighed. "I'm not the one behind all of this. I swear it."

"Right," I said, tears filling my eyes. I believed him. But I'd been here before . . .

We heard the sound of tires on the gravel, and both of us swiveled toward the driveway as Tripp's Jeep crawled to a stop.

"Call Hannah," Wes said, leaning down to pick up the camera before taking a few steps away. "Make sure she got home okay."

I pulled my phone from my pocket as he walked to the Jeep, meeting Tripp as the driver's side door swung open. Their voices drifted toward me, a familiar hum.

As my eyes scanned the words of the text I'd missed, I sighed with the relief. Hannah was okay.

> HANNAH—11:47PM: SORRY I HAD TO BOLT. TEXT
> ME THE NEXT LOCATION AND
> I'LL MEET YOU GUYS THERE
> TOMORROW. LUV YA.

I felt my nerves uncoil as I pictured Hannah snuggled under her yellow comforter, her hair spread out across her pillow.

But it was more than that.

It was Wes, too.

His voice. The look in his eyes. What he'd said about his feelings for me.

I knew it was a huge risk, but I actually believed him.

MONDAY

JUNE 5

CHAPTER 26

11:11 AM

"Thanks for coming with me." Jude was sitting a few feet from the pond, his head hanging low as he tied a series of knots in a long strand of grass. "I almost drove past your house, but something made me pull in the driveway."

"I'm glad you stopped." I wanted to sit by his side and be exactly what he needed me to be, but the emotions from last night with Wes were swirling in my head, mixed in with a fresh wave of guilt over what it all might do to Jude. I'd have to tell him the truth—that I had never gotten over my feelings for Wes—but being honest now, when he was so upset, seemed cruel. "I wouldn't want you to be out here by yourself."

"Maybe it's strange," Jude said, looking up at me with a sad smile, "but I don't want to leave her alone, which makes no sense because she's not even out here anymore."

I shifted my weight from one foot to the other, taking in the way Jude's body seemed to be caving in, crumbling under the stress of being the one to find Leena. In that moment, I hated myself for not calling the police when I found her. I could have protected him.

But I had to protect the girls first. There was a big difference between finding a dead body and being one.

"Wanna sit?" Jude patted grass beside him, his eyes squinting as he peered up at me.

"Sure," I said, folding my legs beneath me and settling down. In reality, it was the last thing I wanted to do. I was jittery and nervous. If I was honest, guilt was the real reason I'd agreed to follow Jude into the woods—after the previous night, I'd hoped to avoid this spot for the rest of my life—but that guilt was also the reason that I wanted to jump up and run away.

"I feel like I'm losing my mind," Jude said.

I almost told him that I did, too. "You wanted to talk?"

"Yeah." He looked out over the water, his fingers looping the strand of grass over itself and pulling one end through the circle.

The police tape blocking off the crime scene rustled in the breeze. For an instant, I pictured Leena there, standing among the flowers and notes and trinkets people had left, her ghostly hands gripping the yellow plastic strip, trying to get our attention.

"I'm sure it's been hard," I said. "Being the one to find her. To see her that way."

"It was awful." Jude's voice broke on the last word. "She looked like herself, you know? Like she was just sleeping. In the moonlight, it was hard to tell that anything bad had happened to her. At least, at first. When I called her name and she didn't move, I think I knew. But I didn't want to believe it. I was so relieved that she was right there in front of me—I tried to wake her up, but as soon as I touched . . ." Jude's voice trailed off.

"You called the police right away?" I asked.

"I couldn't breathe at first with her lying there, her face turned up toward me. My mom thinks I had a panic attack. Anyway, as soon as I caught my breath, I called the hotline for the missing girls and ran back to the farm to meet the police. When the first cop car showed up, I brought them out here. But I refused to stay. I didn't know where you were or if you were okay, so I made them take me back to Jonesy's. I needed to be there waiting for you."

"You're always thinking of me," I said.

"How could I not?" Jude asked with a sad smile. "You're amazing, B."

"Did they start searching right away?" I asked, wondering if Jude had seen any evidence as the police investigated the area. I knew now that there was no chance the killer was going to let me find any of the girls alive. If I was going to catch him, I needed more to go on.

Jude shook his head, then ran a hand through his hair. "I honestly don't know. As soon as I pointed her out, they took me back to the farm. They said something about preserving the scene, but I think they knew I needed to get away from her."

"That had to be awful. Knowing Leena was dead when everyone else was still—"

"Look, I don't want to talk about any of that." Jude turned his face toward me, his eyes red and glossy. I wondered if he'd gotten any sleep since finding Leena. I barely had.

"I thought that's why you asked me to come out here with you." I ran my fingers across his face, feeling the prickle of stubble against my skin. "I thought you were ready to talk about finding Leena."

Jude took a deep breath, turning to face the pond before he spoke again. "I asked you out here to talk about us."

"Us?" I asked. "Why?"

"Maybe I'm losing it. I just—"

"You're not. Finding Leena has to be one of the—"

"That's not what I'm talking about," Jude said, his voice suddenly stronger. "I'm talking about *us*, Bailey. You and me."

Jude looped the strand of grass around itself one more time, pulling the knot so tight, the stalk snapped in half. He balled the blade of grass up and tossed it into the pond, sending a ripple across the water. "Something's going on. I can feel it. But I have no idea what it is. Will you please clue me in?"

I sat there, my lips parted. There was so much I couldn't share. My mind whirled trying to come up with a single thing I could.

"You've been blowing me off, Bailey. You ignored all of my texts the night I found Leena. Last night, I left you three messages but you didn't call me back. You've been distant. I know you're dealing with something with Tripp, but I don't get why—"

"This whole thing with Tripp is a mess," I said, latching onto the lie.

"So talk to me." Jude put his hand on my knee and squeezed. "It's what we do, right?"

"This time is different, Jude. I want to. But I can't."

"It's that bad? I mean, this is *me*."

I thought about that. I had almost told Jude all about the scavenger hunt the night he'd found Leena, as we lay together in the hammock, but then he'd brought up Wes, and . . . I looked at Jude now, reaching up to tuck a strand of hair behind his ear, and I almost spilled everything again.

But then I thought about the girls. The person behind the scavenger hunt had proven he would follow through with his threats. In a way, he was who I could trust the most. I knew exactly what he was capable of, and that meant telling Jude was a risk I couldn't take.

"I *will* tell you," I said. "I'll tell you everything. Just not now."

"When?" Jude's voice was a whisper, but the pain broke through, hitting me deep in the chest.

"Soon. I'll tell you as soon as I can."

"You promise?" Jude asked.

I didn't have the chance to respond. A voice interrupted the balance that had settled between us.

"Bailey!"

"Who is that?" Jude asked.

I shook my head, pretending I had no idea, but that was another lie. I knew who it was before I even understood he was calling my name.

"Bailey!" he called again, closer now. So close I could hear his feet pounding the dusty trail.

"We're not finished," Jude said. "There's a lot more to say and—"

"Bailey!"

I turned just in time to see him round the bend of the trail, his hand reaching up to shield his eyes from the glare of the sun.

"Wes," I said, the word catching in my throat.

"What the hell are you doing out here?" he asked, striding toward me.

"I'm talking with Jude."

"I see that." Wes pulled back his shoulders as he towered over us. "I meant what are you doing *here*? Where Leena Grabman's body was found just two days ago?"

"Give her a break, dude," Jude said, standing and swiping the grass from the butt of his shorts. I stood, too, focused on diffusing the situation. "I stopped at the house and asked her to join me."

"It figures this was your genius idea." Wes shook his head.

"This place is a memorial now." Jude stepped forward, eyes narrowed. "Her parents said it would be okay. What's your problem, dude?"

"Nothing." Wes looked at me. "It freaked me out when I couldn't find you."

"Well, she's fine, so you can go now." Jude's tone was harder than I had ever heard it.

"Problem is," Wes said, "I can't."

"Why not?" Jude slipped between Wes and me. I pulled him back, suddenly worried about where this whole scene might be heading.

"Long story, dude." Wes shrugged. "Bailey, you need to come with me."

Jude smiled, like he knew a secret that would throw Wes way off balance. "Bailey's not going anywhere with you."

"He's right," I said, putting a hand on Jude's shoulder. "I said I'd meet you and Tripp later, so why don't you just—"

"Uh-uh." Wes shook his head. "Now."

"No." The word was as hard and cold.

"I got a phone call," Wes said. "We've got to go."

"No way," Jude said. "I don't trust you, man. She's not going anywhere without me."

"Bailey's a big girl." Wes thrust his chin into the air. "Why don't we let her decide?"

I tried to think how to explain to Jude why I had to leave when he needed me, but seeing him look at me, the lines creasing the skin around his eyes, I knew nothing I could say would be good enough.

"That's it, then?" Jude asked. "You're just going to go with him?"

"I don't have any choice," I said, placing my hand on his arm. "This is life or death important."

Jude sighed, rolling his eyes toward the sky. "I'm sorry. I don't mean to add pressure. It's just been really hard for me since I found Leena. I'm not sure what I'm supposed to do half the time, and—"

"Don't worry," I said, curling my fingers around his wrist and squeezing tight. "We're all a mess. And this will be over soon. I promise, I'll tell you everything. Just give me a few more days." I kissed him on the cheek and twisted away, keeping as much distance between Wes and me as I could.

Neither of us spoke until we were halfway to my house.

"You okay?" he asked.

"I'm not really sure anymore," I said. "How'd you know where I was?"

Wes shrugged. "I've been watching. Just to make sure you're safe."

"So, you're, stalking me?"

Wes laughed, the sound so real and easy it caught me off guard. "You wish."

"Shut up." I looked away. "Did you even get a phone call?"

"Yup."

"From who?"

"Owen O'Brien. He has an update."

"He found something on the footage from school?"

"He found something. But not from the security footage." Wes sighed. "The camera we took from the cave last night? It was BHS property. And there was a video saved to the memory card. I wanted him to analyze the file before I—"

"Tell me," I urged. "I want to know everything."

"That," Wes said, "is exactly why we're going to Owen's house. He's expecting us in ten minutes."

CHAPTER 27

12:07 PM

"You brought the latest clue?" Wes asked, turning onto Main Street, O'Brien's purple-gray house coming into view.

"I have all of them in my purse." A breeze trailed into the car, tossing my hair around my face. "I'm too afraid to leave them anywhere."

"I want to read it." Wes pulled up in front of the house. "But later. We've gotta get in there."

"Only thing you really need to know is that we're supposed to be at Cold Stone at eight o'clock tonight." I said. "Where's Tripp? I figured he was meeting us here."

"Nah. He's chasing some other lead." Wes pushed his door open and stepped into the street, turning back to look at me. "He said he had an idea about how to get you out of this, but he wouldn't tell me until he knew it would work."

"That doesn't sound very promising," I said as I hopped out of the car.

"Don't be so negative. Together, the four of us can outplay whoever's behind this."

"Forgive me if I'm not convinced." I followed Wes up the porch steps. "And we might be down to three. Hannah's only answered one of my texts so far today."

Wes stopped. "That doesn't sound like her."

"I know. I'm trying not to worry." I checked my phone again. Nothing except a text from Jude—one single red heart and the word *sorry*. "I think last night might have been too much for her. Can't say I blame her for being spooked."

"Well, she only has a few hours to pull her shit together. Tripp said he's going to need us all tonight if his plan's going to work." Wes pushed the doorbell and stepped back to my side.

"I texted her earlier, so she knows where to meet us," I said. "She'll be there. I think she just needs a pep talk. And maybe a few scoops of ice cream."

We heard a muffled voice calling from inside the house, "Door's open. C'mon in."

As we stepped inside, Wes gave me a little wink. Dredging up our history last night, calling him out as one of my primary suspects—it hadn't even phased him. Wes was still Wes.

I stepped into the foyer and closed the door behind me, following Wes into the living room. His sky blue T-shirt rippled against his back.

"'Sup, dude?" Wes stepped to the coffee table, holding a fist out toward Owen's roommate, Bryce Winters who, it seemed, lived on the ratty old couch planted in front of the bay window.

Bryce bumped Wes's fist and leaned back against the couch. "How you been, man?"

"Good," Wes said. "I just dropped by to see Owen. Is he in his room?"

"Yeah." Bryce smirked. "But you'd better knock first. He's got company."

My stomach turned, thinking about who might be in Owen's room and what they might be doing, but I had to see the new video Wes was being so mysterious about. I held my breath as I followed Wes past the card table and all the way down the hall, keeping my lips pressed together as he knocked on the door. Owen called us in from the other side.

"Bro," Owen said as we stepped into the wood-paneled room. "Glad you're here."

Owen was seated at his computer, his hair a mess. Just behind him, perched on nest of blankets tangled up on his bed, sat Sylvie Warner. She was wrapped in a towel, little pearls of water dripping from her white-blonde curls, her eyes focused beyond her knees, which she had tucked against her chest as she painted her toenails a deep shade of red.

"You said you found something?" Wes asked.

"Did he ever." Sylvie lifted her eyes from her paint job as she dipped the little brush back in its bottle. "Hey, B."

"Hey," I said, lifting my eyebrows. "I didn't know you and Owen were . . . friends."

"I've known him for years." Sylvie flashed me a smile, then dropped her eyes to her toes and started painting them again. "But we just started hanging out."

"Interesting," I said.

"So I went through the entire video, frame-by-frame," Owen said, "making adjustments to the lighting, clarifying a few background images, shit like that. It took hours—"

"That's an understatement," Sylvie said. "He was up most of the night. But it paid off."

"One thing I *can* tell you, this is genuine, uncut footage," Owen said. "It wasn't spliced. What you see is what you get."

"Fair warning—you're not going to like what you see." Sylvie scrunched up her nose. "I know I didn't."

"Why?" I asked. "What—"

"Check it out." Owen swiveled the computer monitor so it was facing Wes and me. He clicked a little arrow, and the footage began to play.

I could tell two things from the first three seconds of video: the clip had been shot in the atrium at BHS, and the person speaking, hidden behind the camera, had a voice that was velvety soft and oh-so-familiar.

Jude.

My heart felt like it was about to explode.

"I never liked blood," Jude said as he stepped toward a line that extended from the perimeter of the atrium. A crowd milled around him, extending beyond the camera's view. "This is a good cause, though. So I did what I had to do."

I started to wonder if maybe it wasn't Jude, if it was just someone who sounded like him. But then a junior named Kevin something-or-other rushed the camera's lens, holding his hand up for a fist bump as he said, "Juuuuude!"

The single word dashed all of my hopes.

"That was the first thing you needed to see." Sylvie pointed at the screen with the nail polish brush. "Just wait 'til you see what comes next."

Owen fast-forwarded until Jude stepped up to a long table situated along the back wall of the atrium. From her seat behind the table, Sylvie looked up at us, her smile wide and convincing, as she held out a round sticker that said I GAVE BLOOD. WILL YOU? with the American Red Cross logo centered beneath the text.

"You survived?" Sylvie asked from the screen.

"'Course I did," Jude said. "I'm badass."

On-screen, Sylvie tipped her head back, laughing, her eyes all flirty-girl as she licked her lips and leaned forward, pushing her arms against the sides of her chest until she practically popped out of the V-neck sweater she was wearing.

That's where the text usually came in, fading onto the screen in small caps. But this footage had been shot before the text was added.

"You were flirting," I said. "Shamelessly. With *my* boyfriend."

"*That's* what you're choosing to focus on right now?" Sylvie asked, snorting.

The video continued, past Sylvie's goodbye wink, all the way to the glass doors leading to the student lot. The footage ended then, the camera catching Jude's reflection. He'd been wearing his favorite OSU baseball hat and a Rolling Stones T-shirt that I'd seen him in a thousand times.

"So," I said, blinking hard, tears stinging my eyes, "there's obviously an explanation."

"I don't know about that." Sylvie twisted the cap onto the bottle and scooted off the edge of the bed. She stepped beside me, the scent of nail polish twining around us. "But one thing I can tell you for sure is that I remember that day now."

I looked back to the reflection in that glass door, my eyes locking on a face that I had come to know as well as my own. *Jude* had created that awful *Bakersville Dozen* video . . .

"I remember *him*, Bailey. Jude and the camera. The way I was flirting. And the way he was flirting right back."

"Why didn't it hit you before now?" I asked. "With all the time the thirteen of us spent going over the video, Jude just slipped your mind?"

"Memory is a tricky thing, B." Sylvie shrugged again. "Besides, I was trying to remember a monster, not one of our classmates. A monster using his *phone* to record me—that's usually how it's done these days . . . Jude was using the video setting on a digital camera from photography class. Obviously—"

"Oh my God." I stepped back, bumping into Wes. His hands gripped my arms. Staring right at her, my mind ticked forward slowly. None of this felt right. "You're in on this, aren't you?"

"Please, Bailey." Sylvie laughed, tipping her chin up, all those glossy curls spilling down her back. "Get a grip."

"I saw the footage of you stealing the tiara. *You* took it, not Jude. You planted it on her body, too, didn't you?"

Sylvie's head dipped to one side. "I don't know what you're talking about."

I looked at Owen. "Show her," I said. "Show her the surveillance video from the atrium, of her taking the tiara out of the display case."

"About that," Owen said. "The video was compromised."

"Compromised?" Wes asked. "Or erased?"

"Are *both* of you in on this?" I asked, stepping back, pressing myself against Wes. "Because the way I see it, Jude shooting a video is way less damning than seeing that tiara in your hands an hour before it landed on Leena's head."

Sylvie narrowed her eyes at me. "An *hour* before it landed on her head? Jude didn't find Leena until—"

"The day before." Wes's hands squeezed my arms. "She meant the day before."

"Right," Sylvie said, rolling her eyes. "Of course she did. Look, the bottom line about the surveillance footage is simple: no one's going to nail me for something I didn't do. I have no idea what happened to that tiara after I took it to the girls' locker room."

"Yet you're taking drastic measures to cover the whole thing up. I saw you yesterday," I said. "You and Owen. In the woods."

Sylvie sighed, her eyes flicking to Owen and back to me again. "I had to cover my bases, right? I mean, I didn't even know the tiara was with Leena until your precious little *Jude* found her body and started talking. When I saw Owen standing with Tripp and Wes at the memorial, it clicked. He was the only way you could have seen that footage. So I did what I had to do to take care of it."

"Screwing a computer geek so he'll erase damning evidence in a murder investigation?" I shook my head. "I thought you were better than that, Sylvie."

"No you didn't." Sylvie rolled her eyes. "To be clear, I'm trying to keep myself safe. Just like you've been trying to do."

"So, are you going to defend my honor?" Owen leaned back in his computer chair, smirking up at Sylvie. "Tell her I'm not a geek?"

"He's not a geek." Sylvie stepped up behind Owen and ran her fingers through his hair. "He's a total stallion, if you know what I mean."

"That video doesn't mean anything," I said, trying to convince myself as much as anyone else in the room.

"Oh, but it does," Sylvie said. "At the very least, it means that your precious little boyfriend has been lying his ass off since it released last fall."

"What about you?" I asked. "Evidence or not, I know you stole the tiara, Sylvie."

"Come on, now, Bailey. I'd guess that you've already solved that mystery. Just like I've figured out why you came to my house the other night accusing me, instead of going straight to the police with that footage."

"This should be good," I said.

Sylvie looked at Owen, then back at me. She bit her lip, obviously unsure if she wanted to risk saying more. She took a deep breath before the words tumbled out: "It's red and square. It comes with a command. And a threat."

"Holy shit." Wes's voice was a whisper. "Holy fucking shit."

"What?" Owen asked, swiveling around and looking up at Sylvie. "What the hell are you talking about?"

"Little secret. It doesn't really matter anymore, anyway."

"How can it not matter?" I asked. "You're getting them, too? It changes everything."

"It changes nothing."

Wes's hands slipped from my arms as I stepped forward. "I want to see it."

"Sorry." Sylvie shrugged. "I burned it."

"How could you—"

"Part of the instructions," she replied. "You didn't have to burn yours?"

"No. How many did you get?"

Sylvie smiled smugly. "I only got one, instructing me to move the tiara from the display case to locker number 207 in the girls' locker room as soon as the Last Day Ceremony ended. But if you're asking that, it means you've gotten more than one. And you're in deeper than I imagined."

"Sylvie," I snapped. "You have to keep this to yourself. And you'd better keep Owen quiet, too."

"Don't worry. This is what they call a deadlock, right? You know my secret. I know yours. There's nothing for either of us to gain if we go and tattle. I just have one question."

"What?"

Sylvie's eyes went hard, flashing with anger. "What do we do about Jude?"

CHAPTER 28

7:57 PM

"You heard from Hannah?" Tripp asked as he stepped out of his Jeep. He'd parked next to Wes's truck in the parking lot of Cold Stone Creamery. "I thought she was meeting us."

"She is," I said, slipping out of the passenger seat of Wes's truck and shoving the door closed with my hip. I tucked my phone in the side pocket of my purse. "She just texted me that she's on her way. She said we should get our ice cream and wait on the benches outside for her. Took you long enough to get here, by the way."

"Yeah, dude," Wes said. "We've been waiting for at least ten minutes."

"Sorry. It couldn't be helped," Tripp said as we made our way toward the front entrance of Cold Stone. "Did Hannah apologize for bailing last night?"

"No," I said. "I figured she needed some space. Just chill, okay? She'll be here."

"She'd better be." Tripp walked faster. "I need her tonight."

"What's the plan?" Wes asked, stepping into the sugary air of the ice cream shop. "And where have you been all day? I've tried calling you, like, five times. We ran into some major shit at O'Brien's earlier."

"Let's just find this envelope. We'll talk about the rest later." Tripp ran a hand through his hair, his eyes scanning every face in the crowd. The shop was packed, and the line to place an order stretched from the cash register, across the pink-tiled floor, all the way to the entrance. "What'd last night's clue say again?"

"Second to last stop in the hunt," I recited from memory, my eyes locking on Tripp. "Hit the center of town and grab a few scoops. Then head outside and search 'til you find four essentials you'll need to make it to the end: a clue, a map, a promise, and a warning. Happy hunting."

"A clue, a map, a promise, and a warning," Tripp repeated, his lips forming the words over and over as he stared off into the crowd. I wanted to pull him aside and ask him if he was okay. He looked a little wild, his eyes glassy, and he seemed distracted, on edge. He jumped when the bell on the door jangled and a new customer walked in behind us.

Glancing over my shoulder, I saw Jonsey and Lane stepping to the end of the line. The familiar ring of their laughter rose over the drone of the crowd. I did not want to get stuck talking with them, so I ducked in front of Wes.

I thought I was safe as we rounded the cooler, but a minute later, I heard the bell again, and then Jude's voice. He sounded happy. Playful almost, as he teased the guys about wanting to meet up for ice cream. Lane made a crack about something, and Jonsey laughed.

"I'll be right back," Jude said, his voice suddenly serious. The line advanced, all shuffling feet and swaying bodies, and before I knew what was happening, Jude was by my side, his eyes locked on mine. "I was just coming over to see if your brother knew where I could find you. We still need to talk."

And then his hand was on my arm, pulling me out of the line, away from Wes and Tripp. As Jude led me around a corner and into the hall leading to the bathrooms and kitchen, I looked over my shoulder. Tripp was holding Wes back, arm pressed against Wes's chest to stop him from following.

We were alone—just Jude and me in that hallway. His hand slipped from my arm to my wrist, his fingers squeezing like he never wanted to let me go. The back door screeched as he shoved it open and pulled me into the lot behind Cold Stone.

"I need you to explain," he said, twisting me around, blocking the doorway. "Why are you spending so much time with Wes when you promised me you'd stay away from him? Is he the reason you're avoiding me?"

The air conditioning unit buzzed to life, jump-scaring me, its internal fan churning the scent of spoiled milk and rotting fruit toppings from the dumpster sitting in front of it.

"There's something you need to explain before we get to that," I said, hating the fear that made my voice shake. "I saw something today, Jude."

His jaw clenched. "Don't change the subject, Bailey."

"A video," I said, holding my head high, not wanting him to know that I was terrified. At least we were in a semi-public place and Tripp and Wes close by. "It was eerily similar to *The Bakersville Dozen*, but there was a lot more to it. Sound, for one. And new footage that revealed a lot more."

Jude closed his eyes, ducking his head. His hands clenched into fists at his sides, setting off a wave of fear that surged through my body.

But I had to keep going.

"It's not what you think," Jude said. "I didn't—"

"Not what I think? I heard you, Jude—*your* voice. I saw your reflection in the glass doors of the atrium. You were the one holding the camera."

"That's true." He looked at me, his face softer now, his eyes pleading. "I shot the video of Sylvie, yeah. But not the rest of it."

"How am I supposed to believe that? How am I supposed to believe anything you say?"

"I obviously didn't shoot the footage of us, B."

I chewed on my bottom lip, trying to arrange all of the information in an order that would make sense. Nothing fit. "I'm listening."

"I shot the footage of Sylvie for Mr. Brewer. He shoved the camera in my hand when I got to the health rally that day, saying the video would be good for promoting the event next year. I didn't just film Sylvie. I went around the entire rally, getting footage of all the different tables and activities. Look, B, somehow, someone took the footage off of the school camera and added it to that video. But I swear it wasn't me. I would never, ever—"

"Why didn't you go to the police?" I asked. "Why didn't you tell them that you filmed Sylvie's section?"

"I did!" Jude said, his eyes wide. "I went to see Tiny Simmons last fall. He's one of my cousin's friends. He was almost done with training, had his job lined up and all. I figured I could trust him enough to tell him everything. I was scared to death, afraid they'd analyze the video, see me, and think I was behind the whole thing. But he believed me. He took me in and sat with me as I told the story to the detective in charge of the case."

"Oh," I said, tucking my hands into the pockets of my jeans, suddenly feeling very stupid, not to mention horrible for accusing him. "Why didn't you tell me?"

"I wanted to. Really, I did. But the detective told me I couldn't tell anyone. He said it might compromise the investigation, which was the last thing I wanted to do. I hated keeping anything from you but I didn't have a choice." Jude wrapped his arms around me and pulled me to his chest. His heart was beating, loud and clear and fast. He dropped his chin onto the top of my head and I let my body melt into his.

"I understand," I said, my words lost in the whir of the air conditioning.

"Is it like that for you?" Jude whispered. "Whatever's going on?"

"Yeah," I said, my fingers gripping at the soft fabric of his T-shirt. "It's awful, Jude."

"You can tell me. Whatever it is." He looked at me, his eyes shining in the dim light of the parking lot. "You're safe with me."

"I know."

I stood on my tiptoes, bumping my nose against his before he pulled me in for a kiss. The screech of the door opening split us apart.

"Bailey?" It was Tripp, his body outlined by the bright light of the hallway behind him. "We gotta hit it."

"You have to?" Jude asked, his voice a whisper.

I nodded. "I'm sorry."

"We can finish up later." Jude kissed my forehead. "For now, just be safe."

I walked into the chaos of the ice cream shop, following Tripp down the hallway. Wes was waiting, leaning against the drinking fountain as he licked a scoop of black raspberry chip from the waffle cone in his hand.

"Here." Wes handed me a bowl with a scoop of chocolate chunk, then turned, pushing his way out the main door. Tripp trailed behind me as I followed Wes out, deciding to ignore the silent treatment he was giving me. The wooden benches out front were crowded, so we huddled together, whispering.

"You found something?" I asked.

"Yeah," Tripp said. "I didn't want to grab it without you. In case someone's watching."

"We have to figure out what we're going to do. We can't just follow along. Not anymore. We need a solid plan."

"I have a few ideas. But we've gotta get through this first." Tripp thrust his chin at one of the streetlamps—a thick wooden pole covered with black-and-white posters advertising events in the area, handwritten, photocopied. Fluttering at the center was one item that did not match the rest: A bright red envelope.

I walked to the post and yanked the envelope from the tack holding it in place. After dumping my ice cream in the trash, I raced to the parking lot, tucking myself between Wes's truck and Tripp's Jeep before opening the flap and pulling the cardstock free. A small piece of paper fluttered to the ground at my feet. I bent to pick it up, but Wes was there already, eyes locked on a spiderweb of lines that criss-crossed the paper.

"It's a map," he said, his voice tight. "What's the clue say?"

I looked down, the words blurring together. As I read, panic settled deep within my chest:

CONGRATULATIONS!
YOU'VE MADE IT TO THE FINAL CLUE.
IT'S TIME TO HEAD TO THE LAST STOP.

THIS ONE IS OUT THERE,
SO FOLLOW THE MAP.
CAN'T HAVE YOU GETTING LOST.

HURRY ALONG.
THE CLOCK IS
TICK, TICK, TICKING . . .

HERE'S THE PROMISE:
I HAVE
WHAT YOU ARE MISSING.

AND THE WARNING?
IF YOU DON'T PLAY THIS RIGHT,
YOU'LL NEVER SEE IT AGAIN.

P.S.:
CALL THE COPS
AND YOU ALL DIE.

HAPPY HUNTING!

"Am I supposed to understand what that means?" I asked.

"What are you missing?" Tripp asked, leaning against his Jeep. "JJ Hamilton?"

"Well, obviously, but—" My phone vibrated with the ring-tone Hannah had programed for herself. I pulled it from my purse, swiping my finger across the screen.

"You're late," I said. "You texted that you were on your—"

"It's not me texting you, Bailey! Not since I left last night." Her voice was high-pitched, terrified, making my entire body go numb. "Don't do it. Whatever the clue says, stay away from—"

I heard a shriek, then the sound of something slamming.

Next came the breathing, heavy and rushed.

And then the voice, robotic, distorted by the kind of device that I thought was only used in horror movies.

"You want her, come and get her. But you better hurry. She's not going to last long."

The line went dead. I stood frozen, the phone pressed against my face.

"Who was it?" Wes asked. "What's happening?"

I looked at him, panicked.

"Hannah," I said. "Hannah's what I'm missing."

"But I thought—"

"We have to save her. We haven't been able to save anyone yet, but we *have to* save Han—"

Tripp's phone rang. He went pale as he checked the caller ID, then accepted the call. "Right," he said. "I understand." After hanging up, he looked at me, his eyes tired and sad. "I'm sorry. I have to go."

"No, Tripp! You can't leave now. Hannah needs us. *All* of us."

He grabbed the envelope from my hand, placing the clue and the map on the hood of his Jeep and snapping a picture of each.

"Looks like this is out near Laurel Falls. Should be easy for me to find you, right? What I'm doing, B, it's part of my plan to end this once and for all. I can't tell you anything yet, but I'll come as soon as I can." He looked at Wes. "I'm trusting you, man. Keep her safe."

"You know I will," Wes replied.

I climbed into the passenger seat of the truck, silent as Wes started the engine and backed out of the parking space.

As we pulled onto I-675, I gripped the door handle and focused on my breathing. I had no idea what I was about to face. Or if someone I trusted could somehow be in on it. But I was going in, all the way.

Hannah needed me.

And I planned to save her.

No matter what.

CHAPTER 29

9:37 PM

I looked out the window at the trees blurring by. Wes was speeding up a narrow backcountry road that twisted its way toward hills more than an hour outside of Bakersville, spiraling us toward the final location in the hunt. I glanced at him, the glowing lights from the dash spilling across his face, wanting to tell him to go faster. But faster would be dangerous, and he would probably do what I asked, so I kept my thoughts to myself. Hannah needed us.

My best friend had been taken along this very road against her will. All because she had been supporting me. I wondered if she'd been awake, terrified and trying to keep track of time and the distance as she was carried away. Or if whoever had taken her had made sure she would sleep through the trip. Either way, she was somewhere in the hills ahead, hidden away by a person who had murdered four of our classmates and then staged their bodies for me to find.

"I should have known something was wrong," I said, my voice bouncing around the cab of the truck. "It shouldn't have taken as long as it did for me to figure out that she was in trouble."

"You thought she was texting you," Wes said.

"But she wasn't," I said. "Not since she left last night."

"How were you supposed to know—"

"She's my best friend. I should have known."

"You're being too hard on yourself."

"No, I'm not. I was too caught up in you—in the past—to see what was going on right in front of me."

Wes glanced at me from the corner of his eyes. "Too caught up in accusing me, is more like it."

"I'd be stupid not to consider all the angles. It could have been you."

"You can accuse me of a lot, okay?" Wes's voice cracked. "Of being a dumbass last summer, thinking I could just let go and move on. Of letting you push me away at Christmas when I should have made sure you understood how I really felt. Of leading you upstairs to my room, knowing you'd follow, hoping that one more night might be enough to make you see . . ."

"Make me see, what, exactly?" I asked.

"That I wasn't over you. That I would never be over you. You can accuse me of playing games and of not being careful with your heart, but you can never, ever accuse me of trying to hurt you on a level as twisted as this hunt."

I watched the road curve to the left, feeling the tires hug the pavement.

I wanted to believe him. But I couldn't. Not about the hurting me part—I knew he would never put me in real danger. But hearing that he had kept his feelings to himself, that he felt the same way I had always felt about him . . . it didn't feel real.

"You lied to me."

"I never lied."

"But you acted like I had meant nothing to you. As we got closer to the end of summer last year, I was hoping you might change your mind, that you'd at least try to see where things with us could go. But you left for college with barely a goodbye."

"Our goodbye was at the pond," Wes said. "It needed to be private."

"That wasn't goodbye," I said. "It was the end. But it didn't have to be. I was ready to tell Tripp, our parents, *everyone* how I felt about you."

"Yeah, but I'd never been in a serious relationship. I was confused. Scared about how much I was feeling for you. Most of all, I was afraid I would hurt you in the end." Wes chewed his lower lip for a moment, his eyes steady on the road. "Would it matter if I told you how sorry I am? How much I regret letting you walk away? When I found out about you and Jude, it almost killed me."

"I waited for weeks, hoping you'd change your mind."

"I thought I was keeping you safe."

"I'm sorry. I don't get your logic."

"I didn't trust myself," Wes said. "I was heading to college, B. What if I had a stupid, weak moment with a girl and I broke your heart? I would never have forgiven myself."

"It happened anyway."

"I knew how I felt. Those first few weeks, I missed you so much I could hardly stand it. I wanted to wait it out. To be sure I could give you what you deserved before I made any promises. But by then it was already too late."

He looked so sad, his hair falling around the sides of his face, just like it had when he was younger. I almost reached out and touched him, my fingertips burning to feel the silky curve of his lips, to follow the slope of his neck.

And then I remembered where I was. What I was supposed to be doing. This wasn't about Wes. Or me. This was about Hannah. Her life depended on me knowing exactly what to do and exactly when to do it. If I was going to get her out of this alive, I had to let go of everything with Wes and Jude and focus.

"This you and me thing is a mess," I said. "A mess we're going to have to figure out later."

"So you'll listen?" he asked. "If you'll hear me out, I swear I'll be honest. Completely."

"Let's get Hannah home safe," I said. "Then I promise to hear you out. We both deserve at least that much."

Wes sighed. "That's all I can ask for."

The headlights swept across a green sign with five words: LAUREL FALLS LODGE—NEXT RIGHT.

"This is it." My voice shook as I glanced down at the map in my lap.

"Didn't the police search the cabins out here?" Wes turned off the road and onto a gravel path that led to the main lodge and string of cabins, buildings that had been abandoned years ago. We'd been here a handful of times when we were younger— Tripp and Wes and me. Our fathers had taken us fishing in the stream that fed the waterfall. The three of us had skipped past the cabins on the way to the trails, fishing poles propped against our shoulders, while our fathers trailed behind carrying the bait that I absolutely refused to touch.

"Yeah, the police searched up here when the first girls went missing." I said, smiling at the memory of Wes slipping a worm on my hook, promising he would do it every time I asked. "They searched everywhere they could think of."

"And there was nothing here?"

"Just a bunch of empty cabins."

"This place might be a little overgrown"—Wes glanced at the main lodge, a dark building made of thick log walls—"but it hasn't changed at all."

I slid my phone from my purse.

"You texting Tripp?" Wes asked.

"I want to let him know we're here, but I don't have a signal. What about you?"

Wes stopped in front of the main lodge, the truck's headlights illuminating weeds that knotted the pathway to the front door, and pulled his phone from the console.

"Nothing," he said with a shake of his head. "You think we should've called the police?"

"Maybe." I sucked in a deep breath. "Probably. But convincing them that Tiny could be part of this whole thing wouldn't have been easy and it would have taken too much time. Not to mention the threat—I can't get it out of my head. It said no cops or she's dead."

"Actually," Wes said, "it said no cops or we're *all* dead."

"I'm just thinking about Hannah right now. Getting her out of here." I looked at Wes. "We need a plan."

"Simple." Wes shrugged, like it couldn't be more obvious. "We stick together. No matter what."

"Obviously," I said. "I wish Tripp was here."

"He said he'd find us."

"We can't afford to wait. I have no idea what he's doing, but we need to move."

"Okay," Wes said. "So which way do we go?"

I looked out the window, my eyes swimming in the darkness surrounding the cabins. I didn't want to think about how much ground we'd need to cover. There were miles of hiking trails, a stream, and the cavern all the way out by Laurel Falls.

"I guess we go up the path. The clue didn't mention a specific cabin."

"You think we're supposed to go all the way to the falls?" Wes asked, turning the ignition off.

"Don't know," I said, reaching for the glove compartment and slipping my fingers underneath the latch on the door. "But we're gonna need light if we're going out on the trails. Do you have a flashlight in here?"

"Don't!" Wes's voice rang through the cab of the truck.

I looked at him for a second, my fingers pulling the latch on instinct alone, my eyes narrowing with confusion.

And then I heard the thud of something heavy hitting the floorboard between my feet.

"What is that?" I asked, reaching for the rearview mirror, pressing the button on the underside, and hearing a soft click as a white light flooded the space, illuminating all of Wes's secrets.

A handgun rested at my feet, its glossy chrome sparking in the bright light.

"Wes, where did you get that?"

"Tripp," Wes said. "He gave it to me earlier today. Said he had to do something before he could help tonight, so he wanted me to have it just in case."

"You and Tripp have been hunting like three times in your lives. Are you sure you know how to use this thing?"

"We've had some practice target shooting," Wes said. "Nothing fancy—just out at the Jones's farm—but enough that I know how to use one of these things. Tripp stopped by the farm earlier today and said he needed a favor. Brennan Jones handed it over, no questions asked. This whole thing has everyone in town freaked."

"Is it loaded?" I asked, leaning down, my fingers brushing against the metal barrel, wrapping around the grip of the handle.

He answered, but I didn't hear him.

It was like time stopped as my eyes locked on the other items that had fluttered out of the glove compartment, spilling around the gun like a puddle of milky blood.

My brain couldn't quite process what was in front of me—three red envelopes, my name printed neatly on the face of each one in all caps, and at least seven pieces of cream-colored cardstock, all of them blank.

Wes looked down at the space between my feet. "Bailey, I—"

"Shut up," I said, my voice shaking as I pressed myself against the door.

"But, Bailey, I have no idea how—"

"SHUT UP!" I shouted. "SHUT UP! SHUT UP! SHUT UP!"

He pressed his lips together so tightly they turned white.

"You always have an excuse. You can talk your way out of *any-thing*. But not this." I pointed the barrel of the gun toward the floorboard, my heart lurching at the sight of the envelopes, my name, the blank cardstock, all identical to the materials used for the clues that had been left with the dead bodies of my friends.

"It's not me," Wes whispered. "I swear it's not—"

I pointed the gun at him, the barrel shaking in the air between us.

"Stop." I reached for the door handle and jerked it toward me, shoving the door open. "Not one more lie, Wes."

He shook his head, holding his hands up in the air. Surrendering. As if Wes would *ever* surrender to anything.

"I'm not lying." His voice was scratchy. Raw. And his eyes were wild.

I swiveled, hopping out of the truck. Wes reached for the gun, his hand gripping the barrel and twisting it as he ducked toward me. A shot exploded into the night, the sound blasting through my ears as I turned, racing into the darkness, hoping that Wes wouldn't see which way I'd headed. That I would have enough time to get to Hannah, to save her, and maybe even JJ. That all of us would be able to run away from the abandoned cabins before he had the chance to finish whatever sick game he had started.

CHAPTER 30

10:03 PM

I was running away from Wes as hard as I was running toward Hannah. But after a few minutes, I didn't know where either of them were. I wasn't even sure where I was anymore.

And then I heard music.

Hard, thrashing music seeping from somewhere in the darkness surrounding me.

There was another sound, too. A low rumbling that ran just beneath the frenetic pace of all those instruments.

I let it pull me, the vibrations splintering the peace of the cool night air. Clouds blocked the rays of the moon, making it hard to see. My ears were still ringing from the gunshot. But finding Hannah—saving her—was my only concern.

I veered toward the cabins on my right, feeling safer away from the open pathway, and raced past one sagging front porch, then two, and three. Thick patches of crabgrass choked my steps. Crossing into the lawn of the fourth cabin, I heard the *wisk-wisk-wisk* of someone close by, chasing me, and pictured Wes there, the denim of his jeans rubbing together as he swerved in and out of the shadows. I moved faster, my feet ripping through the weeds.

I knew that Wes probably wasn't working alone; even if I escaped him, I'd still have to face someone else. There was no way to prepare, so I had to hope. Hannah might have noticed something that would help us escape safely. But not just us. JJ "Juicy Fruit" Hamilton, too.

I followed the sound of the music all the way to the last cabin on the street, racing around the side of the building and down a small hill that dropped into a wooded backyard. I smelled gasoline near the back porch, then noticed a neon yellow contraption on the ground. It was waist high, metal, with wires that snaked through the weeds and toward the house.

Generator, I thought, picturing a similar machine that was tucked in a back corner of our basement. *The only way they'd have power up here.*

I glanced at a small window in the rear wall of the cabin. Light streamed out through the grimy glass. My heart lurched as I stepped forward, hands shaking as I reached out to grip the sill. The tips of my fingers grazed something lying on the chipped surface of the paint—an old screwdriver that tapped the pane before falling to the bed of leaves below. I cringed, worried that someone might have heard, then realized there was no way. Not over the pumping grind of the music.

I told myself that Hannah would be okay, that JJ was fine, that we would all get away. But I knew the chances of the three of us making it out safely were next to nothing.

As I focused on the scene inside the cabin, my body recoiled.

I realized I had fully expected to discover Hannah dead.

JJ, too.

Just like the others.

But that's not what I saw.

Hannah was sitting in a chair—bruised, dirty, and wildly unkempt—but looking very much alive. JJ was right by her side, shoulders slumped forward, her teeth biting at her lower lip. Her eyes were sunken and framed by dark circles, but they were staring back at me, radiating life.

As soon as she realized I was there, her mouth pulled tight, and she shook her head, tipping it toward a corner of the cabin I couldn't see. The movement was so small, I barely caught it. But I understood the meaning immediately—she was warning me that someone else was there, too.

I wanted to barge in, to pull them out of that awful place. But I had no weapon. Nothing at all to defend myself or the two girls inside, whose lives depended on me. Wes was supposed to be by my side, helping me make these decisions. He was supposed to be part of my team.

I'd have to figure it out on my own now.

I had surprise on my side. Though I'd been baited to Laurel Falls, JJ Hamilton was the only person who knew exactly where I was. With no cell service in the area, Wes hadn't had the opportunity to warn whoever his partner might be. And he hadn't caught up to me yet, so the other guy must be inside, alone. I had a chance. *If* I acted fast. Bending down, I grabbed the screwdriver, pressing it between my forearm and body—hidden, but accessible.

Without another thought, I rushed the door, turning the handle, surprised to find the door unlocked as I made my way into the little room. The music hit me full force as I took in the details—the dim lighting, the white table pushed against a wall, two stained couches framing a fireplace, and a circle of chairs in front of the stone hearth.

Hannah opened her eyes. Her lips were scrunched tight and her chin quivered.

That's when the first blast of fear exploded through my chest.

Hannah had never been a chin-quivering kind of girl.

If she was this afraid, I knew I should be, too.

Then the music stopped, the last notes echoing through the room.

I looked for a place to hide, but there was none.

Footsteps came next, along with a wispy shadow draping the floorboards to my right.

And then the voice—feminine, light, and acidic.

"Please tell me you didn't come alone, B. God, that would be so boring."

CHAPTER 31

10:13 PM

I recognized that voice the instant I heard it.

I twisted around, seeing her, but I still didn't believe.

She was dead.

I'd left her in the cave twenty-four hours ago, her body as lifeless as all the others.

I noticed her hair first, long and brown, falling over one shoulder in a thick braid. She stood there, body straight as a rail, one hand propped on her hip, spangled bracelets that she'd designed twining up her arm.

"Suze," I said, the word coming out high-pitched, confused. "You're alive."

She smiled and gave me a coy little nod.

Suze "I'm Sexy and I Know It" Moore was alive! *Alive* and *well* and standing right there in front of me. Instinct kicked in and I started forward, my arms reaching out to grab her and pull her to me, a surge of relief washing away the horror that had been with me since the cave.

"Bailey, no!" Hannah shouted.

But she was too late. Suze's hands shot out, one latching tightly around my wrist, the other yanking the screwdriver from my grasp and tossing it into the corner. She began tugging me toward the chairs.

"Suze?" Confused, I dug my heels into the floorboards, feeling the grit of dirt scraping beneath my shoes. "We have to get out of here."

She looked at me, her eyes glittering, her hand squeezing me so tightly, I could feel the blood pulsing through my veins. "Well, that wouldn't be any fun."

"We're not here to have *fun*," I said, wondering what had happened to her. I'd heard of the Stockholm Syndrome. But this? This seemed extreme, even for Suze, who liked to push it to the limits.

"Oh, but we are," she said, her head tipping back, her deep, throaty laughter spilling around us. "This is the grand finale. It's what we've been waiting for."

"Stop," I said, yanking my wrist away and scrabbling back a few steps. "You're scaring me."

Suze fluttered her hand in the air, a smile lighting up her face. "And to think, we're just getting started tonight."

"Started with *what*?" I asked, looking to Hannah and JJ, who'd sunk down in their seats.

"Sorry. Can't tell until everyone arrives." Suze propped her hands on her hips, her bracelets jangling as she tipped her head to the side. "That wouldn't be fair."

I looked at the chairs again, counting. There were five.

"Who else is coming?" I asked.

"That's a surprise," Suze said with a wink. "But we won't all be sitting. The chairs are for audience members only."

She clapped her hands, jumping up and down a few times on the balls of her feet.

"This is going to be perfect," she said, her voice trembling with excitement.

I took in my surroundings again, suddenly understanding several things at once. First, Hannah and JJ weren't sitting in those chairs. They were trapped in them, shackles clasped around their ankles, a thick chain stretching from their bare feet to a large bolt fastened into the cabin's floor. Second, there was a staircase in the corner that might be an additional escape route. And third, centered on the kitchen table, was a knife—light gleaming off the metal blade.

"We just have to wait until they all get here," Suze said with a shrug, slowly circling the chairs, her fingers sliding along the smooth wooden armrests. "Then the party can begin."

Hannah tapped her foot on the floor so softly I almost didn't hear it. The rhythm was familiar, a secret beat that we used to clap to get each other's attention back in middle school. I watched her eyes skip from me to the door I'd entered through and back again.

Go, she mouthed. *While you can.*

I shook my head.

Hannah's eyes filled with tears. *Get help.*

Suze started toward me again, that smile still on her lips. "You aren't thinking of leaving, are you?"

I pulled my shoulders back, looking her right in the eyes, but I didn't answer.

I was weighing my options: go for the knife so I had a way to protect myself or go for the door and try to find help. As much as I hated it, I knew Hannah was right. I had to get out before

Suze, who had obviously lost her mind, allowed Wes to chain me to one of the chairs in the middle of the room.

I swiveled, lunging for the door, leaping out of the cabin and onto the back porch. The smell of gasoline washed over me again, and I hesitated, wondering which way to turn.

That's when I saw them staggering out of the darkness, moving as one toward the cabin. Two bodies tangled up in each other, a puzzle that I couldn't piece together. But I knew enough to shout a warning, and when he looked up, his brown hair falling into his eyes as he caught sight of me, I did.

"Careful, Jude!" I yelled, wondering what he was doing there, and how I could be so lucky that he had shown up when I needed him most. An image popped into my mind—Jude following Wes's truck from the parking lot of Cold Stone, tailing us across winding back-country roads and up into the hills. But then it hit me. So far, nothing had been as it seemed. I'd found the envelopes in Wes's truck. Suze was alive, not dead. What if Jude's reason for following had nothing to do with helping me?

I back-stepped, suddenly unsure who to trust.

My eyes tripped over to Wes. His face was a deep shade of red; his eyes shimmered with fear. And then I noticed the arm wrapped around his neck, how his hands were clawing at the muscle pressing against his windpipe, that his feet were dragging behind him, the toes of his gym shoes digging a skittish pattern across the leaf-strewn ground.

I felt myself relax, thinking that everything would actually be okay.

Jude had Wes.

Which meant he was on my side.

Wes wouldn't be able to hurt anyone anymore.

Not Hannah. Or JJ. Or me.

Not bat-shit-crazy Suze Moore, either.

But then I looked at Jude again.

The anger in his eyes burned into me.

And I realized that absolutely nothing had been as it seemed.

CHAPTER 32

10:21 PM

Jude smiled as he dragged Wes toward the cabin and threw him against the outside wall. It was a dark smile, void of all kindness. Wes grunted as his shoulder cracked into the wood, and again as he slid into a heap on the ground, his hands circling his throat as he gasped for air. My reflexes kicked in and I moved to rush to his side, but I caught myself.

"Bailey." Jude tossed his hair out of his eyes. "I'm glad you made it."

Suze stood in the doorway, her palms pressing into its frame, her face full of childlike excitement.

"This is freaking epic," a voice called from the trees at the side of the yard.

I whipped around, seeing her step from the darkness. I had to focus to keep my balance. Seeing dead people, it seemed, had a way of throwing everything off-kilter.

"Em!" Suze squealed, bounding off the porch and across the shadowed ground. "You're back!"

Emily "Teaser Not a Pleaser" Simms shrugged, as though coming back from the dead was no big deal.

"You're dead," I said, my voice trembling. "Both of you. You're supposed to be *dead*."

Suze and Emily tipped their foreheads together and they both started laughing. I felt the cold chill of terror wrap itself around me. I'd gotten it *all* wrong.

"Gotcha, didn't we?" Suze locked arms with Emily and pulled her toward the cabin.

As they approached, I stepped sideways, careful to keep out of Wes's reach. I trusted no one.

"This makes no sense," I said, so many questions tumbling through my mind.

"You want to know what's going on here, don't you?" Emily asked, her lips curving up in a smile, her eyes flat and dark, nothing like the girl I'd once thought I knew so well. "I can practically hear your brain churning with all the new information, wondering who and what and where and when and why."

"It's killing her," Suze said, crossing her arms.

"No pun intended." Emily smirked.

Suze gave a little snort-giggle then pointed down at Wes, who was still tucked into a ball on the ground. "Jude, take care of that, will you? We're going to get your little virgin girl all set up."

"On it," Jude said, bending down and jerking Wes to his feet.

Suze and Emily grabbed me, pulling me toward the doorway. I kicked and scratched, fought with everything I had, but that just made them angry.

As we made our way into the cabin, Suze grabbed a handful of my hair and cracked my head into the doorframe.

Everything faded to black.

CHAPTER 33

10:43 PM

My head hurt. I felt like I was spinning. I wasn't sure where I was, but I didn't want to open my eyes because my stomach was threatening to heave, so I focused on my breath. In and out—slow and steady.

I heard footsteps. Pacing. Somewhere nearby.

The scent of fresh cut wood swirled around me.

"Someone's missing."

The voice was taut, angry, and so familiar it brought back all of my memories in one single flash. I opened my eyes, but just barely, careful to keep my body still. My lashes blurred the scene, but I was able to soak in the details. I was seated in one of the chairs in front of the fireplace. Hannah was across from me, her eyes wide as she watched the others. JJ sat beside her, staring at the floor.

Suze moved like a caged animal, pacing back and forth, the wood floorboards creaking beneath her weight.

Across the room, Jude sat in a chair at the white table, chewing on his nails. His elbow was propped on the tabletop, the knife gleaming just a foot away.

"We're short one player without Tripp. But I think we're inching toward two." Emily was standing next to me, peering down at Wes, who sat in the chair on my right. His body was slack. Blood stained the hairline directly above his left eye and dripped down the side of his face. Worry began to seep into my fear. "Did you have to hit him so hard?"

"What's it matter?" Jude asked. "If he dies, he dies."

"That's not what has me worried," Suze said, her words icy and hard. "Where's Tripp?"

"Dunno," Jude answered, his voice telling me he couldn't have cared less.

"What do you mean, you don't know?" Suze stopped pacing, swiveling on Jude. "You said they've all been following the clues."

Jude shrugged. "He left Bailey and Wes back at Cold Stone."

"And you just let him?"

"What the hell else was I supposed to do?"

Suze started pacing again, faster now. Emily abandoned Wes, crossing the room and leaning against the far wall with one foot propped behind her.

I tried not to panic, but there were so many things working against me. Like the restraints clamped around each of my ankles. Looking at the length of the chain spiraling toward the bolt in the floor, I realized that I might be able to take a few steps if I stood up, but no more than that. Same thing for Hannah, JJ, and Wes.

I tried to ignore the way Wes's head had lolled back unnaturally, and how that meant he probably wouldn't be walking any time soon. For now, I needed to stay still. The longer they thought I was unconscious, the better.

"I put the extra envelopes in Wes's truck before I went into Cold Stone," Jude said. "Do I get any credit for that? It was the perfect set-up. When they pulled up outside, Bailey found them and bolted away. But not before she tried to shoot him."

"Did you say 'shoot'?" Suze asked, her voice low and contemplative.

"Yeah." Jude's hand disappeared behind his back for a moment, then snapped into view, his fingers clasped around the thick handle of a gun.

"Shocking development," Suze said. "I didn't think Bailey had it in her. Though I'm not surprised she aimed at the wrong boyfriend."

I risked a glance in Wes's direction. He was folded in on himself, his head still hanging at an unnatural angle. His left eye was almost swollen shut. I wanted to tell him how sorry I was. But I was afraid I'd never have that chance.

"Well, this puts a new spin on things," Suze said, grabbing the gun from Jude's hand and turning it over in her own. "It's perfect, actually. Now, what about Tripp?"

"The three of them read the clue in the parking lot back at Cold Stone. But then Tripp got a call and took off. I had to choose between following him wherever the hell he was going, or following these two. Figured you'd prefer me out here for the closing ceremony."

Suze pointed the gun at Jude's chest. "Don't fuck with me."

"I'm not. I swear."

"This has to end perfectly. *Perfectly*. Do you understand?"

"I got it," Jude said. "Losing Tripp isn't that big of a deal. We've got Wes. Dead or alive, he's all we need. And now with this gun, it'll be a piece of cake to pin the entire thing on him."

"You think so, huh?" Suze's hand dropped to her side, the barrel aiming toward Jude.

"I do," Jude said, standing from the table, looking Suze directly in the eye. "Especially considering your experience with setting people up."

Suze smiled, tipping her head to one side, waiting for what would come next.

"First, Roger Turley," Jude said, circling Suze slowly. She turned with him, her eyes following his footsteps, hand gripping the gun so hard her knuckles had turned white.

"As if you care about him," Suze said.

"Fine. Turley was a no-brainer. But why me?" Jude asked, his voice raw. "I gave you and Emily a camera that was untraceable. But you switched it out with the one from school before you prepped the cave last night."

"If you know about that," Suze said, "it means Bailey saw the video. And she *actually* confronted you? I'm impressed. I bet that put a dent in the whole 'Cutest Couple' status."

"She thought it was me," Jude said. "She accused me of doing everything."

"Well," Emily said with a giggle. "She's not so far off, is she?"

"Shut up!" Jude said. "We're in this together. We're supposed to protect one another."

"Yeah," Suze said. "But I thought it might be fun to spice things up."

"I planted two dead bodies in the last three days," Jude said. "How 'spiced up' do you need this to be?"

"Hey, guys," Emily said. "I think—"

"God, fine," Suze said. "You caught me. I was planting evidence to cover myself."

"And frame *me*?" Jude asked.

"Sorry." Suze shrugged. "It was a back-up plan. I'm not about to take the fall for this."

"Guys," Emily said, pushing off the wall and taking a few steps toward Suze and Jude.

"It was your idea," Jude said. "The whole entire thing was—"

"Don't pull that shit with me," Suze said. "You were in on this from day one."

"Guys!" Emily said. "Bailey's awake."

Suze sighed, turning and walking toward me. She stood there for a moment, then kneeled down in front of me, her free hand patting my knee. "You're probably a little confused."

I nodded, wondering how to best play this out "Just trying to figure out what the hell is going on."

Suze's pats turned into little smacks, the sting of her hand on my leg biting through my jeans. "Oh, I'll explain all of that. *After* you tell me where Tripp is."

I shook my head. "I have no idea."

"She's lying," Emily said, stepping between Wes and me.

"I'm not." I shifted in my chair, watching in horror as Emily wrapped her hands around Wes's neck.

"Where is Tripp?" Emily asked. "Tell us now, or Wes dies a little faster."

"Tripp wouldn't tell us," I said, my words strung together, tumbling out of me. "He just said he had a plan."

"Lovely. That means we don't have much time." Suze stood and walked to the front of the fireplace, propping her hands on her hips in a way that pointed the gun directly at Wes's face. I wanted to pull him to me, out of the line of fire, but I suspected that trying to save him, might put him in more danger. The only good thing was that the gun seemed to spook Emily. Her hands dropped from Wes's neck and she stepped away.

Hannah tapped her foot again, whisper-soft. When I looked up at her, I saw her mouth the words, *Get her talking.*

I had no idea how to do that, and I had no desire to hear anything Suze had to say. But then I understood—it was our only way out. "We don't have much time for what?"

Suze beamed, her entire face lighting up, life sparking back into those cold, dead eyes. "You have no idea how long I've been waiting for this."

"I don't," I said. "But I'm curious."

"I bet she's dying to know," Emily said with a giggle. "Get it? She's *dying* to—"

"The whole thing started over Winter Break," Jude said. "With you and Wes and your dirty little secret."

Jude's words hit hard, the memory of that night welling up in my mind: Wes leading me up the staircase, my thumb flicking the lock on the door as I closed it behind me, my body tingling as Wes traced his fingertips across every inch of my skin.

"You thought that you and Wes were the only two who knew?" Jude said, crossing the floor and standing directly in front of me.

"Jude," I said. "I'm sorry. I—"

"Sorry?" Jude asked, leaning down, his breath hot on my face. "You're a little slut is what you are."

"Shut up, Jude," Hannah said. "She loves Wes. Always has."

"That true?" Jude asked, his face inches from mine.

"Yes." I blinked away my tears. Anger rose up from inside me, mixing in with all of my fear.

"Cut the dramatics, Jude." Suze rolled her eyes. "And don't ruin the story. It's always best to start at the beginning."

CHAPTER 34

10:53 PM

"It started last summer. At the farm." Suze looked around, her eyes flitting over every face in the room. "All of us were there. It was the night of Jonsey's end-of-summer party, just a week or so before everyone heading out of town left for college."

Jude backed away from me as she talked, circling around the room and placing himself directly behind Hannah. He locked eyes with me, his expression void of all emotion. The change was so complete, I wondered how I could have missed the fact that this version of him existed beneath the surface

"Jude was wasted," Suze said, rolling her eyes. "Sloppy drunk and sulking, sitting under the big tree near the barn, all by himself."

"I wasn't sulking," Jude said.

"Yeah. You were. And when I asked you what was wrong, you told me you'd asked Bailey out and she'd denied you."

I looked at Wes—saw the blood trickling down his face, the knobby lump forming just under his hairline, the swollen eye—and hated myself. They were planning to pin everything on him. All because of me.

Suze smoothed the fabric of her shirt down over her stomach, taking a deep, composing breath.

"So, Jude here, he wanted you," Suze said. "I told him that the only way he could get to you was to take his time. It was obvious that you needed some space to get Wesley "Party Boy" Green out of your system. There was no way he'd be able to deny the temptation of slutty coeds wearing "fuck-me" shoes, getting shit-ass drunk on keg beer. Which meant it was only a matter of time before you were left broken-hearted. And Jude, here, was primed and ready to swoop in and take all of those bad feelings away."

"You're the reason I agreed to go on that first date with Jude," I said to Suze. She had walked up to me in the hallway at school last fall, lockers slamming all around us. "You said all he talked about during science lab was *me*. That he wasn't going to give up, so I might as well give in."

"And it worked," Jude said. "The next time I asked you out, you said yes."

"But Suze didn't do all of that just to make you happy," JJ said. "She worked you, Jude. Emily, too. Just like she works everyone."

"So smart, JJ," Suze said. "Such a shame that brilliant mind of yours only has a few hours left to live."

"You're behind *The Bakersville Dozen*," I said, shaking my head with disbelief. Jude had been right by my side through all of it. And I hadn't suspected a thing. "You and Jude created that video. But why?"

"Those girls needed a reality check," Suze said. "They had everything they'd ever wanted, and it all came to them so easily. That's not how life works."

"So you were jealous?" Hannah asked.

"A little. Maybe," Suze said with a shrug. "But I was angry, too. It wasn't fair. I thought I'd teach everyone a little lesson. I followed the girls for a few weeks, shooting as much footage as I could."

"How'd you get Jude to go along with your plan?" I asked. "He's not stupid. He'd never risk his future at OSU without—"

"You don't know your boyfriend very well, do you?" Suze scrunched her nose up and flashed a wicked smile. "Jude is the ideal accomplice. He's sneaky, but popular—totally likable. And he doesn't care who he hurts."

"That's not true." I looked at Jude, hoping to find a shred of the boyfriend I had known. If I could appeal to that side of him, I might have a chance. "You're kind, loving and—"

"I think I just threw up in my mouth a little," Emily said. "How are you so clueless?"

"Give me some credit," Jude said with a snort. "I played a good game."

"*That* was my ticket," Suze said. "Jude thinks everything is a game. Shit, he only wanted you because he thought you were virgin blood. Of course, the truth was obvious to me—hence '*Like a Virgin*'—but Jude thought you were the ultimate conquest of senior year. So I reeled him in, using you as my bait. When I finally told him my plan, which made his quest for your virginity seem like child's play, he was all in."

"Jude?" I said, my eyes searching his. He looked back at me with a blank stare.

"He's the only reason you made the list," Suze said. "I had nothing against you, Bailey. But Jude thought you'd break sooner if you were facing a particularly difficult situation. He'd be your shoulder to cry on. You'd get lost in the moment. And then you'd give it up."

"How'd that work out for you, Judas?" Hannah asked, swiveling to face him. "Oh, wait. Bailey never gave you what you wanted, did she?"

JJ laughed, the sound bursting in the room.

Jude back-handed Hannah across the face so hard she was nearly knocked out of her chair. She righted herself slowly, taking in a deep breath, and tossed her hair out of her face.

Tears burned my eyes. Jude wasn't Jude anymore. The truth was, he never had been. I couldn't believe I'd been so stupid.

"Keep your mouth shut, Hannah," Jude said. "You were never part of the plan. Don't give me a reason to take you out before this is over."

"But you didn't stop with the video," I said, trying to distract him. "Why move on to the kidnappings? I mean, you could have gotten away with everything."

"We still will," Emily said, bouncing on the balls of her feet like an overeager child. "The plan is solid. We'll come out looking like victims and then go on with the rest of our lives."

"My bet is that this plan of yours has a flaw," Hannah said. "Just like the plan with the video. It got bigger than you expected, didn't it?"

"Sure," Suze said. "I mean, all those hits on the internet? Neither of us could have predicted that. Not to mention the hours of analysis, forcing me to bond with all of the girls. Every whiny, insufferable moment I spent with them made me even more proud of what I'd done—dragging each of them down. But by then, I needed another accomplice."

"Emily," JJ said. "You chose Emily because she was the weakest of us all."

"Wrong," Suze said. "I chose Emily because she hated her step-father."

"We set him up," Emily said with a giggle.

"He never even touched you?" I asked. "And you set him up for rape, kidnapping, *and* murder?"

"He's a class-A asshole. Trust me, you don't need to feel bad for him." Suze waved a hand in the air, dismissively. "I have to admit, planting clues to frame him for the disappearances of the girls was a stroke of genius. We needed the diversion for the cops, and everything fell into place so smoothly. But we still needed Jude."

"Your new plan," I said, my stomach churning at the thought. "The kidnappings."

"Yes!" Suze snapped her fingers. "You people were getting on my last nerve, so I decided to take a few of you out of play."

"But she needed my help," Jude said, circling back to the center of the circle. "No way they could have pulled this off without me."

"Thing was," Suze said, kneeling in front of me. "I was pretty sure Jude wouldn't be down with the kidnappings or my plan for this scavenger hunt. That is until I saw you and Wes sneaking away from the Christmas party. Together."

"You were there?" I asked. "I didn't see you—"

"No, I don't believe you saw anyone that night except for Wes. But I saw you. I followed you upstairs and hid out in the bathroom connected to the hall and Wes's room. I was worried you'd hear when I jimmied the lock with a hairpin, but I shouldn't have been. By then, you two were full-on—"

"I felt horrible," I said, looking right at Jude. "So guilty. I've been planning to come clean, to share everything, and—Wait. When did she tell you?"

"Oh, sweetie, I didn't tell him," Suze said. "I streamed video to him. *Live.* It's like he was right there with me. That's all it took; Jude snapped. He was in. But he had two conditions."

It hit me then. How deeply demented Jude really was. "You picked me?" I asked. "For the hunt?"

"Yup." Jude smiled. "I also picked Wes to take the fall."

"The rest was cake," Suze said. "We were three strong with at least one person to stay here at the cabin and guard the girls as we took them, and at least one person to keep an eye on things in town who could report back here once Emily and I were 'missing' and couldn't risk being seen."

"Your secret rendezvous was perfectly timed," Emily said. "We couldn't have done any of this without Jude. He brought us food and all the other stuff we needed. And, of course, he planted the important game pieces—the clues, the bodies, the—"

"I still don't get it," Hannah said, her words a challenge.

"What's there not to get?" Suze asked, waving the gun in the air like it was a lollipop she'd grown bored with. "We just spelled the entire thing out for you."

"You didn't. You told us what you did, and how you did it, but not why." Hannah bit her lip, shaking her head. "I don't buy it. There's more than that."

"The kidnappings," JJ said. "They staged Emily on a roadside at night, bait for the next person on the list. It worked every time. Leena, Becca, me—we all stopped without thinking, jumping out of our cars to pull her to safety."

"But they got a little surprise," Jude said.

"Sure did." Emily laughed. "I didn't need saving. They did."

"One second, I think I'm bringing someone back from the dead," JJ said, her voice like sandpaper, "the next thing I know, my head feels like it's been cracked open. Then I'm waking up here, shackled like some animal."

"Ugh!" Suze spun on her heel and strutted toward the center of the circle, the chains she stepped across rattling as she pointed the gun toward JJ. "You deserve to be treated like an animal with the crap-ass music you and that loser band of yours plays."

"You're doing this to me because you don't like my music?" JJ asked, her mouth dropping open.

"No," Hannah said. "She's jealous of your recording contract."

"As if I have anything to be jealous of?" Suze paced in front of us, the star of the show.

I watched her feet navigate the tangled web of chains criss-crossing the floor, an idea forming as Suze swiveled in front of the fireplace and retraced her steps through the center of the circle.

I tapped my fingernail on the chair, the same rhythm that Hannah had used earlier. She looked at me, her cheek red and swollen from her chin all the way up to her eye. I hated Jude for that. And I would make sure he paid.

I pointed at Suze's feet as she passed in front of Jude, then thrust my chin toward the chains. Hannah's eyes narrowed with confusion. I sighed, lifting one foot several inches off the floor. JJ caught the movement, looking from me to Hannah and back again, her eyes popping wide open.

No, JJ mouthed. *No-no-no.*

Get ready, I mouthed. *One shot.*

Hannah gave me a single nod, then turned her attention back to Suze.

"You shouldn't have anything to be jealous of," Hannah said. "You have everything you ever wanted, just like the rest of the girls."

"Exactly right," Suze said, glancing toward Emily, who was now standing halfway between the wall and the circle of chairs, as though she wasn't quite sure where she belonged.

"And you're risking it all to prove some point about . . . what again?"

"You need to shut the hell up before you piss me off," Suze said.

"I don't think so." Hannah gave Suze a knowing smirk. "I'm calling you out."

"You sure?" Suze asked, holding the gun up and pointing it directly between Hannah's eyes.

Hannah's body tensed, just slightly, like she finally realized that she was in danger, but she didn't back down. "The only reason you're telling us any of this is because you plan to kill us, right? Pin the whole thing on Wes so you can play the victim when the media vultures come calling offering you all kinds of deals. If I'm as good as dead, I might as well say what I think while I still can."

Suze looked down at Jude, who had propped a foot on the chair next to Wes. "Do you believe this?"

He shrugged. "She's always been a little feisty."

"There had to be a trigger," Hannah said, her voice stronger, louder. "Maybe not for the stupid video. That could have been a serious case of mean girl syndrome. But the rest of it—everything that happened after Winter Break—that stuff was prompted by something bigger."

Suze shook her head, her eyes flashing with anger.

"What's your theory?" I asked, my voice shaking a little as I forced the words out, wanting to help Hannah, to take the focus off her for a moment or two.

"It's pretty simple," Hannah said, standing from her chair, her chain scraping along the wooden floor as she took three steps toward the fireplace, then turned to face the rest of us. "I've been thinking about December—what was happening with each of the girls who were taken—and it hit me."

"This ought to be brilliant," Suze said, circling the gun in the air in a hurry-up-already gesture. But her hand was shaking. Hannah was on the right track.

"December is when the cheerleaders found out they were headed to National Championships in Florida, right? Leena Grabman was captain, so their success was hers."

"That's the same month my band won the talent show," JJ said. "Part of the prize was a recording contract in Cincinnati. We'd just finished the CD when I was taken."

"And Becca Hillyer," Hannah said, "she may have been a train wreck, sleeping with her theater teacher, but in December she found out she'd been accepted to Juilliard. *Juilliard* of all places. That's freaking out of control crazy, right?"

Suze shrugged, the gun wavering in her hand. "Whatever you say."

"Emily was captain of the volleyball team. They'd just won the state championship. And you, Suze. If I remember correctly, you got an acceptance letter of your own."

"Yeah." Suze's face pulled tight, shadows darkening her eyes. I could feel the pressure building.

"Parsons School of Design wanted you." Hannah clapped her hands, her lips parting in a fake smile. "Which might just have been more impressive than Becca getting into Juilliard."

"All of the kidnappings, they're linked by success," I said. "Each and every girl was celebrating a major victory."

"Exactly what I was thinking," Hannah said. "Until I was chained to this chair and had a chance to think, and I realized that part was wrong. They weren't *all* celebrating. Someone had been lying."

"Shut up," Suze said. "Just shut the—"

"If you'd gotten into Parsons, there's no way you would have gone this far. Kidnapping? Murder?"

"Murder wasn't part of the original plan," Suze said. "As the girls were brought in, they woke up to find Emily, and eventually me, chained alongside them. They thought we were victims, too. Until Jude, our masked kidnapper, screwed up and said too much. When Leena figured out who he was, all of the girls started making threats. They had to be eliminated before we could go back to our lives. If it wasn't for them being so nosy—so freaking *mouthy*—we might have all made it out alive."

"That's sick," Hannah said. "Beyond disturbing. But still, you wouldn't have done this if you had a future. Which means there never was an acceptance to Parsons. You'll never have a clothing line, there will be no future buyers, no promise to show at fashion week."

"You're wrong," Suze said. "This will put me in the spotlight. There'll be front page headlines about the victims of the Bakersville case. I'll be a hero."

"No way you covered all your tracks," Hannah said. "They'll find out you're behind this. And then you'll have *nothing* that you'd dreamed for your life."

Hannah kept talking, but as soon as Suze started moving, I blocked everything out, focusing on her feet step-step-stepping across the floor. Time seemed to slow, but I knew she was moving fast, charging toward Hannah with that gun sighted on Hannah's face.

I held my breath.

Focused everything on calculating time and distance and the rate of propulsion.

I had to get this right. For all of us, but especially Wes. He hadn't moved since I'd regained consciousness. I was terrified of what that could mean.

When she was a half-step away, I jerked my foot up to the seat of my chair, wrapping my fingers around the cold metal linking me to the floor, and pulled the chain taut. It caught Suze's ankles perfectly, and she faltered. I swiveled in my chair, sweeping her feet out from under her.

Suze spiraled through the air, arms flung wide, her face a mask of surprise. Hannah tried to duck out of the way, but she had reached the end of her chain, and went down when Suze toppled into her.

And then they were both on the floor, a writhing mass of arms and legs, twisting and shifting in the center of that circle, the gun peeking out every few seconds.

I slipped to the floor, crawling on my hands and knees, and locked my hand on Suze's foot as she tried to pull away from Hannah. But then I felt myself slide backward, a vice-like pressure wrapped around my leg, dragging me across the floor. I kicked, screaming Hannah's name because I couldn't believe that after everything that had happened, I couldn't help her. That got JJ moving—she lunged off of her chair, landing directly on Suze, grabbing her braid and jerking so hard I thought her hair might tear free from her head.

The pressure on my leg tightened. With Hannah and JJ working together, I flipped to my back. Jude was on the floor, reared up on his knees as he yanked my leg, pulling me toward him. His face was blotchy red, his lips pulled back in a snarl, and I wondered for a moment if I was about to be killed by the guy I had spent nearly a year dating.

"You have any regrets?" Jude demanded. "The way you played me? The way you strung me along?"

I had screwed everything up and I might never have the chance to make it right again.

But then he was there, Wes—complicated, confusing, perfect Wes—looming just behind Jude, blood still spilling from the gash just above his hairline, arms raised, the chair that had been next to him arcing silently through the air.

"Jude, watch out!" Emily screamed, her words reverberating off the walls.

But she was too late. The chair crashed into Jude's head and he collapsed on top of me, a dead weight that I couldn't escape until Wes rolled him onto his side.

I heard the grunts of Hannah and Suze and JJ struggling behind me, and I wanted to turn and help Hannah finish what I'd started. But I had to keep track of Emily, who was standing over Jude's body, her eyes wild, the knife I had seen on the table clutched to her chest.

"This isn't right," Emily yelled. "This isn't how it was supposed to go."

And then the cabin echoed with the deafening explosion of the gun.

CHAPTER 35

11:17 PM

I looked to the pile of girls on the floor in front of the fireplace. The stone was spattered with dark spots. I didn't understand where they could have come from until I noticed a puddle of blood forming on the floor, creeping its way toward me.

A scream tore through the cabin—*Hannah!*—my voice razor sharp, mixing in with the echo of that gunshot.

I stared, eyes blinking furiously, waiting for Hannah to pop up and toss some smart-ass comment my way. But none of them moved.

For a moment, there was only silence.

Then thunder shook the ground, and the cabin's door burst open.

"Police!" a deep voice shouted, followed by the crack of the door striking the inside wall. "Everybody on the floor!"

Wes dropped to the floor, shoving Jude to the side before lying next to me.

Men wearing riot gear poured into the room, weapons aimed.

"Get down!" the voices shouted. "Keep your hands where we can see them!"

Emily screamed, throwing the knife to the floor and flinging herself at one of the men. "I'm Emily Simms," she shouted, her voice wild, her fingers ripping through her hair. "They took me. Kept me here. I just want to go home. Can you please take me home?"

The man tucked his rifle against his side, then wrapped an arm around Emily. Her body shuddered with deep, guttural sobs as he ushered her out the door.

"Drop your weapon," another voice called, each word rolling away from him like a heavy stone.

I turned back to the girls and the fireplace. From my spot, face-down on the ground, I saw a sticky pool of blood seeping into the imperfections of the wood, sealing the cracks between the floorboards. A body lay crumpled against the stones of the hearth, and I knew in an instant that it was JJ. She was silent, pale, and very still.

I saw someone else, too, stepping just between us.

She stood solid, her feet planted firmly on the ground.

As my eyes traveled up the curves of her legs, my heart raced.

"I order you," the voice shouted again. "Drop. Your. Weapon."

I lifted my head higher, taking in the entire scene: Suze and Hannah were still facing off, the gun between them, its barrel inches from Hannah's face.

"You didn't even belong here," Suze yelled, her voice shaking. "You screwed up my entire plan. I was going to be famous. Everyone was going to know my name, my story! All of them were going to be talking about my designs!"

"Little secret, Suze," I said, my voice strong, pulling her attention from Hannah, but just barely. My heart hammered as

I watched the gun, which hadn't moved an inch. "Your designs really aren't all that good."

Face pinched with outrage, her hips twisted away from Hannah. Mad determination glowed in her eyes as she swung her arm around toward me, gun slicing through the air.

Then I heard the shot, felt the blast in my chest, the way the bass drums had vibrated every inch of me during the Last Day Ceremony, only deeper to my core.

Suze flew back, a slow-motion spiral, her arms flinging as she fell to the ground. Her head bounced once off the wooden floor, eyes wide open as she came to a rest next to the splayed fingers of JJ's right hand.

"Hannah!" I shouted, pushing off the ground with my hands, dragging the chain behind me as I raced toward my friend and pulled her into a hug. "I thought she was going to kill you."

Hannah grabbed onto me. "That chick was seriously messed up."

I squeezed her tighter. "Are you okay?"

"I don't know yet," she said. "What about Wes?"

I turned and saw a string of men in black traipsing into the cabin, two of them helping Jude stand before leading him outside. A few of them dropped to the floor, checking both JJ and Suze for a pulse, staunching the flow of blood of one, closing the eyes of the other.

But none of that seemed to register. All I could see was Wes, his face so pale it was practically translucent, eyes rolled back, body stiff, jerking spastically.

I dropped to the floor, scrambling closer to grab his hand and slide his head onto my lap.

"Wes!" I shouted, pressing my hand against his cheek. "Wes!"

And then there was another voice, mixing with my own, coming from outside.

"That guy right there just said all clear. You need to get out of the way."

"This is a crime scene. I cannot let the three of you—"

"It's a crime scene you would know nothing about if it weren't for me, Tiny. My sister is in there! Let us through, or we'll find another way in."

There was rushed talking, and then several sets of footsteps racing toward me.

"Bailey!" My mother's voice cracked on the word, causing something inside me to unwind. "Thank God you're okay."

"Mom, help!" I didn't glance up as she swept to my side. I was wholly focused on the way Wes's body continued to shudder and twitch.

"Oh my God, Wes," my mother said, bending over him, her hands pressing against the blood seeping from his head. "Tripp, have you called his parents yet, or—"

"You have to move." My father's voice was as strong as I'd always remembered, but something beneath the surface gave way, and I knew he was just as scared as I was. "Both of you need to back away."

"Wes needs a medic." Tripp squeezed both of my shoulders. "One followed me in, okay, B?"

I glanced up and saw the panic in Tripp's eyes, the tremble of his lips as he repeated himself. "Wes needs a medic."

She was there, pushing her way past Tripp, around my mother, kneeling down at Wes's side, a picture of calm as she murmured a string of sentences to her partner. I caught something about a blow to the head and a rating of nine on the GCS scale. The partner shouted for fluids and a backboard to carry Wes out.

My mother put a finger under my chin, tipping my head back and looking me over. "You okay?"

"Yes," I said. "Fine, but—"

"How long has he been seizing?" the medic asked, her eyes and hands fluttering over Wes as she waited for an answer.

"Two minutes," Hannah said. "Maybe less."

"Hannah," my father said, tears glistening in his eyes as he reached out and pulled her against his side. "Thank God. When Tripp called us, we didn't know what to tell your mom. She'll be here any minute now."

But none of that mattered. *Nothing* mattered, except for Wes. I leaned down and kissed him on the forehead.

"You can't leave me," I whispered. "Not now."

The medic shouted something about finding a tool to break the shackles off Wes's legs, that they needed to prepare him for transport *now.*

Wes's body shuddered a few more times, then fell still, his head lolling to the side. The medics continued to speak rapidly to each other as an officer kneeled behind them using bolt cutters to cut the shackles from Wes's ankles. Hannah and I were freed next. All the while, my parents stared at the shackles, horrified, but that was a blur. The only clarity I had was Wes lying there, as still as all of the bodies we'd found during the hunt.

"He's going to be okay, right?" I asked the medics, my voice hoarse, shaky. "You have to make him okay."

But no one answered me.

"Dad?" I said, tears dripping down my cheeks, watching as Wes was swept away on the backboard, his eyes closed, one hand dangling free as they squeezed him through the doorway and out into the deep night.

My father tugged me from the floor and folded me against him. The frantic pulse of his heart betrayed his words as he told me that everything was going to be okay, just fine, that there was nothing to worry about.

"Wes is strong." Tripp planted his hand firmly on my back. "He'll pull through this."

"You called the police." My words were muffled by my father's shirt.

"He did the right thing," my mom said, her voice soft. "What you should have done from the very start."

"You're right," I said, twisting away from my dad's arms. "But I didn't know who to trust."

My mom's eyes were red and glossy. Tears streaked down her cheeks. Hannah was by her side, wrapped up in her arms. Mom sighed, glancing from me to Tripp and back again. "It was an impossible situation. You all did the best you could."

"I started talking to Tiny the night we found Becca at Timber Park," Tripp said. "I knew he wasn't the one, and you guys wouldn't trust me, so I just had to. He's seen pictures of all of the clues. Followed behind us almost every step of the way. Which means they knew that Suze and Emily were still alive—I guess those two bolted right after we left that set-up in the cave—but I had no idea or I swear, I wouldn't have sent you out here. After I left you at Cold Stone, Tiny brought Mom and Dad in and told us all what they thought was going on. By then, it was too late to warn you, so we just bolted out here." Tripp looked at me, his eyebrows raised. "Sorry I went behind your back. I had to do it."

Hannah pulled Tripp to her and my mother, a tangle of arms sweeping him in. "No apologies. You saved us."

"But what about Wes?" I asked. "We have to follow them to the hospital. We have to make sure they save him, too."

SATURDAY

AUGUST 20

CHAPTER 36

11:30 PM

I stood in front of the fire, watching the flames dance as people circled around me. Music pumped from an iPod dock somewhere nearby. Someone tossed a log into the flames and hundreds of glowing sparks floated up to the night sky. The fire hissed and crackled, popping loudly and making me jump.

"You okay?" Hannah asked, bumping me with her shoulder.

"Yeah," I said, my mind locking on the fact that I was fine. I still had to remind myself of that sometimes, running through a quick mental check to assess my surroundings and myself. It had started the night the police whisked me away from the cabin, and settled in during the hours I'd spent sitting with my parents in the stark, white hospital, waiting for news about JJ. And Wes. Refusing to leave, convinced that I needed to be there, that both of their lives depended on me sticking close. As each passing day took me further away from the terror of the hunt, it was getting easier to trust that I was safe.

"I can't believe we're out of here in three days," Hannah said. "You deserve this, B."

My mother had said the same thing the morning of graduation, her perfume spiraling around me as she pinned my cap in
place, its tassel swinging back and forth as she told me that she
was proud of me for agreeing to go to the ceremony. Of course,
she also added that as proud as she was, Tripp and I were still
grounded for the rest of the summer. Like, can't-leave-the-
property-without-supervision grounded. I was lucky to have
talked my way out of the house for this party, luckier still that
she understood how important tonight was for me.

"*We* deserve this," I said. "No way I'd be here without you,
Han."

Hannah tipped her blue Solo cup against mind and said,
"Cheers to that!"

People stirred behind us, shifting to make room for Jonesy,
who swooped in holding a camping chair above his head.

"Make room," he said, opening the chair and planting it on
the pavers surrounding the fire pit.

The girls swept through the crowd, moving as one, Kelsey
and Carrie on one side, Summer and Beth on the other, while
Amy and Brittany brought up the rear. Centered among them all
was a weak, but recovering, JJ Hamilton.

"You guys are treating me like I'm going to break," JJ said.

"No," Beth said. "We're treating you like you were shot in the
shoulder and lost so much blood you almost died."

"That was over two months ago."

"Barely," Kelsey said. "And this is the first night your mom
has let you out. We promised we wouldn't let you push too hard."

"She's overreacting," JJ said. "And so are all of you."

"You earned this." Jonesy handed JJ a Jell-O shot and gave
her a kiss on each cheek. "Enjoy the evening."

"I would have sneaked out if I'd had to," JJ said, taking the shot and sitting in the waiting chair. She found me in the crowd, flashing a huge smile. "Missing Jonesy's end-of-summer bash? Not an option."

"Agreed," I said, walking to her side. "How've you been feeling?"

"Little pain here and there," JJ said. "Nothing I can't handle. PT ends soon. But I'm sticking around town for the year. I'll take a few classes and transfer later."

I caught a glimpse of Sylvie as she made her way through the crowd, the glow of the fire sparking off her curls.

"Girls," Sylvie said, joining the group with a little twirl. "I can't believe we're all here!"

"The odds certainly were against you," Hannah said.

"You're one of us now, you know?" Sylvie wrapped her arm around Hannah's shoulders, pulling her in. "An honorary member of *The Bakersville Dozen.*"

"You're drunk," Hannah said.

"Maybe a little." Sylvie giggled. "But I meant what I said."

"Well, thanks for the formal induction to the group." Hannah tried to spin away from Sylvie's reach, but Sylvie spun with her, and the two became a tangle of arms and legs. We all started laughing then, softly at first, and then a full-on release. It was the perfect moment to share during our last night together.

Sylvie released Hannah and turned back to the group. "Have you guys heard the latest?"

"Yeah," I said. "Tiny stopped by earlier today and said the news would break soon. Turley was getting clues, too."

"Which explains why he went to the locker room right after the tiara was taken," Hannah said. "They set him up over and over, threatening to take him out with fake evidence, and it worked every time."

"You guys haven't had enough of each other yet?" a deep voice called. I swiveled to find Owen O'Brien walking our way. He swept Sylvie off her feet and twirled her in a circle. They were both smiling, laughing, but the vision made me feel dizzy and a little ill.

It made me think of Jude—the feel of his arms around my waist as he would pick me up and swing me around. Things between us had always felt so right.

I squeezed my eyes closed, reminding myself that Jude was sitting in a jail cell, awaiting news on his trial. The police had piled one charge on top of another.

Emily was in a different jail, in a different cell, awaiting trial, as well.

I wasn't sure if Suze, who had been pronounced dead after being transported to the hospital, was the least fortunate or if she'd gotten off the easiest.

But none of that mattered.

It was over now.

Most importantly, I was okay. The rest of the girls were okay. And they would never be able to reach us again.

I took a deep breath and opened my eyes, searching the crowd.

I found him in an instant, just like always. He was talking to Jonesy's oldest brother, Brennan. A small city of tents fluttered in the night breeze behind them. My heart flipped to triple-speed as our eyes locked. He smiled at me, then said something to Brennan, holding out a fist, which Brennan bumped with his own. And then he was walking toward me.

"Hey," he said when he reached my side.

The corners of my lips curved up in a smile. "Hey."

"You having fun?"

"It's surreal, " I said. "This whole scene. It's amazing to be here, totally free, without any worries in the world."

"No worries?" Wes asked, tilting his head up. The glow of the fire flashed across the skin above his left eye, still tender after thirteen stitches.

"Maybe one," I said, glancing at the fire.

"What's that?" Wes asked.

"I'm not sure all of the stuff my mom bought will actually fit in my dorm room." I sighed. "Combined with everything Hannah has, we could be in trouble."

"I think you'll figure it out," Wes said. "If you can't, you can always call me for help."

"You'd do that?" I asked.

"Of course," Wes said. "I'm always here for you. And with both of us at Ohio State, I'll be living, what, three minutes from your dorm?"

Behind us, JJ said something and the rest of the girls started laughing. It was good to hear them happy. To be part of this night. I caught a flash of Tripp weaving his way through the crowd, following the slope of the grass to where Wes and I were standing.

"Glad you found us," Wes said. "I have a question."

"You need a ride home?" Tripp asked. "I thought you were allowed to drive now. Or did the concussion make you forget you'd gotten your driving privileges back?"

"Very funny. I've remembered almost everything, by the way. Except for some of the stuff that happened out at Laurel Falls— that part is still pretty fuzzy."

"Did I hear someone say Laurel Falls?" Hannah asked, swiveling from the circle of girls to face the three of us. "I think we should declare that place a forbidden topic. At least for tonight."

Tripp turned to Wes and clapped him on the shoulder. "What'd you want to ask me, man?"

"It's not so much a question as something I need to say." Wes took a deep breath, looking from Tripp to me and back again. "I have a thing for your sister. I kind of always have."

Tripp and Hannah locked eyes, pausing for a moment before they began to laugh.

"What's so funny?" I asked.

"Yeah," Wes said. "This is serious."

"As if we didn't already know you two have been pining away for each other for, like, ever?" Hannah asked. "This was basically all Tripp and I talked about last summer, when you two were trying to hide your little fling."

"And you didn't say anything?" I asked, looking at them both. "Why didn't you—"

"It was obvious you wanted to keep it private," Tripp said with a shrug. "Besides, if you guys knew that I knew and then he broke your heart, I'd have to kick his ass. Would have challenged a lifelong friendship. But I think he's proven himself."

"I should hope so," Wes said.

"Just to be clear, I'll still kick your ass if you hurt her."

Wes wrapped an arm around my shoulders. "You won't have to."

"Good. The last guy who fucked with her is looking at life behind bars." Tripp winked at me and then held his cup in the air. "I'm empty. See you guys in a bit."

"I need one, too," Hannah said, grabbing Tripp's arm as she navigated the grassy ground outside of the fire's glow.

Wes sucked in a deep breath and swiped his fingers through his hair. I caught another glimpse of the scar healing just beyond his hairline, pink and swollen, a permanent reminder that he had been so close to losing everything. That I had been so close to losing him.

"We're heading out in three days," Wes said. "College life is crazy busy, what with classes and homework, not to mention football. OSU games are epic, you know."

"Oh, I know," I said.

"So, I was wondering . . ." Wes looked up at me, his eyes glimmering in the light of the fire. "Would you like to go out with me?"

"On a date?" I asked. "Like, a real, official date? Out in public and everything?"

"That's the idea." Wes laughed. "I was thinking Flying Pizza. Maybe a movie."

I looked at Wes, feeling a swell of gratitude to have him there in front of me—his eyes bright, chest rising and falling, hands shaking.

"We can go fancier if you want. That steak place in the center of town is always—"

"No," I said.

Wes's eyes creased with confusion.

"I don't need anything fancy." I placed my hand on his heart, feeling the steady beat beneath the palm of my hand. "But I would love to go out with you."

I stepped forward then, the heat from the fire mixing in with the heat of Wes until I wasn't sure where one ended and the other began.

He drew me into a hug, his breath warm against my neck.

"I love you, B," he whispered. "Always have."

And then I said it, the one thing I regretted never being brave enough to say when I'd had the chance.

"I love you, too, Wesley Green."